D0554280

BLOODY SCOTLAND

BLOODY SCOTLAND

EDITED BY JAMES CRAWFORD

PEGASUS CRIME
NEW YORK LONDON

Bloody Scotland

Pegasus Books, Ltd.
148 West 37th Street, 13th Floor
New York, NY 10018

First Pegasus Books hardcover edition March 2018

ISBN: 978-1-68177-654-5

10 9 8 7 6 5 4 3 2 1

Printed in the United States of America
Distributed by W. W. Norton & Company, Inc.

Contents

Bloody Scotland

Introduction

A number of years ago, I went with a small group of friends to visit the ruins of Castle Campbell in Clackmannanshire. It was a strikingly bright June afternoon: a cloudless sky, no breeze, and the sort of humid, energy-sapping heat that very occasionally and very unexpectedly intrudes upon Scottish summers. The castle sits between two narrow glens in the Ochil Hills, above the small town of Dollar. From the car park, you still have quite a distance to walk – all part of the experience, as a steep path winds up the hillside, with the ruined walls revealed only gradually on approach. That summer the surrounding undergrowth was an uncontrolled explosion of greenery, punctuated everywhere by bright, colourful wildflowers. It was so warm that the castle was blurred in a heat haze. There were no other visitors. We climbed in and out of the ruins, enjoying the dry coolness in the shade of the old stones. The only sounds were our own footsteps, the scratching of grasshoppers, and the lazy hum of bees drunk out of their minds on nectar.

The castle nestles a little in its hillside setting, surrounded by tall trees. When you are there, you can look out and see almost no sign of the modern world. We walked down to the stepped terraces in front of the castle to sit in the sun. And that was when we heard it. *A gunshot*. In the stillness of the day, it echoed off the hillsides like a thunderclap. One of our group screamed at the shock of it. We all looked at each other for the tiniest instant with genuine alarm. And then we started laughing. 'Must be a farmer', one of us said. And we didn't question it beyond that. A farmer doing the sorts of things farmers do; not that any of us really knew what those things might be. And, within seconds, we had relaxed again. We rested for a while, walked some more around the castle, and then descended the winding path back to our car, the gunshot forgotten.

Well, perhaps not totally forgotten. Because that moment of alarm always stayed with me. It teased with possibility. What if it hadn't been a farmer, I wondered? What might we have stumbled upon unwittingly? Who was firing the gun? What – or indeed who – was in its sights? Why was the trigger pulled? The setting that afternoon added immeasurably to the potential for drama: the dog day heat, the stillness, the seclusion. And looming over it all was the castle – called 'Glume' before it was Campbell, and set between the valleys of two portentously named burns: 'Care' and 'Sorrow'. It is a dark, implacable ruin; a survivor; a witness to so much over the half-millennium since it was first built.

So perhaps, in some imagined story, it could have been more than just a witness, perhaps it could have had a purpose too. Buildings and places have ways of getting under our skins, of provoking thoughts, memories and feelings – good and bad. If we had to recall all of the major emotional moments of our lives, all of the highs and lows, and were then asked to plot them on a map,

I suspect most of us would be able to do it remarkably easily. *You always remember where you were when...* Buildings don't pull triggers. But perhaps they can trigger people to pull them. Perhaps.

That day at Castle Campbell came back to me when I found myself talking to the co-founder of the Bloody Scotland Crime Writing Festival, Lin Anderson, and its director Bob McDevitt, in the Authors' Yurt at the Edinburgh International Book Festival in August 2016. 'What if?' I asked them. 'What if we asked twelve of Scotland's top crime writers to write short stories inspired by twelve of our most iconic buildings? What would they think? What would they come up with? What could possibly go wrong?'

This book is the answer.

Prepare yourself for a lot going wrong for a lot of people in a lot of ways in a lot of buildings. Prepare yourself for crimes of passion and psychotic compulsion. Prepare yourself for a 1,000-year-old Viking cold-case, a serial killer tormented by visions of ruins old and new, and an 'urbex' love triangle turning fatal. Prepare yourself for structures that both threaten and protect, buildings that commit acts of poetic vengeance or act as brooding accomplices to murder.

Yes, a lot goes wrong. But, of course, a lot goes right too. Because these stories offer a perfect demonstration of the incredible wealth of creative literary talent in Scotland today. Scottish crime writing has carved out a formidable reputation. Our authors can entertain and they can shock. And they are fearless when it comes to tackling many of the issues at the heart of contemporary society, shining lights into some of the darkest corners.

Bloody Scotland, then, is a tribute to two of our nation's greatest assets – our crime writing and our built heritage. Read these stories and, if you haven't already, go out and visit the structures and sites that feature. Seek your own inspiration from the experiences, let your imagination wander – and, just like our writers have done, feel that electric jolt of excitement at all the myriad possibilities that Scotland's places can offer.

But before that, it's time to relax (not too much), settle down (if you can), and steel yourself for the stories that follow. Take a deep breath. And now read the bloody book.

James Crawford
Publisher, Historic Environment Scotland

BLOODY SCOTLAND

Maeshowe

Orkahaugr
Lin Anderson

'Here is a work for poets; Carve the runes
Then be content with silence.'
George Mackay Brown

Orphir, Orkney, the present day
The runes began to dance before his eyes, their cryptic
tree shapes merging branches one with another. Magnus
glanced at the bottle of Highland Park, registering how
much he'd had since settling down to work. Not enough
to affect his vision. More than likely, he decided, it was
the lateness of the hour.

Rising from his desk near the fire, he went to the back
door and stepped outside. The scent in the house had
been of warmth and peat smoke, but out here his strong
sense of smell was besieged by a salty cold and the sharp
tang of seaweed on the nearby beach. As he passed the
sensor, the darkness was punctured suddenly by the
automatic light springing on to illuminate the dark water,
which lapped just short of the top of the grey stone jetty.

The tide's in.

Had the sea been rougher, or the wind stronger, salt
spray would have been splattering the seaward windows
of his home. Built by fishermen below the high water
mark, the two-storey narrow house was reached by a
flagstone walkway from dry land, with the remaining
three sides surrounded by water when the tide came in.

It was like living on a boat without the swell, something Magnus liked.

As he reached the old fish-smoking shed, the light switched itself off. Magnus paused, giving his eyes time to adjust to the night. Gradually, the whale shape of Hoy became visible across Scapa Flow, then the flatter form of the small island of Cava. A crescent moon peeping out from behind a cloud fashioned a silver path across the water towards him.

There were no lights to be seen on Hoy, but looking westwards it appeared a few folk were still up in his own mainland parish of Orphir. Approaching the midwinter solstice, the Orkney archipelago had entered a time of near constant darkness – the sun rose fitfully after nine, hovering no higher than ten degrees above the horizon, only to set six hours later.

Magnus didn't mind the short days and long nights. Born and bred here, he found the dark season strangely comforting. It was during the long summer days when the sun dipped briefly below the horizon, creating what Orcadians called *simmer dim*, that he found sleep evading him, his internal clock urging constant wakefulness and a mad energy.

In his present post as Professor of Criminal Psychology at Strathclyde University he spent less time on the islands than he would have liked. So much further south, Glasgow didn't experience the same extremities of darkness and light, although Magnus preferred the constantly changing sky of Orkney to the often dreich grey blanket that would lay itself over his adopted city. With his lecture timetable completed, he had returned to spend the midwinter festival at home, and was intent on observing the phenomenon of the last rays of the setting sun entering the passageway of the 5,000-year-old chambered cairn known as Maeshowe – something he'd seen only once before as a teenager. It all depended on the weather of course. A cloudy sky at sundown would ruin everything. Luckily the most recent forecast was good, giving Magnus hope that he might experience that magical moment again.

Then his second stroke of good fortune – the images of the runes, delivered earlier today, courtesy of DI Erling Flett, a boyhood friend as well as a local police officer.

'They were etched on a small, part-broken flagstone unearthed by a local farmer between the Stones of Stenness and Maeshowe,' Erling had explained, 'I've handed the stone over to the archaeological folk at the Ness of Brodgar dig, but I took some photographs of the etchings first. Had a sneaking suspicion you might be interested in them...'

Interested had been a mild description of how Magnus had felt at that point. His fascination with Neolithic Orkney had been fashioned in childhood. Although he'd eventually become a forensic psychologist and not an archaeologist, he'd continued to be absorbed by the structures and symbols left by those who had dwelt on the islands. *His islands*.

The burial mound of Maeshowe, or Orkahaugr in Old Norse, contained one of the largest groups of runic inscriptions known in the world. They were the work of the Vikings. Much like present-day graffiti, the words etched on the inside stone walls consisted mostly of blunt and short sentences, like 'Thorfinn wrote these runes' or, a little longer, as though fashioning the beginning of a story: '...these runes on the Western Ocean with the axe that killed Gaukr Trandkill's son in the South of Iceland'.

Some were written by women, suggesting that the raiding parties that had broken into the ancient tombs hadn't always been made up of just men. Although, as was often the case, and in whatever era, the women were wont to be judged, sometimes kindly, sometimes not. 'Ingigerd is the most beautiful of women' boasted one carving and, 'Many a woman has come stooping in here no matter how pompous a person she was' commented another.

But Magnus's favourite was definitely the straight-forward 'Thorni fucked, Helgi carved' – although the official guide tempered the first phrase when explaining the meaning of the runes to visitors.

Shivering in the night air, Magnus went back inside and, pouring himself another dram, sat back down at his desk. He let his brain be consumed again by the puzzle of understanding the marks that someone in the distant past had felt compelled to cut into stone.

Orphir, 1151

Rognvald Kolson stepped onto the stone quay. Already the short northern day was drawing to a close. It had become plain on the journey that his warriors, a mix of Norwegian and Orkneymen, did not like one another. And they would have to winter here before they sailed southwards to find another sea – landlocked, warm, its shores a feast of fruits and treasure.

Rognvald could only hope that the sets of Vikings would not kill one another in the interim.

If they were lucky, the crew might inspire the verses of one or all of the three Icelandic poets he'd brought along. To die young and in battle and be remembered in song and perhaps in mystical runes was surely pref-erable to a straw death*: grey haired, wheezing and choking in some shut bed in one of the many low, poor stone buildings that fought the wind here and in Norway.*

That self-same wind was now driving in from the

north, bringing snow. Pulling his furs closer about him, Rognvald looked forward to his warm lodgings and the food, ale and female flesh that awaited him there. As for his warriors, they would have to find shelter and winter fare for themselves.

'There.' Helgi pointed at a humped shadow in the distance. 'Orkahaugr. That will be our shelter.'

The others didn't argue. No one argued with Helgi, not if they wanted to live. Not least Thorni, the man who was currently allowed to lie with her. Then there was her sister, Freylis. Smaller, lighter, raven-haired. And, like the raven, when her eyes watched you, it was as though they knew of your past, and your future.

As they crossed the strip of land that led to the ring of giant standing stones, the moon emerged from behind a cloud, and their eyes, accustomed to the night, were startled by the sudden creamy brightness that lit their path. Like everything else that happened in their world, they wondered if the moonlight signified that the Gods had chosen to guide their way. Or were the Gods, instead, illuminating the path to their imminent death.

They stood transfixed for a moment, until Helgi's order drove them on towards the burial mound. As they drew closer, the size of it became clear. Surrounded by a ditch and a raised bank, at first glance there appeared no way inside. Helgi seemed unperplexed by this and reminded them that other Vikings had used it for shelter.

Her reminder didn't allay their fears.

They'd heard the tales of hidden treasure, already plundered from this place of the dead. They also knew of the tale of the last group to take refuge here. How the stones had rung with voices. How one warrior had gone mad with the sound, and the others had fled.

Helgi, sensing their reluctance, issued a further order, assuring them that she had been told by Odin that they should shelter here, so that when spring came, they might travel south to where the women and wine were sweet and warm.

Only Freylis stood back as the others crawled into the mound, her eyes fixed on the standing stone near the entrance from where a raven watched.

'Any luck with the inscription?'

'I sat up late with it, but no luck as yet,' Magnus admitted.

'And the plan's still on for later?'

'If the weather holds.'

'I have it on good authority that it will,' Erling assured him.

After determining that Erling would join him at Maeshowe, work permitting, Magnus replenished his coffee and sat down at his laptop to check the Maeshowe webcams. The main one, above the entry passage, looked down on the back wall of the tomb, the second faced west towards the Hoy Hills to give an idea of the weather conditions close to sunset. The third was located in the east chamber looking out towards the entry passage. When the weak winter sun set between those hills, its last rays would touch the top of the solitary Barnhouse stone, after which they would illuminate the low stone passageway that led into the burial mound's central chamber.

A few seconds of light in surely the darkest of places.

Why the architects of these tombs had striven to make this happen, no one knew. Magnus had pondered this as much as others. Maeshowe had undoubtedly been a place of the dead. Perhaps the light that fell within offered the souls that lay there a way to the afterlife. Maybe that line of light simply promised that winter would be replaced by spring – a symbol of renewal and rebirth.

It seemed every stone structure had been given its place for a reason.

But what about this latest find?

Daylight, however weak, offered a different view of the etchings. His jottings from last night were scattered about the desk. Magnus drew them together. Of the words he'd attempted to decipher, there was only one of which he felt certain. And that word was *death*.

The darkness, like liquid, flowed about and within her. The others had taken to the side chambers, but Freylis had chosen to lie near the entrance. Helgi had tried to order them to reseal the opening with the flagstone, but Freylis had resisted her command, offering instead to be their guard. Seeing her younger sister's fierce expression, Helgi had wisely agreed, then, summoning Thorni, had climbed into the nearest of the three side chambers. Freylis could hear them even now, Thorni grunting his pleasure while Helgi urged him on.

Freylis crawled back along the stone passage, until the sounds of their lovemaking were blanketed by the walls. From here she could see a little of the sky, clear now and scattered with stars. She knew that Thorni had no choice but to do as he was bid, but it didn't make it any easier to listen to. Freylis was aware that her sister had chosen the tall Viking because he had first appeared interested in Freylis. As Shieldmaiden and leader, Helgi had to be seen to take what she wanted. If not, her place would be usurped – and swiftly.

And she believes I may be the one to do that, *Freylis thought.*

The noises had ceased, to be replaced by snores. Freylis continued her way along the passage. Emerging into the cold, sharp night, she rose, axe in hand, to find the raven awaiting her, its eyes bright with certainty.

Magnus noted the raven on his way to the car. Perched on the porch roof as though awaiting his exit, it cawed loudly when he appeared. He knew much about the raven's place in Norse mythology. How Odin was often pictured with a *hrafn* – a raven – on each shoulder. Called Huginn and Muninn, they were dispatched each day, their task being to bring back news of hanged men and those slain in battle.

As a boy Magnus had been both fascinated and scared by such stories. He had always disliked, even feared, ravens – for their sharp looks, for the way they'd watch you while they picked at the flesh of some dead animal. 'Do you know what you call a group of ravens?' his grandmother had once asked him. 'An unkindness.' They were thought to signify that something unpleasant or evil was about to happen. Orkney folk history was full of such tales, where the appearance of a raven on the roof of a crofthouse, or one seen flying into the west, was a portent of sudden death.

As he drew away from the house, Magnus watched in his rear view mirror as the bird followed him briefly, before winging its way skywards.

Driving towards Maeshowe, Magnus noted how clear the sky was, how still the air. From the road, Scapa Flow appeared as smooth as a mirror. It looked as though Erling's forecast was right, provided it lasted until sunset.

He arrived at the parking spot at Tormiston Mill, but there was no sign of Erling's police car. *Must have got stuck at the station*, he thought. His friend could always watch it on the webcam – but it would be a poor substitute. The light was already fading. Magnus walked quickly in the direction of the large grassy mound.

Despite the starry sky, Freylis felt the soft touch of snowflakes on her face. She was cold and would be better off inside, but still she waited, her back against the upright stone, in the hope that Thorni would appear to wrap his furs about her. So often he had come to her after lying with Helgi. On the ship sailing here and before at home in Norway. But they hadn't been careful enough, she thought. Surely Helgi had sensed Thorni's desire for her sister and had sought to thwart it.

Freylis fingered her axe, its blade so sharp it could cut stone. The raven had gone, or its inky blackness had melted into the night. Its presence here could, she acknowledged, have been the eyes of Odin watching over her. Or a signal of impending death. Freylis wasn't afraid to die, in fact she would welcome it, provided it happened in battle. She, like the others, wanted her story told in poem and song and in the runes.

At that thought, an idea came to her.

The stone she leaned against had a smaller partner which lay flat in the earth before it. Crouching, Freylis began to score its surface with her axe.

The mound looked deserted as Magnus approached. He hadn't expected to be alone to view the sunset, but he wasn't complaining. Usually it was visitors to the island who showed the deepest interest in the spectacle. Orkney folk had lived with it all their lives.

Glancing to the west, Magnus registered the weak sun approaching the horizon. Despite the clear sky over the hills of Hoy, he felt something white and wet touch his cheek. Turning east, his heart sank as he spotted a dark mass on the eastern horizon.

Snow.

His watch told him it was ten minutes until sunset, still time surely before the bank of cloud swept in? Further flakes began to appear, tossed this way and that in what was definitely a rising wind. Swearing under his breath, Magnus ducked and entered the long low passageway.

Emerging into the main chamber, he was swallowed by darkness. Using the light of his mobile, he made his way to the back wall and settled down to await the arrival of the final rays of light.

She had chosen to fashion a raven, with rough lines for feathers, a sharp beak and one eye side-on. Freylis had always felt an affinity with ravens, perhaps because of her own dark colouring, or the keenness of her eye, even in poor light. And like the bird, she could read what people were thinking and anticipate what they might do, which was as good as knowing the future. It was a skill that had kept her alive until now.

But my sister isn't easy to read, *she thought.* Helgi does what is expected of her as a Shieldmaiden, but I do not know her thoughts.

A faint sound from within the mound caused Freylis to pause and shift position, her axe hand ready. She caught his scent before she saw him and her heart upped its beat. Emerging from the passageway Thorni rose, tall and broad against the sky. Freylis watched as he sought her scent and, finding it, he turned in her direction. As he approached, Freylis rose from behind the stone to greet him.

Magnus glanced at his watch again. Surely it was close to, if not already past, sunset. Yet no line of light crept from the blackness of the passageway. The snow clouds must have reached the west in time to cover the setting sun, he thought. There was no point in staying there in the dark. Disappointed, he made to rise. As he did so, he was startled by a smell – not of the cold stone of the mound, but of a human.

Was someone in here with him?

Magnus swung his mobile's light round the main chamber. It was empty, although the smell was growing stronger. Standing motionless, he focused entirely on the odour, attempting to analyse it. There was no hint of decomposition. Though pungent it came, he was sure, from a living, perspiring human being. Then he caught something else. Sharply metallic, like fresh blood. Disturbed, Magnus made for the first of the side chambers, persuaded that someone was in there and that they might be hurt.

As he did so, the sounds began. Strange, eerie, resonant. Magnus had read all about the unique acoustic properties of Maeshowe. A chanter or drum being played in the main chamber might be swallowed by silence, yet the noise it made could suddenly appear from one of the side chambers. But that wasn't what was happening now. Rustling and breathing sounds surrounded him. Magnus knew that he was among people. Sleeping people.

Were his sense of smell and the acoustics playing tricks on him in the dark? He felt like a boy again, flinching at the sight of a raven. He wanted to leave. He directed his mobile's torch at the entrance passage. But it was no longer open. Instead, it was partly covered by a large flagstone.

Their eyes met. Freylis didn't step forward, waiting instead for Thorni to come to her. And come he did, enveloping her in a bear-like grip, crushing her to his chest. As heat flowed from his body to her own, Freylis realised how cold she had been.

She was glad of his body and his warmth, registering too that he either desired her, or his earlier desire for her sister had not yet abated.

'Hrafn,' he whispered into her hair. 'It is done.'

As he drew her down behind the stone sentinel, Freylis laid down her axe.

Magnus manoeuvred the flagstone back, perplexed by how it had got into that position in the first place. As cold air flooded in from the passageway, he took a deep breath, ridding himself of the scent of blood and sweat. Emerging into the night, he was surprised to see that the sky was clear again and filled with stars, the snow clouds gone. His mobile's light gave out on his way back to the car, despite the fact that he'd charged the battery fully before leaving home.

As his eyes grew accustomed to the night, he stopped, turned round and looked back to the mound. According to his watch he'd been in there for almost two hours.

'What just happened?' Magnus asked himself aloud as he started his car. Time, he knew, could evaporate when he was working, or when he sat outside watching the waters of Scapa Flow. Had he spent that long trying to analyse what he was hearing inside the mound? What he'd smelt in there? There were stories of people losing their sense of reality when visiting such structures. The burial mound had been built to house the dead, their dark isolation being the first step into the afterlife. So why had he heard and smelt life inside the tomb?

As he drew out into the road, something hit his windscreen with a thump, causing him to swerve. He immediately thought of a gull, but there had been no flash of white. Magnus braked and, drawing into the side of the road, got out to see what he'd struck.

He had to walk backwards to find the body. The raven lay dead, its glassy eye staring up at him. Something in that pose told Magnus what he'd been striving to see the previous night.

Freylis gazed up at the starlit sky. She was growing cold again. She could feel the heat that Thorni had brought, seeping out of her body. She thought of his eyes hard on hers, his warm wet touch on her lips. He had loved her, but love had not been enough. She watched as Thorni walked away, back down the passage to the tomb. When winter was over, he would go south to the sun, where the women and wine were sweet and warm. Would Helgi go with him? Or was she, too, destined to stay on these islands? Her hand reached out, seeking the hard handle of her axe. Her strength was ebbing quickly, but she would finish what she had started. She would tell what had happened.

Magnus laid the sheet of paper alongside the photograph, fitting it to the broken edge of the flagstone. On it he'd drawn what he believed were the missing letters and the remainder of the rough sketch.

Now seeing it complete, Magnus sat back, a wave of emotion washing over him. He was looking at a gravestone.

The word preceding 'death' was surely *Hrafn*. The name that followed was *Thorni*. And the drawing, side on, with its one eye staring out at him, was a raven.

The Hermit's Castle

Ancient and Modern
Val McDermid

Alan asked me to marry him right here, on the edge of the cliff. There was a glorious sunset at his back, smudged bars of scarlet and gold and bruised plum, the colours reflected in the ruffled surface of the gunmetal sea. I couldn't see his face because of the radiance behind him and I wondered what he was up to, getting down on one knee on the uneven rock. I thought he'd dropped something. But the next thing I knew was, 'Ellie, will you do me the honour of being my bride?'

I only hesitated because my mouth was too busy grinning. 'You bet,' I yelped. Then I yanked him to his feet and squeezed him so tight his breath exploded in a loud, 'Oof!'

Of course, I never told Colin any of that.

Serendipity. The dictionary defines it as the 'occurrence of events by chance in a happy or beneficial way'. And serendipity was what brought us to this place.

Our summer holiday that year was a cycling tour of the North West Highlands. We'd driven up from our home in Manchester with the bikes mounted on the back of the car. We left the car in Ullapool and set off. We'd spent weeks planning our routes, poring over maps on the living room table, googling points of interest on the way, deciding on the youth hostels and B&Bs we'd stay in overnight. We'd given the bikes a thorough service and worked out the absolute minimum of packing. We were good at that; it wouldn't be the first time I'd cycled up a hill with a pair of pants pegged across the top of a pannier, drying in the sun.

We were blessed with one of those spells of good weather that makes people agree that if only you could guarantee the sunshine, nobody would ever bother with going abroad. It's a sentiment that resonates even more these days. When I was a kid, Scottish holidays were as memorable for the awfulness of the food as they were for the depressing frequency of the rain. Apart from the glorious fish and chips bought from busy counters in tiny shop fronts filled with the reek of hot fat, mealtimes were an ordeal.

Not these days. That holiday, Alan and I ate like kings. From the dirt-cheap local lobster and chips in a pub in the middle of nowhere to the millionaire tiffin we picked up from a stall at a village market, we stuffed ourselves with food that brought smiles to our faces. Just as well we were cycling long hours every day or we'd both have come home the size of houses.

That afternoon, we'd fetched up in Lochinver, a village in Sutherland that straggles along the shores of a three-legged inlet of the loch that shares its name. For a small place, it's got a lot of options where you can spend your money. Pubs, restaurants, a bookshop, a pottery, a couple of galleries. And an award-winning pie shop – which, as far as we were concerned, meant no contest. I chose pork, chorizo and manchego; Alan went for savoury lamb, on condition we swapped halfway through. We were always good at sharing.

We ate sitting on a bench in the sun, our eyes feasting on a stunning view of twinkling blue water and dramatic rocky shores. Our silence was companionable; although we'd been together for just under five years at that point, we always had plenty to say to each other. We saw a pair of ravens circling and swooping above the rocky point. 'You don't get that in Cheadle,' Alan said.

I laughed. 'You don't get any of this in Cheadle.'

Pies finished, we set off on the last four miles of that day's route. We were booked in for the night at the youth hostel in a tiny hamlet called Achmelvich at the end of a twisting, undulating single-track road. It was hard work in the sunshine, but when we reached our destination, we knew it had been worth every straining turn of the pedals. Achmelvich consisted of a scant handful of croft cottages, the youth hostel and a caravan site. Plus one of the most spectacularly lovely beaches we'd ever seen. We were too early to check in to the hostel so we locked up our bikes and headed for the sea.

We breasted a low line of dunes then white sand spread before us between the two rocky arms of the bay. The sea glittered in the afternoon light and the soft whisper of waves grew to a gentle shush as we walked down to the water's edge. We walked the length of the bay, rapt. At the far end, a rocky outcrop was hunched above the sand. I could imagine the fun kids would have clambering over it, seeing it as a castle or a pirate ship. But, this afternoon, we were the only people around. For the time being, it was our private beach. I couldn't help saying a small prayer of thanks for so special a moment.

At the end of the bay was a gate that led to the caravan site. Alan checked the map and we saw that beyond it lay a headland we could clamber over to look out across the sea towards the Hebrides. There was still plenty of time before we could settle in at the hostel so we set off across the rocks. 'Lewissian gneiss,' Alan panted scrambling up an awkward incline. He always knew stuff like that. He was the best man to have on a pub quiz team if you wanted to scoop the rolling jackpot. We had friends who brought him in as a ringer for just those occasions. Mind, as a result there were some pubs in South Manchester we couldn't go back to…

There were patches of bog between the rock escarpments and I swear the sheep were laughing at us as we unerringly picked the most awkward route across the rocks, drawn on by the sparkling promise of the sea ahead.

Then we crested a shoulder of the hillside and both stopped in our tracks. Ahead of us, on the edge of the cliff above a steep-banked inlet in the promontory was something so unexpected I wondered if I was hallucinating it. But a quick glance at Alan's face told me he could see it too.

A miniature fortress, geometric concrete shapes apparently growing out of the rock, topped with what looked like a periscope facing out to sea. There were small square holes in the concrete walls, blank eyes that my imagination filled with gun barrels pointing our way. It was completely incongruous, straight lines against the irregular humps and bumps and treacherous slopes of the rocks.

'What the hell is that?' I said.

'I've no idea.' Alan unfolded the map again. 'There's nothing marked on the map. And I didn't see anything about it when we were checking out our route.'

'Let's take a look.' We descended slowly, fascinated

by the sight. I almost missed my footing a couple of times on the way down, so intent was I on our destination. I didn't want to take my eyes off it in case it vanished like Brigadoon.

As we grew closer, it grew less ominous. It was about nine or ten feet tall, and the holes looked as if they'd once held glass bricks. The concrete had been mixed with shells and pebbles from a small shingle beach we could see twenty or so feet below, which added to the camouflage effect of grey concrete in a grey and black and green landscape. From the landward side, there was no obvious entrance, but we could see where a path had been worn round the far corner.

Alan was a couple of steps ahead of me and he called, 'Careful, it's really narrow here, you could easily slip and fall.'

I saw what he meant when I followed him round the corner. The path was barely wide enough to plant my feet side by side. When I looked up, I saw a narrow doorway leading inside the building. Alan had already disappeared inside. The doorway gave on to a narrow passageway that curved round like a snail shell. It was a tight squeeze then suddenly there was a wooden lintel and I was inside a tiny chamber like a monk's cell. 'Wow,' I said, turning around, taking it all in.

Not that there was much to take in. A concrete bed platform with a low lip, just deep enough for a heavy-duty sleeping mat. A fireplace like an oven with pigeonholes alongside it and a ledge, presumably for firewood. Though where you'd find firewood in an area so exposed – there were no nearby trees – I had no idea.

'That thing that looks like a periscope? It's the chimney. It's got a right angle bend at the end to stop the smoke blowing straight back down. That's very clever.' Alan was a builder specialising in sustainable homes; he knew about things like that. 'And that entrance, it's the same thing. Curving round like that means the wind can't blow straight in either.' He nodded, pursing his lips approvingly. 'Very impressive.'

All the same, there was no glass in the windows, no signs of occupation. Nothing except a graffiti tag sprayed across one wall. Not even beer cans and used condoms, which there would have been if this extraordinary structure had been in Cheadle.

'It'd be hard living here. No running water. Not even a nearby stream. You'd have to carry all your water in with you.'

'Or come in by boat.' I pointed in the direction of the shingle beach. 'You could bring a little boat right up to the shore there. It's not that far.'

Alan laughed. 'Humping water thirty feet up the hillside? Rather you than me. And there's no sanitation.'

'There's the sea.'

He laughed. 'It's not the Med, Ellie. It's the Atlantic. It'd freeze your bits and tits off eleven months of the year.' Then he moved closer and pulled me into an embrace. 'Nice and private though,' he muttered between kisses. Then he pulled away and headed back outside. 'Soon be time to get into the hostel,' he said. 'And then we can maybe find out what the hell this is.'

I followed more slowly. I felt a strange attraction to the concrete pillbox on the end of the point. Who had built it? And why? And how come it seemed to be a secret from map-makers and tour guide writers alike?

The hostel was surprisingly quiet, considering the weather. There were three geology students from Edinburgh up to climb Suilven and the three Corbetts of Quinag; a quartet of German bikers; and couple of sinewy cyclists doing the North Coast 500, a gruelling ride that we'd decided was more pain than pleasure. We'd bought some smoked fish, onions and potatoes in Lochinver earlier and made a basic fish stew, followed by a couple of rhubarb and apple pies from the pie shop.

Later, we sat on a bench outside with a view of the beach and lured the warden to join us with the half-bottle of Talisker we'd brought with us. He was a big bear of a man in his mid-thirties, shaggy of hair and beard, dressed in a plaid shirt, khaki cargo shorts and a pair of battered work boots. His arms were covered in colourful tattoos in complicated Celtic designs. His name was Martin, and he'd moved up from Tyneside to run the hostel, which seemed to me to be pretty close to the perfect job.

After we got past the preliminaries, I asked the question we really wanted the answer to. 'We walked out to the point this afternoon,' I began. 'What on earth is that concrete pillbox doing out there?'

Martin chuckled. 'So you found the Hermit's Castle?'

'Is that what it's called? What's it for? Who built it?'

'Both good questions. To be honest, the answers are a bit unsatisfactory. But here's how the story goes.' He shuffled around on the bench so he could see us better. 'Back in the early 1950s, a young man arrived here in Achmelvich. An architect from Norwich and, by all accounts, he'd run away from his life because he was having some sort of breakdown.' Clearly, this was not the first time Martin had told his tale. He'd eased into it with all the comfortable familiarity of a favourite armchair.

'He didn't have much to do with the locals. He bought a little open boat down in Lochinver with an outboard motor. And he started buying bags of cement as well as the usual stuff that campers go for – bread, eggs, fish, tea, milk. He had a three-gallon drum of water that he filled up at the fishing pier. And wood. Apparently he bought some fishing boxes from one of the trawlers.'

'Did people not wonder what he was up to?'

Martin shrugged. 'Back then, a lot of the land round here was owned by the kind of absentee landlord who employed people to do all kinds of nonsense. So if they thought about it at all, they just assumed it was another one of the laird's stupid carry-ons. And because he was going in and out by boat, none of the locals really saw anything. You can't see the thing till you're right on top of it. He was camping out there in a tent, out of sight and out of mind.' He chuckled. 'Not just his own mind.'

'I can't believe nobody was curious about what he was up to,' Alan said.

Martin shook his head. 'What you've got to remember, man, is that up here back then, it was like the middle ages. It was virtually feudal. The laird was the law and it didn't do to question him. So if a man wasn't causing any bother, best to leave well alone. So your man, he made his frames out of wood from the fish boxes and he cast his concrete and he built his little castle. It took him the best part of six months.' He paused for dramatic effect.

I let him have his moment then said, 'Then what?'

'He slept in it one night, then he went back to Norwich and never came back.'

'I told you,' Alan said. 'No sanitation. The fatal flaw.'

'Or maybe he was cured,' I suggested. 'It was therapy and it worked. He knew he could face the world again.' Then something struck me. 'If he didn't tell people what he was doing, how did they know what he'd done? And that he'd gone home?'

Martin smiled. 'Most people don't ask. I wondered that myself when I first heard the story, but actually the answer's the least interesting part. He sold the boat back to the fisherman he'd bought it from in the first place. He told him what he'd done and how he was heading back to Norwich to pick up where he left off.'

'You'd have thought he'd have come back,' Alan said. 'Just to see what had happened to it.'

Martin finished his dram and set the glass down on the bench. 'For all we know, he might have done. He might have come back and stayed in this very youth hostel and hiked out to the point to check it out. But if he did, he never let on to anybody round here. Serious walkers and wild campers sometimes use it as a bothy. Who knows? He might have done that for old times' sake.' He stood up and stretched. 'Now I've got my chores to get done before I can call it a day.'

'What time do you lock up?' Alan asked.

'It's supposed to be ten o'clock, but I don't generally bother till getting on for midnight. It stays light so late at this time of year, it seems daft.'

'So if we went out to the point to watch the sunset, we'd still be able to get back in?'

Martin grinned. 'Some nights I don't bother locking up at all. It's not like we're a hotbed of crime out here. Whatever time you come back, it's canny.'

So we hiked back out to the point, our path lit by a sunset whose colours ranged dramatically from violet to lemon yellow, shifting with every passing minute, splashing random shades on the rocks and the sea and the etiolated fronds of cloud that drifted lazily across the sky. It was a remarkable show. If we'd filmed it, nobody would have believed it wasn't artificially enhanced.

We sat for a while on the hillside above the Hermit's Castle, then we walked down. Close up, I could see that there were dozens of little shells incorporated in the concrete. Although it was such an oddity, this geometric outcropping among gneiss that had been shaped and scoured by millennia of weather and wear, the pebbles and shells gave it an unexpected organic connection to the landscape. It was an extraordinary thing to have imagined and then conjured into being, but in a funny kind way it felt as if it belonged here. Even more oddly, I felt a connection to it too.

So, although I was genuinely gobsmacked when Alan got down on one knee and asked me to marry him, it seemed curiously appropriate. When I pulled him to his feet and hugged him tight, I'd never been more at home anywhere on earth. We melted into each other's embrace and without discussing it or thinking about it, we slipped inside the Hermit's Castle and fell on each other with an urgency that took no account of hard surfaces or tight corners.

When we surfaced, panting and exhausted, we realised we were losing the light. We hurried back across the treacherously uneven rocks before the dimming of the day made it too perilous to consider. As we walked back up the track to the hostel, we held hands in a tight grip. Something had shifted in our relationship, moving the intensity up a gear. We both knew without the need for words that we'd sealed something out there at the Hermit's Castle. Something that would last a lifetime.

I never told Colin any of that either.

* * *

Who knew that a lifetime would be so short?

We never even managed the wedding. Eleven months after the night at the Hermit's Castle, Alan was dead. He was cycling to work, at a site a couple of miles from our home, down the busy A56 near Old Trafford. It's a complicated and confusing series of junctions, and a van driver realised at the last minute he was in the wrong place so he cut across two lanes of traffic without warning. Brakes screeched, horns blared, but Alan was on the far side of those two lanes, unsighted by a people carrier and he kept going. The van ploughed into him, mangling man and bike, and sliding sideways into a bus shelter.

When the paramedics arrived a startlingly short time later, there was nothing for them to do except pronounce life extinct. For a long time afterwards, I felt my life had gone the same way. Alan was the love of my life. I know it's a cliché but it's also the truth. We shared a sense of humour, an outlook on the world, a common set of values. Our tastes in films and music and books overlapped, but there was enough leeway for each of us to have our own personal preferences that we indulged on our own or with friends. We weren't joined at the hip but there was never a day apart that we wouldn't rather have spent in each other's company.

After he died, bleakness descended on me like a blanket. Not one of those soft snuggly baby blue ones; the rough, prickly grey kind that makes your skin itch. All that kept me going for those first few months was the prospect of the trial. I lived for the day when the man who had destroyed our future would stand in the dock and face the consequences of his recklessness. The police officer I spoke to about making a victim impact statement said that on a charge of causing death by dangerous driving there was a maximum sentence of fourteen years in jail but in this case it would probably be more like eight or nine years. It wasn't a fair exchange for what I'd lost but I decided that I could live with that. So I opted not to make a personal statement because I couldn't face going through everything I'd lost. Not with a stranger.

If I'd known how things would turn out, I'd have poured my heart out on the page and screamed it out in court like a demented fishwife. But I didn't know, and I didn't speak, and maybe things would have been different if I had.

Probably not, though.

The first time I saw Colin was in court. I was sitting near the back of the public gallery. Friends had warned me about the way the press would focus in on me and I didn't want to be on show for them. Where I was sitting, it would be an effort for them to turn and stare at me and I thought the judge wouldn't stand for that. So I was sitting anonymously by myself when they led him into the dock.

It was a shock to see him in the flesh. He didn't look like the photo in the local paper. They'd snatched it on his front step when he opened the door to them, and he'd looked unshaven and bleary, like a man struggling to negotiate a major hangover and failing by a mile. Today, though, he was a man scrubbed up for a night out. Clean shaven; eyes bright and free from dark shadows, unlike mine; dark hair freshly barbered and sleek as a seal's; collar and tie and a suit still pressed from the dry cleaners. He looked more like someone who worked for the legal system than someone who was about to be nailed by it.

Shock enough, you'd think. But there was more to come. And from the least expected direction. The prosecution barrister stood up and told the court that the defendant had agreed to plead guilty to the lesser charge of causing death by careless or inconsiderate driving. In the light of the guilty plea, he went on, he urged the court to sentence him to no more than two years imprisonment.

What had happened to the trial I'd been promised? What had happened to eight or nine years? It made no sense to me. I felt faint and my ears were ringing so loudly I barely heard the judge hand down 18 months in jail and a two-year driving ban. I felt physically sick and I could barely stand after he'd been led away.

Outside the courtroom, I spotted the policeman I'd spoken to about my victim statement. 'What just happened in there?' I stammered. 'That's not what you told me to expect.'

He had the grace to look ashamed, the colour rising up his neck and in to his cheeks. 'I didn't know myself till this morning. His barrister came to the CPS with the offer of a deal. Saves a trial, and that saves money.' His words were bitter and he shook his head, his eyes following the prosecutor as he swept along the hall without a backward glance. 'And that lot can never resist a result they don't have to work for.'

My legs gave way then, and only the strong arms of the policeman saved me from crashing to the marble floor. He steered me to a bench and sat with me while I tried to make sense of what had happened. The life of the man I loved had been bartered away for next to nothing, for the convenience of the court. Nobody gave a damn about Alan. What was the death of one good man weighed against saving the system a few quid?

The next time I saw Colin was almost a year later, spotting for a gym bunny doing bench presses. Ten months in a low security jail didn't seem to have caused him much grief. He'd bulked out through the shoulders and the legs from working out in the prison gym and, I guessed, in his cell. According to my friendly police liaison officer, Colin had walked straight into his job at the gym when he walked out of jail because his uncle was the franchise owner.

I signed up for a year's membership. I was willing to play the long game. I didn't think there was any chance of Colin recognising me. Since the trial and the handful of blurred photos in the press, I'd had my hair cut; I'd had laser surgery so I didn't need glasses any more; and I'd lost so much weight I'd had to buy a whole new wardrobe. Grief seems to take you one of two ways. Alan's sister went in for comfort eating and ballooned three stone. I lost all interest in food and only ate because the alternative was falling over.

I chose Colin to perform my gym induction and set my exercise regime. I didn't flirt. I forced myself to talk to him in a relaxed and friendly way. Deferred to his knowledge and admired his skills. Over the next three months, I found excuses to talk to him about my programme, my goals and my achievements. Gradually, we became more friendly, both of us telling only part of the truth about ourselves. Both lying, though for very different reasons.

In the fourth month, having established his taste for *The 1975*, I turned up at the gym with a pair of tickets for a gig in Leeds later that week. 'I was going with my pal Denise but her mum's gone into hospital and she's had to go back to Stoke to take care of her dad,' I said. 'Then I remembered you saying you like them, and I wondered if you wanted the spare ticket?'

Of course he did. He even offered to drive us over the Pennines for our night out.

I won't pretend it was easy to go through with it. There wasn't a moment when I let go the knowledge that I was with the man who had taken Alan from me. At one point I had to go to the loo and throw up, I was so disgusted with myself for being there with him. But I had a plan. The long game. Whatever it took.

And six months later, there I was in the North West Highlands again. Not a cycling holiday this time. No, we were driving round, Colin and me. Taking our time, staying in B&Bs, going for walks. My flesh still crept when he touched me but I was used to it by then and I could fake it better than any BAFTA-toting actress.

One night we stayed in Ullapool. Fish and chips and a walk along the harbour. Whisky nightcaps in a busy bar. Then up the next morning and a walk up towards the Falls of Kirkcaig. We didn't go all the way; Colin was plagued by the midges and anyway, in spite of the muscles and the gym, he wasn't really that fit when it came to beasting up hills.

We'd booked in at the Culag Hotel in Lochinver, but I suggested a drive up to Achmelvich. 'There's an amazing building right out on the point. It's only a short walk out of the village but you'd never know it's there.' And I told him the story. 'I went there once with a friend of mine, years ago. I'd love to show it to you.'

Colin grumbled a bit, and my heart was in my mouth in case he refused. But he gave in. Appropriately, it was another spectacular sky that greeted us when we got out of the car, but this time it wasn't glorious colours but dramatic storm clouds rolling in. 'Are you sure about this?' he said. 'It looks like it's going to chuck it down.'

'That's miles away out at sea,' I reassured him. 'We'll be there and back before the first spit of rain.'

We scrambled over the rocks. I led the way; I remembered it so well from before. Colin trailed behind, occasionally muttering when he planted his foot in a suck of bog, or slipped on a treacherous piece of rock. And then we crested the final hillock and there it was. The Hermit's Castle.

'Wow,' he said.

Thank goodness, I thought.

We scrambled down and I pointed out the shells and pebbles embedded in the concrete.

'Amazing,' he said.

We rounded the corner of the building, heading for the doorway. I let Colin go ahead of me and just at the narrowest part of the path, I called his name. He half-turned, awkward in the narrow space. I swung my arm back and smashed him in the side of the head with the sharp-edged chunk of stone I'd picked up on the beach at Ullapool.

I saw the blood on his temple and the shock in his eyes as he staggered, his arms windmilling helplessly. A small push in the chest was all it took to finish the job. He tumbled backwards down the cliff, head first, bouncing off the unforgiving ancient Lewissian gneiss. He didn't even cry out.

I peered over the edge. He was sprawled at the water's edge, his head half-submerged. I'd checked the tide tables and I knew the high tide would cover him within the hour. I settled down to wait, my back against the unyielding concrete of the Hermit's Castle, watching the storm come ever closer.

In spite of its modernity, it inhabits a primitive place, a place of rock and water. Modern justice failed me, so

I reverted to the primitive kind. 'Thou shalt give life for life, eye for eye, tooth for tooth, hand for hand, foot for foot, burning for burning, wound for wound, stripe for stripe.' Amen to that, Colin.

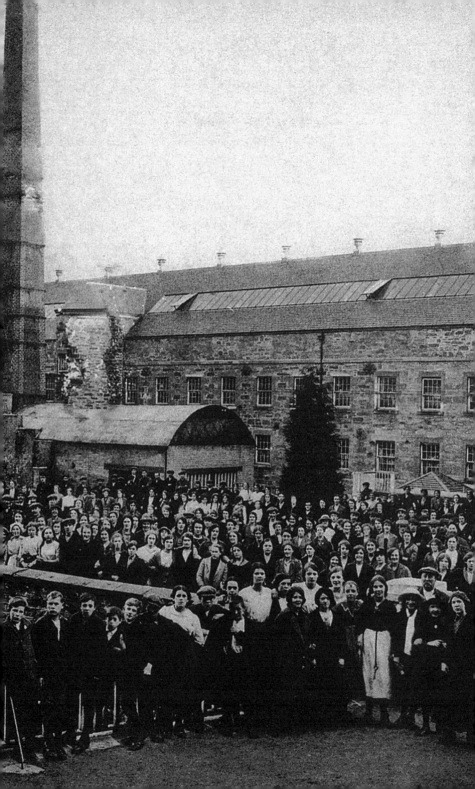

Stanley Mills

Kissing the Shuttle
E S Thomson

When I was six years old my father showed me the tunnel cut through the rock. 'Your great grandfather built this,' he said. 'He spoke only the language of the islands, but he knew what was being asked of him when they put a shovel in his hand and sent him down into the earth.' I watched the water racing out of the dark hole. It was black – not clear, like water should be – black and cold as the ground it had surged through. 'Black with the souls of the men who died digging it', my father used to say, 'and as cold as Mackenzie's heart. There's never been a foreman at Stanley as cold and hard as John Mackenzie.' By the time I was seventeen my father's hatred had solidified into something as unyielding as the stones on the hillside, and as capricious as the river.

From the foot of the brae, at the gate to the mills, we could watch the Tay rushing past. Unstoppable, slate-grey, tumbling around the peninsula as the land fell away, swollen with the rain that poured from the skies and the water that drained off the land. By the time it reached us at Stanley, it had coursed all the way from the southern Highlands, through the lochs and glens some of us had once called home, and it raced and boiled as though filled with all the rage and sorrow of those lands. A narrow curving weir, built out into the flood, scooped up an armful of the Tay and hurled it into the tunnel my great grandfather and his fellow workers had sliced through the rock. As my father and I walked across the yard from the workshops, we heard Mr Mackenzie telling the factory inspector about it as they stood outside the Mid Mill. My father made me stop, and pretended to adjust the burden I carried so that he might listen.

'Yes,' said Mr Mackenzie, 'the Duke of Atholl dug the tunnel right through from the falls up at Campsie Linn – brick-lined all the way. The Tay drops twenty-one feet as it passes around the headland. The waters are harnessed to power the wheels that drive the mills here at Stanley.'

'The Duke of Atholl didn't dig anything,' said my father.

Fortunately Mr Mackenzie didn't hear. The inspector looked uninterested. It was the buildings that concerned him, the buildings and the machines inside, not the mill lades and the river – though we would not have one without the other. He blew a breath into the wintry air and watched it bloom before him.

'Does it freeze?' he said. 'The mill lade? What happens then?'

'Sometimes it does,' said Mr Mackenzie. He shrugged. 'Then we go curling on it.'

The water in the lades was as smooth as a mourning band by the time it reached the mills, a shining ribbon of silk tamed by the flat bottom of its brick-lined bed as it curved behind the low buildings of the North Range. Giant black cogs and studded wooden gates drew it to a halt before the wheel pits. Sometimes, in the summer, we saw the silver flash of a trapped trout glistening in the dark pool at the sluice gates. My father caught one once. He killed it with a stone. It was a pale and fleshy thing in his hands, a reminder of what happened up at the top of the Mid Mill. I had to look away.

The lades passed under the road and into the wheel pits – two beside the Bell Mill and two beside the East Mill. A boy died down in the water, right beneath the windows where I worked, crushed and drowned while helping to fix a broken bucket on the East Mill's wheel. 'Should've been Mackenzie,' my father had said. 'It was him who sent the lad down there. For two pins I'd hold *him* under the water.'

'Jenny McRae said John Mackenzie was in Glasgow all week,' I'd said. '*He* didn't send Tom Rennie into the wheel pit, it was Tom Rennie's da' –.'

'Should've been Mackenzie. He's the foreman. He's responsible. Should be him drowned down there.' He'd not looked at me. 'Jenny McRae said so, did she? Well, well.'

I'd thought of Mr Mackenzie drowned and floating face down as the wheels turned above him, his head pulped by the blows of the metal-edged buckets. Perhaps things *would* be better if he was dead – my father seemed to think so. I'd peeped into the wheel pits. It was hard to imagine that they had not always been there, those great curving slopes of wet stone, slime-green and slippery, dripping and dark as the giant wooden blades that swept over them. They drove the gears that worked the machines crammed into the hulking buildings – including those that my father tended, for he was over-looker to nearly one hundred looms on the top floor of the Mid Mill. Two of those looms were mine, and I worked them every day from half past five in the morning until seven at night. Five floors beneath our feet the water ran and ran. I could feel its power and fury in the thrum of the belts that drove the shuttles on our looms back and forth with a vicious clack and rattle. After that, it escaped beneath the mill and back into the Tay. But I could never escape. Not from him. None of us could.

The Mid Mill was only recently re-opened. Destroyed by fire – as is often the case with mills, so my father said – it had taken two years to put it right again, though Mr Buchanan, the owner, said it would take more than a few flames to put *him* out of business. Mr Mackenzie insisted that a water tank be fitted on the roof of the Bell Mill, the building that ran adjacent to ours, so that fires could be attended to quickly and efficiently with the necessary resources to hand. I heard him laughing with the inspector about it.

'Yes,' he said, 'despite the greatest river in the kingdom flowing right around our ankles, it seems that a good part of the Mid Mill still managed to burn down.'

My father heard him too. 'I doubt whether Isobel Douglas and Jean Reid are laughing, for they both lost sons to the blaze,' and he scowled at Mr Mackenzie, who didn't notice as he was pointing to the new brick-built water tank.

The factory inspector shaded his eyes as he peered up, and then dropped his gaze to watch the wheels turning. I could tell at a glance that they were running sluggish. It had been raining for days and there was every likelihood that the river would back right up into the wheel pits and prevent the wheels from turning altogether. The inspector, who had no doubt seen hundreds of water wheels, seemed to be thinking the same. 'How many days' production do you lose a year?' he asked.

'It varies,' said Mr Mackenzie. 'Sometimes thirty, sometimes fifty.'

'Unfortunate,' said the inspector.

'For who?' muttered my father. 'It makes a change to get a day off.'

'But we get don't paid when the water stops the mills,' I said.

'Hm,' said my father. 'No doubt we have Mackenzie to thank for *that* state of affairs too.'

In fact, I'd heard that Mr Mackenzie had told Mr Buchanan that we *should* be paid when the wheels wouldn't turn, as it was hardly our fault if the rain came down and the Tay rose up, and it was no less than Mr Dale or Mr Owen would have done when they'd run the place, no matter how long ago *that* was. I opened my mouth to say as much – but Mr Mackenzie caught my eye, and I closed it again.

'Well, well, Tam McGregor,' he addressed my father. 'Don't you have work to do? Take that stuff inside.' He never said much – not to my father, at least. My father said it was because John Mackenzie didn't have the courage for a fight. It seemed to me that it was probably because my father only sneered at Mr Mackenzie when he was out of earshot. *I'm twice the man he is*, he used to say to anyone who would listen – apart from Mr Mackenzie himself. *If I'd had his opportunities, his luck, I'd be something better than a miserable foreman like him.* Now, he tugged his cap, his face stony at so public a rebuke, and stalked into our building. Resentment seemed to boil inside him like hot treacle whether Mr Mackenzie spoke to him or not. The McGregors had always been weavers, he had often told me, though not in big places like Stanley. He said weavers were once respectable people, skilled people with money and status, not children and barely competent young women like me. But that was before the mills came. Before men like Mackenzie, whose only talent, he said, was ordering people about.

Mr Mackenzie took the factory inspector by the elbow and led him away, his head bent towards the other man's ear, his hand over his mouth. Even though we were outside, the noise of the place filled the air with a constant clatter. They were now too far away to overhear, but I saw him glance at my father. Perhaps he was saying that he had not been the same since my mother had left. That had been years ago now.

'Come along then, Annie!' my father cried. 'Don't stand there gawkin'!'

I followed him inside.

Our building – the Mid Mill – was built along the riverbank, and was as tall and wide as a barracks. Our closeness to the water kept everything damp, which was good for the cotton, though in summer the sun blasted its southern face, so that the rooms with the carding engines and the spinning machines were raging hot, and we had to open the windows wide to catch any breeze. The north side lay in perpetual shadow. At the base of the mill, the wheels turned in their dark and shaded pits. Above them row upon row of windows stared in blank indifference. No one looked out. The windows were there to let the light in or the heat out, not to allow our gazes to stray from our work. In the roof, the line of north lights that ran from east to west told where we toiled over our looms, beneath bright but sunless skies so that we might easily see any imperfections in the cloth. My father fixed the looms and kept them running smoothly. There were others housed in low sheds behind the East Mill, but I was not lucky enough to work there.

Within, the noise of the place was like a blow to the head. When I had first started work as a weaver, when I was ten years old, I thought it might be possible to touch the sound with my fingers, for it had felt like a physical, tangible presence. But I had got used to it quickly enough, and now I hardly noticed the air trembling and the walls ringing with the din of wheels and gears turning belts and shafts, and machines rumbling and rattling. Once, years ago, Elspeth McInnes got her hair caught in the shuttle. A great bloody hank of her scalp and hair was torn out, though we didn't hear her screams because of the noise. At Stanley Mills, on the weaving floor, no one's screams could be heard.

We were allowed home for lunch – we could not take our piece and jam at our machines – and then streamed back to work, down the brae from the village and into the mills. I ran up the stairs with the other girls. My father would already be at the door, where he stationed himself every morning and every afternoon, watching the women file in after breakfast or lunch, noting which of them was the last to arrive. He treated me no differently, and he took me away from my machines the same as he took anyone else. When the others realised this, they had looked at me pityingly, though they said nothing. Now, we hung up our bonnets and stood before our looms. I saw that Jeanie Gilchrist was late again. He'd make her pay for it – but only when Mr Mackenzie wasn't looking. And yet perhaps she would not suffer today, for had I not been with him when Mr Mackenzie had told him to get back to work? I had heard the reproach and I had seen my father's face as it was uttered – though it was no less than he deserved. I knew him better than anyone, and I knew how he would slake his sense of inferiority, and his anger, and I felt my stomach knot inside me at the thought.

Later, on the way back from the privy, I met Mr Mackenzie on the stairs. This time he was alone.

'How are you keeping, Annie McGregor?' he said. His voice was mild and soft. Even though there was no one around to listen to us he brought his face as close as a lover's to my ear so that I might hear him above the noise. And yet he had no need to do so, for I could read his lips well enough. We all could read lips, there was no conversation to be had otherwise.

'I'm very well, sir,' I said.

'Are you crying, child?'

I said I was not, that it was just the air full of cotton dust that made my eyes water. He nodded. 'I think you have just come from your father,' he said.

'No,' I replied, perhaps a little too quickly, for he smiled grimly and said 'No?' in a questioning way, as if he didn't believe me. He offered me his handkerchief.

'It was made a long way from here,' he said. 'I'm afraid we produce nothing so fine at Stanley.'

But we were paid by the piece and I had already been away from my looms for too long.

'Mr Mackenzie,' I said, using the backs of my hands rather than his handkerchief to wipe my eyes, 'please let me get back.'

'You tell that father of yours I'm watching him,' he said, suddenly stern.

'Yes, Mr Mackenzie,' I said. But I knew I would say no such thing, for no one could be watched all the time.

The Mills were constantly changing. My father said that when he was a boy there had been only one water wheel. Now there were four. Some years earlier, when he had taken over the place, Mr Buchanan had ordered a North Mill to be built, enclosing the wheel pits and the gas works in a dark cramped square bounded on all sides by the tall mill buildings. Not ten years later he had torn the North Mill down, so that only stumps of stone jutting from the East Mill told where it had once stood. The lades were always needing repairs, for the winter weather caused cracks to appear and the stonework to rupture. The flues that heated the buildings, drawing hot air upwards from fireplaces in the lowest levels of the mills, had to be maintained too, and the bearings in the wheel pits replaced whenever they became worn and caused the wheels to shift. That winter, the stonework in the pit beside the Bell Mill had shattered due to the force of the water and the constant turning motion, and it had thrown the wheel off-kilter. The grinding of it against the masonry was terrible to hear, and the broken stones were to be replaced with wood. I heard Mr Mackenzie complain about the size of the task and the difficulty of working in the slippery wheel pits in the cold weather, but it could not be helped. Other jobs were to be tackled at the same time – one of the flues in the north wall of the Mid Mill needed work. It had been blocked off years ago at the top, and the fireplace at the bottom bricked up. But the old flue had become prone to damp, and a great dark patch had appeared on the plasterwork near the looms. Now, workmen had torn a hole in the wall revealing part of the flue behind the brickwork. Its blackened lining was exposed against the whitewash on the weaving floor like a dark and angry sore. My father complained that it wouldn't do to have a great sooty hole like that beside a working loom, even though Mr Mackenzie said he would cover the hole with canvas sheeting, and promised to seal it up as soon as the work was done. 'It won't take longer than a day, two at the most,' he said.

'Smoke smuts won't come out at the bleach works,' said my father.

'Then stop the looms,' replied Mr Mackenzie. 'Stop these ones close by and cover them up.'

'But the women are paid by the piece,' said my father. 'They will have nothing for two days.'

'That cannot be helped,' said Mr Mackenzie, in front of all the women. '*They* can thank you for the stoppage.

And *I'll* thank you to remember who's the foreman, Tam McGregor, for it isn't you.'

My father halted the looms, as he had been instructed, and went about his business with a furious face. Those girls whose machines were silent found other work about the mill that day, and they smiled as they left for the weaving sheds beyond the East Mill. My father's knuckles turned white as he gripped his hammer. The stoppage of half a dozen looms near to the open flue made no difference at all to the din of the room, and the roar and clatter of the place seemed to burl and buffet us, as if we were surrounded by the whirling fury of his rage and resentment.

There was plenty for my father to do. Two of the looms kept sticking, and a third needed its reeds replaced. The leather straps on some of the older machines were in a poor state of repair, worn and soft-looking as they thwacked the shuttle back and forth, and he had promised to replace them weeks ago. One of the stopped looms had been troublesome for a while, and he might just as well have opened it up while he had the chance and fixed that too – but he didn't. Instead, he watched the men working on the flue, shaking his head as they made the hole even bigger to allow them to re-block the chimney, and in no time at all it was as wide as a fireplace and as tall as a man. When they disappeared down to the workshops to get some new bricks to block up the hole, he went over and jabbed at their work, loosening what they had done so that some of it fell out and spilled all over the floor. He took to pacing amongst us, then, criticising our work and stopping machines here and there on the most flimsy of pretexts, making us wait while he pretended to fix something, before starting our machines up again. And all the while I saw his lips muttering and cursing. We kept our eyes on our work as he stalked up and down, for we knew what was coming.

He chose Mary Golspie that day – the youngest at only fifteen years old – and he took her, as he always did, into the store room that overlooked the wheel pits in the shadowy corner of the East and Mid Mills. Not two months ago they had found a body down there, floating in the water, for the river was so high in December that the corpse had not drifted out beneath the building into the Tay. It was Mary Golspie's older sister. Mr Mackenzie had told the Fiscal and her family that she must have slipped, and banged her head as she fell, making it impossible for her to cry out, for she was no doubt dead before she even hit the water. He said she had surely died quickly, and without pain. He said this so that she might be buried properly, and with dignity, but all of us in the weaving room knew what had really happened. We all knew that Jane had worked alongside Mary, that she had been a pretty girl, that both her parents were dead, and that she had been one of my father's favourites. We also knew that she had killed herself in fear and desperation at my father's tyranny. John Mackenzie knew it too, I was sure, though he said nothing.

At first my father used to make excuses – some fault or other in the mechanism of the loom that needed it to be stopped, and then he would take the girl into the store room to find 'a spare part'. If a girl objected, then he took her anyway, but he would let her machine run and run until the thread broke and the weave was spoiled, and so she took twice as long to catch up once she came back. Flora Campbell had resisted him forcefully at first, and had almost lost her job because of it. But every one of us needed to work, and there seemed nothing we could do to stop him. Latterly, he had given up stopping our looms, finding us more compliant if we were threatened with the destruction of our work and the fouling of the loom – a situation that we alone would be blamed for. We lived and worked in fear of him, and he knew it.

And so he took us away: whoever he wanted, whenever he wished. No one could hear what happened in the store room, half-hidden amongst bales of cotton. The roar of the machines blotted out all cries, and we were deaf to anything but the crack of a hundred shuttles being smacked through the warp, the turning of the drive belts and the quick, rhythmic *lift-and-drop-and-lift-and-drop-and-lift-and-drop* of the loom reeds. But we knew what he did. All of us knew. We knew that he would stuff the girl's mouth with a piece of fabric woven on one of our own looms; that he would bind her hands with a strip of cotton, and grease himself with the same whale fat he used on the machines so that he might hurt her in ways she would never dare to describe. And if we complained? No one would listen – we were women, after all, and of little value to anyone if we did not keep up our work. Besides, none of us ever got pregnant; that was not his way, he was far too clever – and far too brutal – for that.

The others looked down at their work, their faces impassive, as Mary was led away. The girls nearest to me looked over to catch my eye – but I was no different to them, I knew what happened in there as much as they, and I had no words to say in his defence. How could I? My father had done the same to me. They hated him, of course they did, but not as much as I.

Mary Golspie wept as she walked back to her loom. I saw two droplets of blood on the floor where she had passed by, scarlet and thick and as big as pennies, smeared by the hem of her trailing skirts. My father stood and looked out at us with his hands on his hips, and he smiled. And then all at once he was no longer standing there at all. I heard nothing because of the noise, but I saw him jerk suddenly, half spin around and then fall sideways, collapsing onto the floor with his arms and legs awry. Three of us, who had seen him drop, stopped our machines and rushed over to where he lay – and then we stood still. I held out my hands to keep the others near me, taking their fingers in my own as we looked down so that they would not touch him, would not show him any compassion. We did not stoop, or kneel at his side, but just stood there, staring down. None of us spoke. None of us could have been heard if we had, for the belts and the drive shafts kept turning overhead, the floor kept trembling beneath our bare feet, the echo from the walls hard and flinty with the clatter of the pickers striking against the metal-tipped shuttles over and over again. Beside him, on the wooden floor polished smooth by machine oil and the passing back and forth of so many feet, lay one such shuttle, six inches in length and bloody at the end. The side of his face – the cheek below his right eye socket – was bleeding; the skin sliced open to expose the bone beneath in a gash of white and crimson. The lips of the wound seemed to have drawn back, pulling it open like an obscene second mouth.

It was uncommon, if the machines were well-cared for, for such an accident to happen, but a sloppy overseer deserved what he got. It was not the first time the shuttle had flown out of the loom when the leather strap that bound the picker had snapped, though it was the first time that it had found its mark. We watched as the blood leaked from his face into the floor. Was he dead? Perhaps the white stuff I could see was brain as well as bone. And yet, would the blood flow so profusely if he *was* dead? I was sure it would not. And then I noticed a pulse throbbing in his neck and I knew he was no more dead than I, and I felt a terrible sense of injustice welling up inside me – how close we had come to being liberated!

Were we meant to call Mr Mackenzie and have our persecutor taken up to the infirmary? He would be back amongst us in little more than a week and what, if anything, would have changed for the better? Had the shuttle been but two inches higher, I thought, it would have plunged into his eye, perhaps into his brain, killing him instantly. Beside me, I saw my father's blood mixing with a splash of little Mary Golspie's. Some of the others noticed it too, and I saw their faces darken.

It was not long before the men returned from the workshop. They brought with them a truckle of wet cement and some new bricks, and they laboured as fast as they could so that they might get out of the place and away from the dementing racket of the looms. They asked where my father was, mouthing the words as if I were deaf. I shrugged that I did not know.

When I walked home that night, back up the brae to the village, I was wearing my father's boots under my skirt. No one noticed. Later, I went out and I threw them into the Tay.

The next day, the men came back to plaster the wall. By the following morning when the plaster had dried, and been whitewashed, there was no evidence that there had ever been a hole there. Mr Mackenzie came up to look at the job. He ran his hand over the plasterwork and inspected his fingers, and seemed satisfied enough. He looked out of the window at the wheel pits, and at the men swarming about down below, at the lifting gear that had been brought in and the carts and horses standing around. The inspector was waiting over by the gate house, scribbling in his notebook. There were plenty of things for a foreman to fret about, trying to keep the mills as productive as possible while one of the wheels was not working, and I saw his shoulders lift and fall as he sighed. He turned to me.

'Where's your father?' he mouthed.

'I don't know, Mr Mackenzie,' I replied.

'Perhaps someone's bricked him up inside this wall.' He grinned. 'I'd be tempted, if I were you.'

I smiled, as I was supposed to, and watched him walk away. How simple he made it sound! And yet it had taken six of us to do it, six of us working in silence as the looms roared and rattled around us: six of us to bind his hands and feet and stuff his mouth with rags, to clean up his blood and force him into the derelict flue. Our fingers were quick with his bindings – had we not spent our lives knotting and tying? We could truss him as fast as we could thread any shuttle. But then we had struggled, for his shoulders would hardly fit and his knees bent and wedged tightly against the bricks, his boots catching on the stonework so that eventually I had torn them off and tossed them aside. We had stuffed bricks and rags in after him, filling the hole as the workmen had done, mopping the blood from the floor with old sacks and pushing them up there, before stepping away to admire our handiwork. We were afraid of being caught, very afraid, for what would become of us if we were found out, even those who had helped only with their silence? But what was done was done.

And so we waited: would he move his knees and ankles and slip back down? Would the workmen look up and see the soles of his feet protruding from the stuff we had rammed in after him? We had no sleep until the hole was bricked up and its scar painted over. I wondered, sometimes, what he had thought when he awoke in that dark confined space, tightly bound and gagged, with the stink of blood and whale grease in his nostrils from the shuttle, and the pain of where we had pushed it. Did he die screaming? No one heard him if he did.

The Forth Bridge

Painting the Forth Bridge
Doug Johnstone

He was already awake when he heard the rush of the 6:20 heading south. Checked his bedside clock. On time. The first trains of the day were usually on time unless the weather was bad, it was the later ones that slipped, work on the line or technical faults. He lay in bed and listened to the whoosh of the approach resolving into the click-clack of wheels on rails as the train headed away.

He waited. Looked at the clock. Anticipated. Were the sounds already reaching his ears from the other direction but too quiet to hear? At what point could you say that you heard something? Then he was sure. 6:27, the first train north, bang on time. He tried to pick out the rhythmic clack, some order in the chaos. Angled his head and felt the gristle in his neck grind. But it was only once it had passed that the sound resolved again, clarity replacing the inchoate grumble.

He thought about the people on those trains, each with their own life, heading into a new day. Sometimes it overwhelmed him, the billions of stories going on in the world that he wasn't part of. Suddenly being confronted by all those people could be shocking.

Especially recently, since he didn't go out so much. But that was going to change today.

He pulled back the covers and placed his feet on the cold laminate. It was a big day. When you waited for something for so long, it was hard to believe when it finally arrived.

He squinted as he turned onto Battery Road and took in the view. The Albert Hotel to his right and beyond it the two road bridges, the new one almost built, suspension cables like a spray of needles slicing the sky. Already the traffic on the nearer road bridge was thrumming, a calm sound in the distance, almost indistinguishable from the shush of waves on the stony beach in front of him.

But looming over everything here was the Forth Bridge to his left, the colossal, blood-red lattice of struts and supports, cantilevers and spans. He loved the vocabulary of the bridge, had learned it when he was on one of the painting crews a few years back. He smiled at that whole cliché about painting the Forth Bridge. People used it as shorthand for a thankless, never-ending task, but it was never true that they started at one end as soon as they finished the other. In reality, some areas needed more patching up than others. Actually, that was a better metaphor for life. And anyway, that super-durable paint they used last time meant they wouldn't need to do it again for twenty years.

He walked down the road as it curved under the bridge, gulls cawing overhead, briny air stinging his nose. The monstrous tubular supports were overwhelming from underneath, the sun blinking through riveted steel girders and panels. He was glad they weren't painting it any more, it was nice to see the bridge without the bandages of scaffolding that shrouded the main spans for so long.

A rumble overhead, heading south. He checked his watch. The 8:28 on time. Annie would be on her way to school in Abbeyhill now. He pictured her in the navy blue uniform, her multi-coloured backpack, swinging her lunchbox. He hadn't seen her in a while, wondered if she still preferred culottes. She was strong-willed, didn't go for skirts or dresses, he liked that. He pictured her walking round the back of Meadowbank, crossing London Road with her mum, heading to school. But then he thought about Carol, and Derek, and the flat the three of them shared on Marionville, and he shook his head.

He stopped at the Private Road sign and looked at the Network Rail portacabins. A couple of workers in orange hi-vis suits and white helmets were smoking outside on the dirt track, about to begin their maintenance shift up top. They got up there by a discrete scaffolding staircase hidden round the side of the stone support for the northern approach viaduct, either that or the rusty old hoist on the leg of the north span, depending where they were needed. These guys were real engineers, not like him, just a handyman. He hadn't been able to hold down work, with one thing and another, for five years. Of course that had been the start of all the trouble.

He came out of his dwam and checked his watch. Time to move. He walked back along Battery Road, glancing at the sign for St James Chapel. There was no chapel left, just a tiny padlocked graveyard with half a dozen ramshackle stones. He saw the block in the crumbling wall with the carved message:

THIS IS DONE BY THE SAILERS
ON NORTH FERRIE, 1752.

But the first 'R' in Ferrie had eroded and looked more like an 'A'. He imagined a place called North Fearie.

He began up The Brae, six minutes to the train station at the top of the hill. The road zigzagged past an ancient spring with an old plaque and he stopped before the bend to take in the view. The three giant cantilevers and suspended spans were like squatting Buddhas holding hands, his own wee flat on Helen Place in amongst the jumble of old and new roofs cowering below. The bridge created a communal spirit in North Queensferry, they all lived in its shadow and felt pride towards it, as if they were its guardians.

An icy wind swept down the platform. It reminded him of being on the painting crew, the 50 mph gales hurling down the Forth at them, whole work days lost to the weather.

He looked past the other platform to the playground of North Queensferry Primary, a square Victorian building with a good reputation. Annie would love it. The kids were lining up waiting to go in, flashes of maroon jumpers and cardigans among the winter coats. He would need to sort uniform for Annie, but she could wear whatever she had for now.

He stared at the mosaic on platform two, depicting the bridge and the town in looping, abstract shapes, made to celebrate the bridge's centenary. He walked to the end of the platform nearest the bridge. There were four warning signs pinned to a board, no access, safety briefings needed and so on. Then finally:

Passengers must not cross the line.
Warning.
Do not trespass on the Railway.
Penalty £1000.

He looked at the concrete by his feet. There was no line to cross.

From here the bridge was end-on and looked like nothing much, maybe just a monument to some forgotten hero. A long intercity came thudding from that direction, the sun behind making him shield his eyes. The train powered through the station without stopping, heading for Perth and beyond. He caught a glimpse of a family at one table, spread out with snacks and comics, parents smiling, a boy Annie's age peering out at the blur of life.

Just as the train disappeared into the tunnel to the north, his own train trundled out and eased to a stop.

He shoved his hands in his pockets, scuttled down the platform and got on.

He was too agitated to enjoy the view from the bridge, buzzed about what was coming. He stared at the island of Inchgarvie between the flicker of the bridge struts, the tanker terminal beyond, a woman walking her dog on the sand at Whitehouse Bay. Three minutes and they were already slowing down for Dalmeny. It was never long enough.

After Dalmeny they ran through fields and passed a tree nursery, saplings stiffened by supports. He thought of when Annie was born, holding her in his arms at the hospital, a full head of hair already, blinking at him, red-faced and wrinkled.

The track skirted the back of the airport. A Flybe twin-prop swung in low from left to right. For a moment it looked as if it was on a collision course with the front carriage, but it was just an optical illusion. He heard the roar as the plane disappeared above the train then re-appeared, wobbling as the wheels touched tarmac. He thought about the people on board, where they came from, where they were going. More peopleshock.

He breathed deeply and got his phone out. Checked the time as they came into Edinburgh Gateway. Scrolled through and called Carol. Voicemail. He hung up. He had his phone set so that his number was withheld. She would work it out, but by then it would hopefully be too late. But he needed to make sure she was in the Monday morning sales meeting as usual otherwise this wouldn't work. Her not answering was perfect.

Past the Jenners Depository and the alien mothership of Murrayfield then into Haymarket, the train busier now. They slipped into the tunnel and waited under the rock of the city for a signal. He felt trapped for a moment, did that breathing thing he'd practised, tried to feel his heart slow down, and the train bumped forward into Waverley Station.

Looked at his watch. Twenty-four minutes since he got on at North Queensferry.

He strode out the Market Street exit and onto the Royal Mile, heading east down Canongate through the tourists. This walk should take twenty minutes but he had to weave onto the road around a gang of teenage Italians with backpacks, then a Nordic family in water-proofs and headbands. This would be slower on the way back with Annie. Maybe best to get a taxi if he could, just in case. He'd tried to think things through but you always had to allow for contingencies.

Past Holyrood Palace and round Abbeyhill, the garage on the left and the railway over a barbed wire fence to his right. It always amazed him about Edinburgh, two minutes round the corner from a palace and you were surrounded by rundown flats and a crappy concrete playground for a crumbling school. No fit place for his daughter.

The knot in his chest tightened. He swallowed twice, his mouth dry, kept walking. Confidence was key. Be positive and confident and others will go along with you no matter what.

Annie would be in class, still a while until morning break.

He pushed the button on the old door, put on a smile, breathed.

He was buzzed in and strode to reception as if he knew what he was doing.

An obese woman wearing a home-knitted cardigan and a Help For Heroes badge frowned at him.

'I'm here to pick up Annie Stevens in 3A for a doctor's appointment,' he said.

'And you are?'

He looked quizzical as if the question was redundant.

'I'm Ross, her dad.'

Heroes looked at a sheet of paper on her desk. 'I don't have a note of it.'

Ross shook his head. 'My wife was supposed to phone first thing.'

Heroes looked again at the sheet then back at him. She held his gaze for a long time. He felt his palms itch but didn't move to touch them. He was smiling but had been holding it so long it felt like a grimace.

'So will I just pop up and get her from class?' he said.

'It's normally Annie's mum we deal with.'

'Carol was supposed to phone you. I thought it was

arranged. You know what it's like getting out the house in the morning.'

An older boy with his hair gelled was passing, and Heroes watched him until he was nearly through the double doors to the right.

'Nathan?' she said, making him turn. 'Can you pop up to Mr Ireland's class and tell him Annie's dad's here to take her to the doctor?'

Ross waited at reception, felt Heroes' gaze on him, scuffed his toe against the old linoleum, threw a confident smile her way once or twice. He resisted the temptation to look at his watch. He stared at an anti-bullying poster, a cartoon block of cheese and carton of milk talking to each other. He didn't understand it.

The double doors swished open and there she was, already older and taller than last time he'd seen her. How did time slip away? Her blonde hair was in a tidy pleat, Carol's work, something he'd never mastered. She was wearing a skirt.

She had a look of confusion when she came through the doors, replaced by a smile when she saw him.

'Daddy.'

She hurried into a hug. He squeezed her but let her go, it couldn't look as if they hadn't seen each other in months, this had to seem like an everyday thing.

'Hi, honey,' he said, touching the top of her head. 'Come on.'

He guided her so that his body was between her and Heroes, so that she couldn't get a proper look. He turned to Heroes and beamed.

'Thank you.'

She watched him with narrow eyes.

He pushed the door, imagining her picking up the phone and calling Carol at work.

Good luck, she'll be in that meeting most of the morning.

'Taxi.'

He was lucky, a black cab rattled down Abbey Mount just as they reached it. It was a sign, everything was going to be OK.

'But I don't understand,' Annie said as they got in.

He spoke to the driver. 'Waverley, please.'

Then he turned to her. 'Put your seatbelt on.'

He leaned over, helping her insert the latch in the buckle. The skin of her hand was so smooth, a tactile memory jabbed him, holding that hand on the first day of school, trying to keep his emotions from his face so that she wouldn't worry at being deserted.

That bond had been taken away by Carol, by this Derek guy, by the courts. But not any more, bonds can be repaired, strengthened, just look at the bridge, over a hundred years old and stronger than ever.

'I was a bit naughty,' he said, smiling. 'We're not going to the doctor, we're going on an adventure.'

Annie smiled. 'With Mummy and Derek?'

'No, this is a Daddy day.'

The edge came off her smile but she still looked like she trusted him.

He resisted the urge to ask about Derek. At least she wasn't calling him Dad.

The taxi rumbled up the Royal Mile. It would've been quicker to go along Calton Road and in the back way but Ross hadn't specified. He was about to suggest nipping down New Street but he saw it was one way now. When did that happen? Why did nothing stay the same?

They sat at the lights by the White Horse, engine throbbing.

'Where are we going?' Annie said.

'We're going on a train,' he said. 'Won't that be fun?'

'Oh.'

His stomach lurched at her tone. Something came to him.

'Then we're going to Deep Sea World. You've been before, remember?'

Annie frowned. What was memory like for a seven-year-old? He'd been fascinated by that watching her grow, how you could guide kids to remember things a certain way. They had a picture of Annie as a baby on the mantelpiece of their old place, eating her first solid food, a mess of green mush around her mouth and hands. Annie had seen it every day, then after a while had claimed to remember the photograph being taken, though she was only six months old at the time. If only adult memories were so easily manipulated.

He wondered if Carol was turning her against him. Judging by Annie's welcome at the school she was still on side, but that wouldn't last forever. Eventually she would take her mum's side. He couldn't allow that, couldn't let the relationship with his own daughter be tainted.

'What's Deep Sea World?'

The taxi had turned along Jeffrey Street, almost there.

'They've got all sorts of great stuff. Weird fish, seals and massive sharks. You go through a tunnel and there's sharks all around you.'

She frowned. 'You're in the water with them?'

The taxi pulled up outside the Fruitmarket Gallery next to Waverley. He got money out and handed it over.

'No, darling, it's safe. I'll look after you.'

He checked his phone. Nothing. So far so good.

The train cu-chunked along the track heading out of

town. The same graffiti and building sites he'd stared at on the way in, but this time everything seemed sharper, had an edge to it.

Annie burped. Fizzy juice was a treat, something Carol frowned at, so the Irn Bru was going down a storm.

'Look, Dad.'

She held up a hand with Hula Hoops on each finger, then began sucking them into her mouth.

He looked down at his wedding ring. He presumed Carol didn't wear hers any more.

He tried to remember the chain of events that had brought him here but it was like staring at the sun, you couldn't look straight or it hurt. After the painting job he'd tried to find work but it drained him, life drained him, one damn thing after another, and the arguments with Carol about money and motivation turned to arguments about bigger things, their feelings for each other. She claimed he was abusive but he'd never laid a hand on her, he wasn't that kind of man. Psychological abuse, she called it, and the courts agreed, they always side with the mother. The deal they cut for visiting rights wasn't fair, so when he'd tried to see Annie more often he was accused of stalking, harassment. How could you stalk your own daughter? He just wanted to spend time with her, be part of her life.

He felt his phone vibrate in his pocket.

It had started.

By Edinburgh Gateway he had eleven missed calls.

He didn't take his phone out of his pocket, what was the point? He knew it was Carol, and maybe the authorities too. The police. He was disappointed that they'd found out so soon but it couldn't be helped. If he got his phone out he was giving his time over to their shit when he should be spending time with his daughter.

He looked around the carriage. An elderly couple with their coats still on, sharing a flask of tea. Two gangly teenage boys with headphones, tapping on laptops. A balding, saggy guy in a suit with paperwork spread over the table in front of him, marking passages with a green highlighter. A backpacker couple staring out at the airport runway and the brown fields beyond. Just people living their lives without interference, without the hassle and stress of an ex-wife calling every two minutes.

He focused on Annie, ignored the buzzing against his leg.

'Let's play a game,' he said.

Annie smiled. 'I Spy.'

'OK, you go first.'

The train shuffled north picking up speed, now free from the buildings of the city, surrounded by patches of trees and muddy grass.

'I spy with my little eye, something beginning with "p",' Annie said.

He frowned theatrically and looking around him.

'People.'

Annie's smile grew as she shook her head. 'No.'

'Potatoes.'

'Where are potatoes?'

'In that field, maybe.'

She shook her head.

His mind churned over. Pain, passion, prosecutor, parent. Police. He looked around the carriage but nothing had changed.

'It's easy,' Annie said, running the vowels out long and teasing.

He wanted to capture this moment, take his phone

out and snap a picture of her smiling, the sun lighting her face, the two of them off to live new lives together, heading into the future as a family. His phone buzzed again and again in his pocket.

But you couldn't capture moments, they were already gone. Annie's whole life so far, seven years of moments accumulating to crush him. There was no such thing as quality time, just time, just being with your children to see them grow up. And that had been taken away from him.

He shook his head. 'I give up.'

Annie's eyes widened as she pointed at the sky. 'It's plane, Daddy. So easy.'

He shook his head and smiled.

Capture this moment in your mind, Ross.

Sunlight flickered across the carriage as they passed a copse of silver birch, then they began slowing for Dalmeny.

He tried to breathe as normally as he could, and let the smile fall from his face because it was beginning to feel forced.

The train's deceleration didn't help, he wanted to be speeding away from here. They were so close to the bridge he could sense it. Once they made it over the firth they would be safe. He remembered night shifts on the painting crew, the camaraderie despite the cold and dark, holding on to the feeling that the bridge would look after them, protect them from harm.

He tried to focus his thoughts as the train stopped.

He looked at a spread of newly-built family homes, the station car park full of commuters' cars, everyone living their happy family lives.

A middle-aged couple got on and sat at the table opposite. The man had a drinker's skin, the woman a smoker's cough.

'Look, Daddy,' Annie said, pointing out of the window behind him. 'Policemen.'

He turned and saw a flash of uniform at the other end of the platform. He pressed his face against the window, saw officers shuffling up the steps.

'Fuck.'

The couple looked at him and Annie then frowned at each other.

The train jolted forward, easing along the tracks, heading north.

'Did they get on?' he said to Annie.

She looked confused.

'I couldn't see,' he said. 'Annie, did the police get on the train?'

Her face fell at the tone of his voice. 'I don't know.'

'Are you OK?' said the drinker across the aisle. He directed it at Ross but then lingered a look at Annie.

'We're fine, thanks.'

Ross stared at Annie for a long time, worried that she might start crying. He looked both ways along the carriage then stood up.

'Come on.' He took her hand and pulled her out of her seat.

'Where are we going?'

'I'll tell you in a minute.' He pushed her ahead of him down the carriage, not looking back.

The train was on the southern approach viaduct now, the land dropping away either side. South Queensferry was down below, the jetty where the *Maid of the Forth* was moored, the Hawes Inn and the Railbridge Bistro on the seafront.

The rhythm of the train was steady, slow going over the bridge. Sunlight glinted off lorries on the road bridge like trout in a stream.

He glanced back down the carriage as they reached the end. Tried to see into the carriage behind. Thought he caught a glimpse of uniform. He stared a moment longer, saw a police radio in a hand, heads bobbing as they made their way up the carriage.

'Shit.'

'Daddy.'

How had they found him so quickly?

He pushed the button to open the door then stood in the end of the carriage outside the toilet. He looked back. The police had entered the carriage they'd just left and were talking to Drinker and Smoker.

He ducked back round the corner and stared out of the window. The walkway zipped by, then one of the maroon bothies. The mesh of struts and supports flickered past, making him dizzy.

He pulled the emergency cord.

The wind hit them first. Out here over the water a hundred and fifty feet below, it was like being whipped in the face.

He huddled Annie to him as he strode north along the walkway. His steps thudded on the patched-up concrete, reverberating up his legs, and he imagined those vibrations spreading all around, through the handrails to the trusses and girders, as if he was a single entity with the bridge, one vibrating being.

He saw the gulls below on Inchgarvie. When he worked on the bridge a peregrine falcon had nested on the southern cantilever, and he remembered once watching as it dived to take a pigeon out of the air below him. He wondered if its nest was still there, if it still patrolled these skies.

He heard voices from behind. He glanced back. Three

police officers were running along the walkway in his direction.

He looked at Annie. She had tears in her eyes and snot bubbling from her nose. No wonder she was scared, being chased by the police.

He picked her up and pressed her to his chest. He heard her breath catch. She was facing backwards, looking over his shoulder at the police officers, but that couldn't be helped.

He passed the midpoint of the bridge, came out the second cantilever onto the last suspended span. He was closer to the north end than the south now, closer to the future than the past.

He saw movement up ahead and wondered if it was a train. But as he ran on the motion resolved itself into four more police officers coming from the northern viaduct. These weren't like the plodders behind him, they were armed, tasers, handguns and one with a rifle.

And behind them, Carol. Even from this distance he could see she was still beautiful, still strong. Her hair was cut in a bob and she'd lost weight, she looked good in her business suit even though she was running in heels. You could tell what sort of character someone was by how they reacted to difficult circumstances. She was grace under pressure.

He thought about the scaffolding staircase hidden behind the viaduct support. The officers were in the way. The hoist on this span was closer but there was still no way he would make it. In the old days they used to have trapdoors that came up from the maintenance level underneath the track, but health and safety saw them all bolted shut years ago.

'Daddy.'

'It's OK, sweetheart, I've got you.'

He jumped onto the track and clambered over the rails, one set then the other, then up onto the other walkway, using a hand to steady himself. The police from both sides followed across the rails then approached along the walkway from either side.

Nowhere to go.

The sound of Annie crying and snorting in his ear was horrible. If only they'd left the two of them alone. The weight of her was hurting his arms, making his back ache, she was too big to carry any more. She used to love it as a toddler, following him around the house with her arms out, pleading for him to sweep her up, hold her close to his heart.

Carol pushed past one of the officers who cursed at her. She never did what she was told.

'Ross, my God,' she said.

He suddenly couldn't picture how he came to be on the bridge, as if his memory had been wiped. He tried to think back through the morning but it was all fog.

'You look good, Carol.'

She held her hands out. 'Give her to me, please.'

Annie lifted her head. 'Mummy.'

She struggled in his arms but he managed to hold her. When did she get so strong? She would soon be a sulking teenager, then an independent young woman, then she would pick a husband who wasn't good enough for her, then she would be a mother of her own. How to explain all that, how to express it.

'How's Derek?' he said.

'Put her down.'

Carol's face was puffy with tears, the skin on her neck flushed when she was upset, all the things about her he recognised so well. And the same with Annie, the mole on her shoulder, the patch of eczema behind her knee that flared up in winter, the way she went cross-eyed when she wanted to act daft. All that knowledge would be lost one day.

He looked behind Carol at the police marksman. He couldn't get a clear shot with Annie's head next to his. He saw the other officers, waiting, like he'd paused the world. No one could go on with their lives until he gave permission.

He turned and looked down at the water. Grey and sludgy, a shimmering sliver where the sun caught it. The vast expanse of it heading out of the firth was too much to comprehend. He looked over the railing. There was a clear way down, a slim gap between the crossed bars and ties.

He turned back to Carol.

'I'm sorry,' he said.

The marksman took a step closer, steadied himself.

'Ross,' Carol said. 'Please.'

He heard something. A familiar rush of noise. He looked behind Carol and saw an intercity coming along the track heading south. He tried to think what time it was, picture the timetable. The 10:42, running a few minutes late.

Annie shoved against his ribs, pushing her body away from his.

'Daddy, put me down.'

He stared at her for a long time, his eyes wide, trying to take in every detail of her, the sinew in her neck, the stray hairs falling from her pleat, the missing baby tooth on the right.

He looked again at Carol, then beyond.

Then he put Annie down. She ran to her mum.

He watched them together for a moment. Then he looked around at the bridge, the solidity of it, the reliable order of its shapes and structure stretching in each direction forever. He looked at the water below, then at the marksman still aiming at his head, then the approaching train.

He closed his eyes and listened as the rush of the train's engine grew louder. He tried to hear the rhythm of the wheels, tried to get a sense of its connection with the bridge, but it was just noise, nothing but noise.

Bothwell Castle

The Last Siege of Bothwell Castle
Chris Brookmyre

'I am not a workaholic,' Catherine McLeod tells herself, striding into the station on brisk but quiet feet. Yes, she is choosing to go into work on a day off, a bank holiday no less, but she has her reasons. There's a certain calm to be found here, comparatively. She's just spent a fortnight in Greece, which she shouldn't complain about, but given how much of it involved listening to her two sons arguing with each other or moaning in unison at her, she is aching for the comforts and privileges that rank confers and motherhood doesn't. She knows her team can argue and moan even more relentlessly than Duncan and Fraser, but the crucial difference is that when she tells cops to shut up and get out of her face, they tend to comply.

Cresting the stairs, Catherine hears the familiar clack of keyboards accompanied by a low hum of conversation, which quietens for a beat as she comes into view of the open-plan bullpen. It is the moment that they notice the boss has turned up a day early, but Catherine reckons she is the one who feels the greater lurch in her stomach. It is ridiculous. She is a woman in her forties, married with two kids, a Detective Superintendent with dozens of officers ultimately answerable to her, and yet she still gets that hollow, insecure feeling when she's back after any substantial absence. It is the same one she used to get at school, but not like returning from the holidays, when everyone had been away: more like going back to class after illness. It's a fear of being uninformed, of what she alone might have missed.

She recovers from it a sight quicker these days, not least because, in this situation, she is the headmistress. When she asks what she needs caught up on, they'd better bloody well tell her.

Beano turns on a heel, swift in presenting himself. If it were anyone less reliably diligent, she'd suspect he was trying to cover up something.

'Boss,' he says, trying to make the surprise in his tone sound bright rather than alarmed. 'I thought you weren't due back until tomorrow.'

'Yeah, but *entre nous*, I feared I might kill my family or myself if I spent one more day cooped up with them. So I thought I'd come in, get a heads-up on what's been going on before I start back properly tomorrow. Also, I want you lot to always be thinking you know not the day nor the hour when the master shall return. Or what kind of mood she might be in. So give me the "Previously on…" and make it succinct.'

Beano takes a moment, looking like he's retrieving and editing a fortnight's data in real time.

'Well, the big headline is a break-in over the weekend at the old Johnstone Engineering Works in Blantyre.'

'But that's been closed for years. I thought it was scheduled for demolition.'

'It is.'

'So what the hell were they stealing?'

'All of the explosive charges that were supposed to bring it down.'

'Jesus Christ. That place was huge. The size of two city blocks. That's how much explosive is unaccounted for? How many people have we got looking?'

'I'm not trying to trivialise it, but this may not be what it appears on the surface. See, the demolition was being handled by Mint-Dem, which has been officially awarded a DAF rating.'

'DAF?'

'Dodgy as fuck. They're run by a guy called Bobby Minto. He's balls-deep in drug connections. I reckon if we dig we'll find that the security outfit supposedly guarding the Johnstone Engineering site is owned by somebody linked to Minto. I'm just on my way to look a wee bit deeper. My theory is it's an insurance job, and that once the cheque has cleared, all that explosive is going to quietly reappear in Mint-Dem's inventory.'

'Sounds about right. Anything else?'

'Trying to think back to when you left. Were you here when the Collinton thing came in?'

'My last day, yes. Classics professor found hanged. Set fair for a verdict of suicide, I recall. First such valediction I've ever seen written in Latin. Bloody academics. I recall being impressed that you were able to translate it, though probably at the cost of the unreconstructed Rangers fans on the firm marking you down as a bead-rattler. What's the update?'

'That the death was revised to suspicious.'

'Christ. You're telling me there's a whole new murder case on the books?'

'Yes and no.'

'How so?'

'I wasn't about to rely on my Higher Latin from fifteen years ago, especially since I only scraped a C. I ran a copy of the note past my old secondary-school teacher for the fine details. According to her, I had got the gist right regarding why Collinton was killing himself, but she told me there was no way he had written the note. It was full of mistakes.'

'I thought the handwriting on the suicide note had been verified.'

Beano gives her an odd smile.

'We brought in his boyfriend, who is a graphic designer. Right handy with Photoshop, apparently. We'd spoken to him before because he was the one who found the body, but we sweated him properly this time. He caved in less than an hour. On the books and off the books rapid.'

'Kudos. I look forward to reading the reports.'

Sanny can see Sid making his way towards the bus stop. He's brought thon canvas tube affair like Sanny asked him, got it slung over his shoulder, though it's folded up, only about quarter the size. You can fit all sorts inside that thing once it's unfolded. Sid stole it last week when some guy came into the school to do a presentation about drugs. It was for these pop-up banners he was using. When the presentation was over and he was packing up, the dude spent ages trying to work out what he'd done with it. That's the thing with Sid. Sanny likes to think he's a fly enough thief, but he's nothing compared to the wee man. Sid could steal the eyes right oot your heid and you'd be standing there for ages trying to suss how come suddenly you can see fuck-all.

'So whit's the script?' Sid asks.

'We're going to Bothwell.'

'Bothwell? Fuck that, man. I don't want to be spending money on a bus fare. Two bus fares, in fact.'

'We don't need tae spend anything,' Sanny tells him. 'Look. I've swiped travel passes.'

'Fae where?'

'Aff two glaiket-lookin' students. Pair of them hingin' aboot Central Station like a fart in a trance. Here ye go.'

Sid takes the pass and examines it, screwing his nose up at what he sees.

'Cannae use this. Looks fuck-all like me. Boy in the photie's no' even the right colour.'

'Whit you talkin' aboot? Cunt's got a sun-tan, man. And as if the bus driver's gaunny look at it twice, apart fae checkin' it's in date. It's no' fuckin' passport control. Free travel, man. We can go anywhere.'

'Well, if we could go anywhere, why the fuck would we want tae go tae Bothwell, on a day aff as well?'

'Bothwell Castle.'

Sid looks unimpressed.

'Whit, can you no' wait for a school trip?' he asks, then his expression softens as he susses it.

'Oh. I remember noo. Place your da' used to take you.'

Sanny's grateful his pal gets it, but isn't comfortable dwelling on this.

'Aye, but that's no' the reason. There's some big cairry-on doon there the day, for the bank holiday. Battle re-enactment, siege engines, archery displays. Gaunny be fuckin' hoachin' wi' tourists, man.'

'I get you noo,' Sid says. 'Easy pickin's.'

'Exactly. And that's how I asked ye tae bring the tube. I reckon we could pick up a bow an' arra.'

'Yass,' Sid says, miming firing arrows. 'I'd be like fuckin' Legolas.'

'And I'd be like William Wallace,' Sanny replies.

'Legolas was better.'

'Aye, but William Wallace was real.'

'And Legolas wasnae?'

'Legolas was in *Lord of the Rings*. It was a film.'

'Aye, and so was *Braveheart*.'

'Not with dragons and trolls and orcs, for fuck's sake.'

Sanny gets a wee buzz as they come around the bend and into sight of the place. He hasn't been here since he was nine, before his dad went inside. It brings back how he felt when he first saw it. He had been picturing some gloomy grey fortress like Stirling or Edinburgh, both of which remind him a wee bit too much of the Bar-L now. He hadn't been ready for the colour, for the redness rising out of the green, so bright and vivid even on a cloudy day.

It's even more colourful this morning. As he predicted, the place is totally hoaching. There are dudes walking about dressed as knights and soldiers, jugglers in jester outfits, women in medieval dresses with their diddies spilling out. Of course, not everybody got the right memo. He also sees some blokes in flowing black robes, the material billowing around in the breeze, their faces covered in golden death-head masks. He recognises the get-up from thon film about Spartan warriors, the one starring that mad cunt fae Paisley. It's not quite in keeping with the appropriate historical period or even geographical region, but then there's weans dressed as Spider-Man and Power Rangers, wee lassies done up like her out of *Frozen*.

Most eye-catching is a replica siege tower. Essentially it's like a giant ladder on wheels, with the platforms inside protected on three sides by wooden boards, and a hinged gangway at the top like a portable drawbridge. It's swarming with weans, climbing all over it like wee monkeys, totally ignoring the shouts of their parents to get doon aff it or at least be careful.

'This is only a half-scale replica of the engine brought here by the English in 1301,' some tour-guide dude in a knight's outfit is saying to a group of tourists. 'In the thirteenth and fourteenth centuries, there was siege after siege, with the castle changing hands back and forth. The Scots had spent fourteen bloody and sapping months laying siege to the castle in 1298, only for the English to recapture it inside a month three years later with the aid of their mammoth siege tower known as the Belfry.'

Sanny catches Sid pure gawking at it. They share a grin, both thinking the same thing. Sid comes right oot with it, though.

'Just think of the places you could tan wi' that.'

There is an archery demo going on to the right of the castle's entrance, the area cordoned off for safety. There are two targets set up beneath the castle walls, a bloke holding a bow as he gives instructions to a group of teenagers. Sanny and Sid watch for a bit, taking in the portable frame where the spare bows are hanging, and noting how everybody's attention is on the targets when the instructor gives the all-clear to shoot.

Sid unfolds the canvas tube. There's a bow inside it within seconds, then it's slung around his shoulder again like it was never off. Never got any arrows, but they can try again later.

Sanny is pretty sure somebody over near the siege tower just watched the whole thing, but the key is to look like you've nothing to hide, like you were meant to be lifting whatever you've just knocked. Sid is always perfect at that, strolling along giving no impression he's

in a hurry to get away. That said, it always helps to clear
the scene, so Sanny suggests they do a wee circuit around
the castle so they're out of sight by the time the instructor
gets back from yanking arrows oot the targets.

'Robin Hood,' Sid says as they walk around beneath
the towering red walls.

'What about him?'

'Was he real?'

'Probably not.'

'Whit aboot Jon Snow?'

'Dragons again.'

'Fuck's sake.'

The castle is on the edge of a plateau, looking down
steep slopes to where the Clyde flows below. There are
trees screening off what lies beyond the far bank, but
Sanny remembers the view from the Great Hall and the
big tower when his da took him up there. It had a funny
name: the Donjon. Sounded like it should be under the
ground but you could see for miles in every direction.

'Naebody could get the drop on you if you were in
here,' Da told him.

He used to climb the outside walls when he was wee,
the damage of the centuries creating a thousand hand-
grips and footholds. There's scaffolding up around a lot
of it now, warning signs specifically telling you not to
get too close. Towards the south-west corner, there is
some kind of tarpaulin affair covering a section where
the Donjon meets the outer wall. He can't tell if they're
shoring something up or excavating.

The knight who was talking about the siege engine
comes around the corner with his tour party. He's
carrying a foam sword, holding it up for them to follow
him.

'I think we should join the tour,' Sanny suggests.

Sid screws up his nose, not exactly coming in his pants at the prospect of a history lesson, but he doesn't get the purpose.

'You might no' fancy it, but I reckon everybody else will find it riveting, if you know what I mean.'

Sid checks out the group of tourists standing in front of the guy, staring wherever he points the foam sword. Now he's on board. The guide won't be pointing it towards anybody's pockets or handbags.

'The castle was initially constructed by Walter of Moray,' the knight is saying as they shuffle into place among the group. 'It is believed to have been designed by Enguerrand III de Boves, Lord of Coucy, and consisted primarily of a Keep, known as the Donjon, intended to be the main lodging within a greater castle complex. The projected castle was never completed, as construction was interrupted by the invasion of Edward I in 1296.'

'Yep,' says a fat bloke with an American accent. 'Builders always got an excuse why they cain't finish the jawb.'

Sanny had clocked him for a Septic even before he opened his mouth. Boy's gone double denim, jeans and jacket, with a trucker-style cap up top. It's totally unacceptable.

The guide responds with a wee chuckle, then signals with the foam sword that it's time to move on.

'Now that I've whetted your appetites, it's time we took a closer look at the Donjon from the inside.'

When they come back around to the main entrance, they have to wait at the gate, as there is a steady stream of people exiting. They are all heading for the grassy field between the castle and the car park, where most of the men and women in costume are mustering. The re-enactment is going to be starting soon, by the look of it: just whenever they can clear all the weans from the siege tower.

Sid gives Sanny an inquiring look.

'Reckon we'd do better among the crowd?' he asks quietly.

'Naw,' Sanny reckons. 'There's Yanks, Japanese and all sorts in this group. Overseas tourists tend to carry a lot of cash 'cause they don't want to be hunting for a hole in the wall when they could be gawking at statues or whatever.'

'Got ye.'

The group takes a hard right once inside, heading towards the main tower. Sanny spots the guys in the *300* outfits again, hanging about just inside the walls next to the ticket office. Maybe they've got some kind of surprise role in the re-enactment.

'Now, the word "donjon" mutated into dungeon in common usage,' the guide says. 'And when we say dungeon we think of some dank and grim underground prison chamber. But Walter Moray's Donjon was one of the most luxurious lodgings in all of Scotland. There were opulent family apartments on the top floor, a reception hall for favoured guests on the floor below and spacious store rooms on the lowest level. If you look up at the walls, you will see a series of regularly spaced holes. These were for the beams supporting the upper floors.'

All of the tourists look up. Neither Sid nor Sanny miss the opportunity.

With his eyes focused on what he's doing, Sanny suddenly hears the guide react in an angry voice.

'Hey. What do you think you're playing at?'

Sanny and Sid plunge their hands instinctively into their pockets, keeping their heads down while composing their best innocent looks. Sanny can't help stealing a glance at the guide though, which is when he sees that they aren't the target of his outrage.

One of the blokes in the gold masks has closed the gate and appears to be locking it. The other two are already marching along the wooden walkway leading into the Donjon.

'Excuse me a moment,' the guide says, then starts striding out to meet them, pure raging.

That's when they pull their robes back and break out the AK-47s.

Catherine has skim-read a couple of reports and completed a quick triage on the email backlog that was waiting for her. She has done enough to ensure she won't feel like she's coming in cold tomorrow, and is about to leave when she sees Zoe Vernon urgently waving to get her attention.

'Boss, there's something you need to see.'

Catherine registers the anxiety on the faces of the officers gathered around Zoe's desk as she approaches.

'Switchboard lit up with about fifty calls at once. Then this came in,' Zoe says, cuing a video.

A few seconds later, Catherine feels a chill run through her as she recognises the black flag, the iconography, the Arabic text and the fuck-awful music that always book-ends an Isis video. She braces herself for things she won't be able to unsee, but what chills her most is the fact it's been brought to her attention right here, right now. This is not something she's catching a clip of on the news after the fact. It's something she is going to have to deal with.

It begins with a hand holding up a *Daily Record* – a first for Islamic State, surely – confirming that it was taken this morning. A caption says 'Crusader Castle Boswell', and a timestamp states that this was ten minutes ago. She has no reason to doubt it. The footage is not quite a live stream, but as good as.

'They mean Bothwell, I'm assuming,' Catherine says. 'Did it have a link to the crusades?'

'I don't know,' says Zoe. 'I think it's just their standard term of abuse for anything ancient in Christendom.'

'Do we have officers on the ground yet?'

'En route. Two minutes out.'

The camera tracks along a sandstone wall, too fast to focus, then it spins and swoops crazily before stabilising. It is looking down into a sunken chamber. She recognises it as inside the base of the main tower, the Donjon. She took Duncan and Fraser there a couple of years ago. It looked different then, primarily because it wasn't containing a group of hostages, all identically dressed in robes and gold masks.

The view pans up to show a similarly masked and robed figure covering them from above with an AK-47. It then pans down again, picking out a second gunman on the floor of the chamber.

'How many are there?' Catherine asks.

'Fifteen hostages, three gunmen,' Adrienne Cruikshank replies.

'What's with the costumes?'

'Persian Immortals. From the movie *300*,' says Zoe.

'Yeah, I got that. But why are the hostages wearing them?'

'So that when our marksmen get there, they can't risk a shot.'

'They're settling in for the long haul then. Shit.'

It gets much worse, though.

The camera follows the lower gunman to a recess in

the outer wall containing a grey plastic box. It zooms in as he briefly lifts the lid, long enough to reveal what is inside without disclosing it to the hostages. Then the camera retreats to the main courtyard where it pans and zooms around the walls, pan and zoom, pan and zoom, picking out grey box after grey box. Each of them contains an explosive charge: cumulatively, enough to bring down the Johnstone Engineering works. Enough to bring down two city blocks. Enough to bring down what's left of Bothwell castle.

'You are prisoners of Islamic State,' the gunman tells them. The boy's accent is weird, not one Sanny can place. Doesn't sound like one of those home-grown jihadis anyway, though Sanny doesn't think there's been any from Lanarkshire so far. Can't imagine someone saying: 'We will rain death down upon the infidel' in a Glasgow accent, without adding 'ya cunts'.

'Allah is merciful. Do as you are instructed and you will not be harmed.'

Sanny doesn't recall Isis ever being particularly merciful. He and Sid trade looks, both bricking it. The boy tells them to line up, and he feels his guts turn to water. He can't take his eyes off the AKs, the stocks gripped by black-gloved hands. Masks and gloves: no faces, no fingerprints.

'Aw fuck, man, this is it,' he says.

But the gunmen appear to be carrying out a headcount. There are thirteen prisoners, including the tour guide. Lucky for him, as it turns out. They unlock the gate and tell him he can go.

'Inform the authorities,' the boy says. 'Let them know we are in control.'

The rest of them are then marched to the Donjon, where

they descend to the bottom of the tower. As they emerge from the narrow spiral of the stairway, Sanny sees three more figures in robes and masks, seated against the wall, not moving, not speaking. Immortals, that's what they were called in the film. They were the baddies. But it's not three more gunmen. Turns out it's three more hostages.

In the middle of the floor, next to the well, there's a big canvas hold-all, like for fitba strips. It's full of more robes and masks.

'Put these on,' the gunman commands. 'Like those three men there.'

It's a different boy from upstairs; Sanny can tell by his voice. Another strange accent.

The boy hands out the costumes, his rifle slung around his shoulder by a strap. Sanny clocks the American eyeing it, but then he glances up and sees he's covered from the platform above. Instead Double Denim settles for giving Sid the stink-eye as he pulls on the robe. It's pure obvious what he's thinking. Obvious he's not going to keep it to himself either. He's probably never seen a Paki in the wild before.

'See, The Donald was right,' he mutters. 'This is what happens when you open your borders to unfettered immigration by Muslims.'

Sid glares back at him.

'Hey, fuck you, ya Septic cunt.'

'What did you call me?'

'Aye, Sid, you've got to watch your language wae the Septics,' Sanny explains. 'They take offence tae the word cunt.'

'No, goddamit, the other word,' he says, raging. 'Septic. What's that shit about?'

'Septic tank. Yank.'

This doesnae go down well either.

'I ain't no Yankee. I'll have you know I'm a proud Georgian. I'm from the South.'

'The south of whit?' Sid asks.

'The Southern states,' Sanny tells him. 'Sure, the ones that got pumped in the Civil War.'

'Silence,' says the gunman who is handing out the robes. 'Do not move. Do not speak. And give me your phones. All of you.'

This provokes a load of moaning, like the prospect of handing over their mobiles is worse than the prospect of imminent death. It also provokes a bit of discomfort in Sanny and Sid, for reasons that might become all too apparent.

The gunman moves round collecting them, counting as he goes. Then he comes to the Septic.

'I ain't got it. Don't know what the hell's happened to it, neither. I swear.'

'Oh, for God's sakes, Chuck, you must have forgotten it on the bus again,' says his missus.

'No, Martha, damn it, I had it ten minutes ago. Took a picture of that siege tower.'

The gunman frisks him to confirm. He's not the only one to have mislaid his mobile, either. There's a French woman cannae place hers either.

Sanny and Sid get frisked too, having both truthfully claimed not to own one. The boy pats them down but doesn't check the canvas tube. Why would he, though? Nobody would keep their mobile phone in there.

Next thing is they get their hands tied with those plastic strip efforts, then get told to sit on the ground, away from the walls. Sanny wonders why the first three hostages get to stay where they are, but it's not like he's going to ask.

Chuck is still simmering: apparently more pissed-off at Sid than at the terrorists.

'Guess you're one of those moderate Muslims we keep hearing about then, huh?' he says, not letting it lie. Sanny's guessing his civil war remark didnae help either. 'Maybe you can appeal to your buddies here, then. Ain't we always getting told Islaahm is the religion of peace?'

That's how he says it: Islaahm.

Sid ignores it.

With everybody seated and restrained, the gunman walks over to a recess in the wall, where there's a grey box sitting. He opens it for a second, then shuts it again. As he lifts the lid, the sleeve of his robe rides up, enough to show some skin above the end of his black glove.

Sid clocks it too.

'Looks a bit peely-wally to have come from unfettered immigration,' Sid says quietly.

The approach to the castle has been cleared of civilians, officers creating a perimeter extending to the Clyde. The tour guide who raised the alarm has briefed Catherine on everything he witnessed. He has accounted for twelve of the fifteen hostages seen on the video as having been with him when they were taken, and confirmed that there are three gunmen.

An armed response unit arrived a couple of minutes before Catherine, but they have been told to stand fast and remain out of sight for the time being. Nobody wants to risk escalating things until they know what they are dealing with.

It is a waiting game now.

The scene looks incongruously peaceful, nothing unusual other than the sight of Bothwell Castle looking so deserted on a sunny day. And, of course, the Isis flag flapping from a pole atop the Donjon.

Catherine's mobile rings, the caller identified as DS Anthony Thomson.

'Beano, I'm afraid you can call off your search for those explosives,' she informs him. 'They aren't going to show up back in Mint-Dem's inventory after all.'

'Yeah, I heard. Yet everything else I'm turning up is corroborating the dodgy-as-fuck hypothesis. Turns out the security outfit *is* linked to Minto: it's owned by his brother-in-law.'

'What's dodgy about that?'

'His brother-in-law is Darren Scanlon.'

Now she gets him.

'Dangerous Daz,' she says. 'Lanarkshire drug-dealer turned property developer.'

'Him and Minto are seriously in cahoots. Seems last year Mint-Dem was hired to do a partial demolition on an old seventies-built extension to this lovely big sandstone villa Scanlon was renovating. It was in a conservation area, so there were strict limits on what he could do. That's until Mint-Dem screwed up knocking down the extension: did so much structural damage to the building that there was no option but for it to be condemned as dangerous.'

'Ordinarily I'd have suggested that would make for awkward family relations. But I'm guessing Scanlon was neither angry nor surprised.'

'Nope. There's no way he'd have got permission to demolish the villa if that had been the plan he submitted, but suddenly Scanlon was clear to build a whole new block of luxury flats on the plot.'

'Noted, Beano. But unless Isis have started forming alliances with Lanarkshire bams, we aren't going to be pinning this one on him.'

As she terminates the call, she sees Zoe waving her across, holding up an iPad.

'They've issued a statement, of sorts. Same email account as the video was sent from.'

Catherine grabs the tablet. It is a simple message, text only. No videos, no fanfares, just words.

This former crusader castle is now part of the caliphate. Do not approach where you have no dominion. If we see anyone violating this order, we kill a hostage. Our demands will be presented at midday.

'Adrienne did find a crusader link to the castle,' Zoe informs her, her tone grim with import. 'De Coucy, the French noble thought to have designed it, also designed Château de Coucy in Picardy. It was a noted stopping-off point for knights of all nationalities on their way to the crusades. And these fuckers love their symbolism.'

'Hmm,' Catherine replies.

'What?'

'Since when did Isis issue demands? They usually cut straight to the bloodshed. And why are they making us *wait* for their demands?'

'Maximise media attention before it kicks off?'

'Possibly. I don't know. But something about this doesn't smell right.'

Sid hasn't said anything for a long time, which is not like him, and Sanny doubts it's simply because he's been told to shut it by a nutter with a machine gun. It would usually take more than that.

It's hard to be sure what Sid's looking at, what with the masks and everything, but Sanny gets the impression he's been studying the gunmen closely, like he does when he's planning on some thieving and he's working up to a move.

'Aye,' Sid eventually says, finally breaking his silence. 'Awfy peely-wally right enough.'

'What did you say?' Chuck hisses. Paranoid fud just assumes Sid's getting wide with him.

'Not talking about you, mate. Talking about them,' Sid goes on, looking up to the gunmen on the platform above and raising his voice to get their attention. 'I'm saying, Chuck here might be an ignorant bawbag, but he does have a point about Islam. A true Muslim shouldn't be threatening innocent people with guns. I mean, does it no' say in the Hadith that if the donkey chases the lamb oot the farmyard, then the true shepherd must forgive him, for he cannot help his nature?'

'Silence,' one of them replies.

'Can you deny it, though? Do you even *know* that passage?'

'Of course I know it. But you understand nothing. Do not speak again.'

The gunman turns his back, like he's dismissing Sid.

'Fuck was that shite?' Sanny asks quietly. 'Donkeys and lambs and shepherds?'

'I'll tell you whit that shite was. I don't know aboot Robin Hood, Jon Snow or Legolas, but I know this much: *these* cunts arenae real. I just made that shite up and he doesnae know the difference.'

Sid looks up to the platform again.

'Haw, whit part of the Arab world do yous hail fae? Lochee? Tannadice?'

The gunman raises his weapon with a swirl of his robes, coming up with a rapid, swinging motion until the barrel is pointing down over the barrier. Everyone recoils, gasps echoing around the chamber in sudden terror at what might happen if he pulls the trigger.

'Silence. I will not warn you again.'

He lowers the rifle, and though he didn't fire, something does issue from the muzzle, falling from the platform to the floor of the pit. Only Sanny notices it, and only then because it lands in the folds of his robe. It's a tiny plastic ball the size of a rolled-up snotter. It's just a totey wee thing, but it changes the whole picture.

Zoe's phone buzzes, puncturing the tense silence.

'Seriously?' she asks, a moment after answering. 'Yes, patch it through. Yes. Hello. Yes. Absolutely. I understand. Let me transfer you to my boss.'

Catherine looks at her inquiringly as she hands over the mobile.

Zoe gestures to the castle, her voice suddenly quiet as though irrationally afraid someone might overhear.

'It's from inside.'

Catherine checks her watch. It's ten minutes until noon.

'Them?' she asks.

Zoe shakes her head.

'Hello, this is Detective Superintendent McLeod.'

The voice is quiet, furtive, someone trying to be discreet about the fact that he is on the phone.

'Aye, very good. Fuck's sake, makin' a secret SOS call here and the number of times I've been transferred, it's worse than tryin' tae fuckin' cancel Sky.'

'Who is this?'

Two minutes later, Catherine hands the phone back to Zoe, having instructed the caller to keep the line open even if he has to conceal the phone again. There's no question he's legit. He is describing things only somebody in there could know.

'So what's the script?' Zoe asks.

'The script is that we've got three chancers in there

who know bugger-all about Islam and may very well be holding fifteen people hostage using airsoft replicas.'

'BB guns?' Zoe confirms, incredulous.

'It doesn't change anything at this stage. Can't risk sending in the ARU on the basis of this one account.'

'Yes, but if the guns are fake, does that mean the explosives could be also?'

'No. We have high confidence that the explosives are real. In fact, we even know where they probably came…'

And suddenly a number of things click into place.

Catherine calls Beano back sharpish.

'That conservation area, it wouldn't be Bothwell, by any chance?'

'Correct. Scanlon owns a lot of property in the area. I think he lives there, in fact. Or Uddingston, can't remember.'

The castle is halfway between the two.

Zoe is waving the iPad again.

'Email,' she states.

It is noon.

We demand that the British Prime Minister make a statement outside 10 Downing Street apologising for all British war crimes in Islamic lands. She must make this statement by three o'clock today, or we will destroy this crusader castle.

To demonstrate that Allah is merciful, we will release the majority of the hostages. The rest will remain prisoners of the caliphate.

'What are they playing at?' Zoe asks. 'They will release the majority of the hostages? Why?'

'Give me that a minute,' Catherine responds, taking the iPad.

She plays the video again, skipping forward to the

footage of the hostages assembled down in the bottom of the Donjon. Then she plays it once more, pinching to zoom in on one specific section of the group.

'A substantial majority,' she states. 'They're going to release exactly twelve, count on it. And they're not playing: the plan is to level the place. As soon as all the hostages are clear and we've been inevitably commanded to pull back again, they're going to blow the explosives.'

'With themselves and three hostages inside?'

'No. There won't be anybody inside.'

Catherine shows her the iPad.

'See these three against the wall? They don't move. According to the kid, they were already there when the other hostages got brought in. They're dummies, just robes and masks.'

Zoe catches on.

'So these jokers are planning to waltz out pretending to have been the first hostages taken?'

'And as soon as they are clear...' Catherine says, not needing to elaborate.

'Which means there's somebody else out here watching this, holding the detonator.'

'Maybe even someone who lives nearby.'

'Why would Scanlon want to level Bothwell Castle?'

'So he can buy the land and build on it. It's the most desirable location in the area, which is why there's been a castle on it for seven hundred years. He blows it up, then Islamic State claims responsibility.'

'How can he be sure they would do that?' Zoe asks.

'Somebody leaves an unflushed jobbie in a toilet these days, Islamic State claims responsibility. Everyone says boo-hoo, then Scanlon comes in as a concerned local developer, with a plan that is sympathetic to the place's legacy. Maybe even incorporate some of the surviving foundations. Ultra-high-end luxury development. He could make millions.'

'How could he be sure the land would be sold to him?'

'The usual way. Backhanders to some, intimidation to others.'

'Bastard.'

Catherine allows herself a smile.

'What?' Zoe inquires.

'Bastard indeed. Scanlon is as ambitious as he is ruthless. And to be fair, he's smarter than many of his peers. But crucially he's not smart enough to realise that's not saying much. I've always reckoned it was a matter of time before his eyes got bigger than his belly, and it looks like today's the day.'

'So what's our move?'

The gate opens twenty minutes after the message was sent out. Catherine has her people waiting to intercept the hostages as they file through the gate, all of them identically dressed, hands restrained with plastic wrist ties.

'Please remain calm,' she tells them, conscious of their anxiety to get away from their captors. 'We have to search everybody before we can proceed.'

Their robes and masks are removed and they are patted down one by one. It takes a couple of minutes, at the end of which three are left and the rest are being escorted swiftly to safety.

'What you keeping us back for?' one of them asks. 'There's terrorists in there.'

'Who's holding the detonator?' she asks them.

'Whit?'

'You heard. It was quite a clever dodge you pulled with the costumes and the dummies, and putting yourselves in plastic cuffs was a smart touch too. But you couldn't part with your mobiles, could you? See, the gunmen took everybody's phones off them, so the way I see it, anybody walking out of there carrying one is guilty.'

'I don't know what you're talking about. There was a lot of folk in there. They must have lost count and forgot to search us.'

'Maybe. Will I go and ask them? I can give them a shout, see if they're listening. Actually, I won't bother. But here's what I will do. See, I figure if I push you back inside and lock the gate, the person holding the detonator will suss his plan's been rumbled. At that point, he has absolutely nothing to lose by pushing the plunger. You guys are the only evidence we have against him. If he blew you up, we'd have a hard time proving what really happened, and he knows it.'

'You cannae do that. You've no evidence we've done anything. That would be murder.'

'Fucking watch me,' Catherine tells them.

She gives the nod and the three of them are bundled inside, Zoe pulling the gate closed with a slam.

While everyone was being searched, Catherine had sent in an explosives tech to disarm the charges, but these arseholes don't know that.

'Oh, and by the way,' she adds. 'The first one to cough and tell me who put you up to this is the only one who gets to cut a deal.'

They all answer at exactly the same time.

The polis in charge comes over to where Sanny and Sid are standing, out on the main road. There's polis vans blocking off access in both directions. The pair of them have been kept to one side, away from the other hostages.

She introduces herself. McLeod. She's the one Sanny spoke to on the phone.

'That was a very brave thing you both did. Alexander Sinclair, right? And Siddiq Sayed?'

'Sanny.'

'Sid.'

'Very brave. But now I need you to give up the phones you stole.'

'What you talking about?' Sid replies.

'It's the same as I told the three numpties we just lifted: anybody walking out of there holding a mobile is guilty.'

'It was oor ain phones we planked in the canvas bag,' Sid insists. 'So they never found them.'

Sanny knows it's useless. There are some polis you know right away you can rip the pish ootay and some who've just got your number.

'Okay,' Sanny admits, handing over the mobile he used to call 999. 'But we found them, we never stole them,'

'Found them,' she repeats. 'Sure. I'm happy to run with that, today. You're the heroes of the hour, after all.'

'So will there be a reward?' Sid chips in.

'Of sorts. I'll speak to Historic Environment Scotland about giving you free memberships, for life. Visit any of their sites, any time.'

'I meant cash.'

'I know, but I can offer something better. You've just earned your immortality. This place has been captured and lost and captured again all down the centuries, but history will show that in the last siege of Bothwell Castle, it was taken back by Sid Sayed and Sanny Strang.'

Sanny beams, thinking what his da will say when he tells him.

Sid looks pretty chuffed too.

'Does that mean we'll be knighted?'

'Don't push it, wee man.'

Kinneil House

Sanctuary
Sara Sheridan

The fog clung to the grass. 'It should roll,' Linda thought, but it didn't. It just hung there, as if the world had stopped.

'The weather's a great bluffer,' Mrs Pleitch said as she tied a scarf round her hair and slowly did up her coat before making for the door. Mrs Pleitch's hair didn't look as if it needed protection. It looked as if it was set in stone.

'I've put the dustsheets on the clothes-horse,' she told Linda, pointing in the direction of the makeshift pantry. 'For the conservator,' she added, as if an explanation was needed. Linda nodded, her eyes drawn again through the window to the thick white view that now obscured even the lights from the cottages further down the track. Mrs Pleitch paused as if she had something to add. She looked at Linda – poor, chubby Linda who had taken the caretaker's job because she'd had to come home.

'I'll be back same day next week,' she said and then, with her handbag over her arm, she opened the door and disappeared into the weather as if she had fallen into a marshmallow.

It was silent here. The walls were thick. They had

given her the job because they were worried about break-ins. They had tried installing CCTV but it kept cutting out and in the end the trustees had been converted to the idea of a caretaker. Kinneil was like that – it felt as if nothing had changed at the old house for an age – staircases led nowhere and the roof was gone in places. The house was a hotchpotch of wings and additions from hundreds of years ago, all in different states of repair. Linda sighed. She'd rigged up a television in the old kitchen – one of the few places with a modern plug point – but it was too early to switch on the set and it felt too little like home. Instead she flicked on the kettle. The house creaked. Down in Bo'ness everyone would be getting home from work. She wondered if perhaps she should wrap up, take her bike and pop down to the pub for an hour or so. She was allowed breaks. But then she imagined the lull in the conversation as she walked in. The whispers of 'Look who's back.' She cursed herself for what she felt stirring – memories of the little girl whose heart beat fast just at the thought of crossing the playground. She should have got over that by now. She should have been beautiful and married and a mother and living in a big city like Glasgow. But she was here. Back where she started. Or nearby at any rate. She grimaced as the kettle clicked off. The thick chrome rail over the stove reflected her distorted image – thinner and more glamorous.

Her bedroom had once been servants' quarters, near the kitchen, down in the half-basement. Except for the rounds she was supposed to make, the grand part of Kinneil was out of bounds.

'It's dangerous. Be careful,' the trustee who'd shown her the old place had said. The house smelled of oil from the boiler and wood shavings. The rooms were mostly unfurnished and some parts were almost derelict – people just came to see the murals and walk in the grounds. Linda comforted herself that it was cosier here, in the small pale-green room in the basement with a camp bed and a single small light.

'Are you sure?' the man had checked when he showed her the accommodation.

'I'll take it,' she'd jumped in.

She wondered if he'd questioned her tone or considered her desperation. At least it was somewhere to stay. Now she sat on the single bed, sipped her tea and dunked a digestive. She was about to pick up the magazine she'd bought at the bus station when the basement window above her shifted. A black shape banged suddenly against it and made her jump. Her heart pounding, she glanced across the puddle of light between the bed and the door. Then the black shape bumped against the glass again and she realised what it was.

'Hello, pussy.' Relief softened her voice. She put down her cup and slipped the catch, letting a damp green-eyed cat jump into the room. There were no dogs allowed in the house at Kinneil: there was a sign at the entrance and another in the museum shop. But no one had mentioned any other animals, she told herself as she scratched the cat's head. 'Who are you then? Want to be my friend, do you?' The cat purred, turned a couple of times and sat comfortably on her feet as she fed it a piece of biscuit.

When she woke the cat was gone. She cursed herself for dozing off. It was the middle of the night now, but then it felt like that the moment it got dark at Kinneil. Hundreds of years ago the rooms would have glowed golden with candlelight – all night, maybe. There must have been balls and parties – the bright lights of the

Palace at Linlithgow only a few miles away. The guide-book she'd skimmed through hinted at intrigue. Glamour. Royal assignations. Not now.

Beyond the bedroom door, the hallway creaked and Linda felt herself stiffen but there was nothing for it. She couldn't leave a cat on the loose – what if it peed on the displays upstairs or scratched the antique wooden panelling? She searched in her bag for the torch they'd given her. Then, taking a deep breath she fumbled through the bedroom doorway. The thin light washed towards the kitchen in one direction and towards the stone spiral staircase in the other. She cursed under her breath as she realised the connecting door to the main house had been left open. The torch's feeble light stood little chance in the unlit rooms. This was why the house was only open in the summer. The electric light was patchy, leaving most of the abandoned apartments in authentic historical darkness. In the oldest parts there were no lights at all – no floors in some places either.

'Pussy?' Linda called upwards. And again. 'Puss?' No hope.

Tentatively, she started up the stairs. There was no bannister and she took it slowly, keeping one hand on the cold stone wall while the other gripped the torch. Her steps echoed on the flagstones when she reached the top. 'Pussy?' she said again and cast the light ahead of her. It didn't reach the end – the old place was a labyrinth, falling in and out of repair as you walked round it. Some doors were bolted, which she had been told was for safety. Now and then there was a flash of wall, a slice of one of the ancient murals for which the house was famous, or a gaping fireplace, unlit for decades, that seemed to rush towards her leering like a toothless old man out of the darkness. She thought she caught something moving ahead but the torchlight couldn't find it. 'There's no ghost here,' she told herself, with her heart pounding as more shapes emerged. But Linda knew that people brought their own ghosts. At least it's warmer up here, she thought. The heating came through grilles set into the floor. Conservation in action. She passed a couple of pieces of masonry on display. She reeled as the light hit them, they looked as if they might keel over. It was hopeless and in the end she panicked and rushed back downstairs, too afraid to look behind her. She slammed the heavy kitchen door, scrambled for the light switch and sank into the chair in front of the stove. The cat would come back when he was hungry.

In the morning the fog had disappeared but the grass was stiff with frost. Linda woke up and, right enough, the cat was mewling. She got out of the chair to open the door and he nonchalantly rubbed against her legs. It felt almost domestic. As she stretched her stiff shoulders, she considered buying cat food from the Spar on the main road. And some cream too. 'What shall I call you?' she asked, as she stroked his dark fur. 'Are you a Harry, do you think?' Then she noticed something in the cat's mouth. Cats brought presents. It was a sign of affection. She knelt, expecting a mouse. Kinneil was full of them – worse, there were probably rats in an old place this size so close to the burn. Or perhaps Harry had found a sparrow in some far corner. The cat dropped the tiny piece of flesh onto the stone at her feet and Linda squinted. There wasn't any fur. Or feathers. Only a smear of blood. Tentatively, she flipped over the offering and recoiled. 'Jesus!' The cat, sensing her distress, darted away. 'God.' Linda had never been much of a believer. Even as a child. Not since her mother died. She crouched down and peered. There was no mistaking. Harry had brought her a finger. A human finger. Or part of one. As she looked up, she realised it must have come from somewhere in the house.

Her hands were trembling. In town, they'd always said Kinneil was haunted. At school they'd told each other stories and dressed up as the Kinneil ghost at Hallowe'en. Linda remembered Jean Blake saying that a woman had killed herself here. 'A proper lady, all posh she was,' Jean lisped, her ten-year-old eyes bright with delight. 'But a madwoman. She jumped out a high window into the ravine.' Lady Alice was said to haunt the garret at the top of the house and to clump up and down the staircases in boots. Jean claimed to have seen her. 'She had white wings like an angel.' The little girl swore on her life that one winter's night she'd spotted Lady Alice flying from the top of the house through the ragged trees. Linda wondered momentarily if Jean still had a lisp and, for that matter, if she'd bagged herself a husband. Then her eyes fell back to the stone floor. This wasn't a ghost's finger. She had to do something.

The light was breaking. Linda pulled her coat from the back of the chair. The oldest part of the house would be cold away from the stove and the reaches of the creaky boiler. Then, carefully placing the finger on the kitchen table, she set off to search. Crossing the threshold was like walking through an invisible curtain into a fridge. The antique glass in the windows distorted the trees across the lawn so that the branches jutted at crazy angles. There was talk of planting an orchard – Kinneil had been famous for its apples – but, she thought, that would only mask the view. High above her the staircase ran into nowhere, fireplaces built into walls, the floors long gone. If someone was here, dead or alive, they must have got in somehow. And it was her job to find out which of the windows or doors had been breached. There was a jumble of entry points from old canon holes to padlocked doorways.

The house was in shade, a contrast to the crisp morning light outside. With the old place empty, it should have been easy to search. The floor was rough, though, a mix of old stacked stones and half chopped wood piled here and there. Sometimes there was only mud and rubble. Even where it was paved there were fissures between the slabs that seemed to descend into absolute darkness. Other rooms were almost perfect, as if the occupant had left only moments ago and simply gone for a walk. They'd briefed her about the history and what was safe and what wasn't, but she hadn't really paid attention. Linda only wanted somewhere to stay – somewhere she could save a little money while she decided what to do. Kinneil had been built for a different kind of woman, she thought. A woman whose long skirt swished as she paced the galleries – someone who knew how to lay a fire and milk a cow. 'You don't know you're born,' her father used to say. 'In the old days we had to look after ourselves.' Well, that's what she was doing now, she thought, as she peered into an empty cupboard and listened as her footsteps echoed all the way up to the leaky roof. She tried to warm to the old place – the house was as empty as she felt, and as abandoned. She was going to be here for months. Maybe it would come to feel like home.

Crossing back into the restored wing, Linda stopped in the hallway and tried to remember when she had last felt at home anywhere. Maybe as a child, when she'd lived on the edge of Bo'ness. There had been fields beyond the back door. Open spaces to walk and explore without fear, not like the school playground. Ten years had passed since she'd left the old house. It wasn't that she hadn't tried. Maybe some people just didn't belong anywhere. The flat in Hawick hadn't felt like home. Jim hadn't wanted it to. 'That's over,' she comforted herself. 'That's done.' She pressed on, fearful of what she might find.

The rounds took forty minutes and she found nothing – no signs of a break-in, no blood and, thank god, no body. When Linda got back to the kitchen, the cat was curled smugly on the formica table and the finger was gone. She shooed him onto the floor and checked to see if she could find it anywhere. Harry licked his whiskers and settled in front of the boiler. Linda flopped into the chair, feeling a mixture of relief and unease. She cringed at the thought of reporting it to the police. To Shuggie. He had always thought she was batty. 'Linda Loser,' he'd taunted her at school, raising his thumb and forefinger to his forehead when she'd crowded the hallway to find out her results. She'd got three exams. But you needed maybe six or seven to do anything worthwhile. Everyone knew that. Shuggie'd got five and went into the police. She wondered if there had been any murders since he joined the force and if he had had to deal with severed fingers or worse. Bo'ness wasn't that kind of town. He'd probably ended up policing a bit of shoplifting. He'd have done that for free while he was at school. Shuggie loved catching people out. Telling them off. He'd told her off all the time. Bullied her, truth be told. Linda's shoulders curled at the memory. She'd changed since then. Perhaps I imagined the stupid finger, she thought as she stared at Harry.

Outside there was a flash of movement and she sat up to see a white van pulling up at the top of the dirt track. She brushed her hair behind her ear. On the mantle there was a small square mirror and she checked her face. She hadn't washed yet. Hadn't had breakfast. But the rap on the door was businesslike and she knew she had to answer. On the doorstep, a young man smiled. He wore a navy padded jacket and a red scarf.

'Cold day.' He nodded towards the boiler encouragingly. 'I'm Mark Lamont.' He held out his hand. There was an awkward silence. 'The conservator,' he added.

'Oh no,' Linda stepped back to let him past. She'd forgotten the dustsheets. 'We're not ready. Sorry.'

'Nobody's ever ready for conservation,' he smiled. 'What's your name?'

'Linda.'

'Work for the Trust?'

'Yes.'

Mark took off his scarf. 'Doesn't look like there's much caretaking needed round here. I thought the old place was all but empty.'

'They're worried about break-ins. Vandalism.'

'It's a nice wee town though Bo'ness?'

'Oh it is,' Linda found herself nodding. 'But there was some trouble. Graffiti, you know. And some kids got in. They didn't want it to get worse.' She followed his eyes to the kettle. 'Cuppa?'

'Parched. And I'll need a look around.'

There weren't any biscuits left. Linda realised she was hungry as she poured tea into two mugs and offered Mark the sugar.

'Are you from round here?' he asked.

Linda made a non-committal sound. 'Where are you from?' she tried to distract him.

'Edinburgh. Born and bred.'

'And you're a... ?'

'Well, I trained as an archaeologist.'

'I thought that archaeologists dug stuff up.'

'Oh yes. Some do. All sorts of things. Even bodies, if they're lucky! Bet there are loads around here. I mean, there's part of a Roman wall in the grounds isn't there? But we'd never get permission to dig that. No. I specialised.'

'Specialised?'

'In paint. I'm a paint specialist. Historic paint.'

She wasn't sure what to say so she handed him the mug of tea.

'So do you come from round here, then?' he asked again.

'I only came back recently. I was living in Hawick,' she admitted.

'Working down there?'

Linda shook her head. 'Husband,' she lied. Jim hadn't wanted to get married. 'All but name,' he always said. 'It's only a piece of paper.' In the end that made it easier to get away. He'd had his name on the flat. On the bills. It wasn't as if she had befriended the neighbours. It was just a bus ticket. She'd looked after herself. That's all.

'Ah well. Home now, eh?' Mark said.

Linda shifted her stiff shoulder. The bruises were healing. 'Come on. I'll show you,' she offered.

Scooping the dustsheets off the drying rail she led the way up the spiral staircase to the murals. Mark stood back with his tea steaming and let out a low gasp. 'I can't believe they almost knocked the old place down.' Linda looked blank. 'In the 1930s. Before the Trust got hold of it.'

'Oh. Right.'

'I mean, there are Roman remains here. James Watt lived in a cottage in the grounds. It's crazy. Did you hear the story about the ghost? Lady Alice Lilbourne?'

She nodded.

'A mad woman. ' He tittered. 'No. The real story is here.' He leaned in to peer at one of the murals. 'Right here on the wall.'

Linda put down the dustsheets. 'Why?' she asked.

'Why what?' He wasn't paying attention.

'Why isn't she the story? The woman? I mean why is it these old things? They're not even finished properly. It's never the woman who's the story, is it?'

'Well, Mary Queen of Scots would probably disagree. I didn't have you marked for... '

'What? What didn't you have me marked for?'

'You know. A feminist.'

'A woman, you mean?'

After that he didn't chat so much. Linda confined herself to the kitchen. At lunchtime she went to the high street and bought food. On the way home she walked the long way to avoid the police station. Back at Kinneil she watched television until the conservator left, banging the door behind him.

It was late when she heard it. The telly was off and she was sitting beside the stove drinking cocoa. The noise was distinct. A bald scream. A shriek really. Linda was in her pyjamas with an old dressing gown wrapped around her frame and a pair of fluffy brown slippers on her feet. She had finally unpacked her things – what little there was. She wondered if the noise was an animal. It might be. Outside the darkness was almost absolute with no more than a sliver of moon. She switched off the kitchen light and peered through the glass. Then there was another scream and she realised that, although it came from far off, it was from the other direction – somewhere in the house. She snapped on the light again and scrabbled for the torch. As she turned away from the sink she grabbed the bread knife. Just in case.

Closing the door to the main house behind her, to make sure Harry wouldn't follow, Linda called into the darkness.

'Hello,' she shouted. 'Anyone there?'

Then she stopped. What if there was someone? Was it a good idea to let them know she was onto them? What if they responded? No such luck. The silence was excruciating. She wondered if she had hallucinated the scream? Perhaps it was only a bird. She began to walk, her soft-soled steps magnified in the silence, her dressing gown trailing over the freezing flagstones. Her breath clouded ahead of her. She was becoming familiar with the haphazard layout, in darkness and in light. At the murals, Mark had laid out the dustsheets and left a box on the floor. It seemed to contain a range of small instruments. They glinted in the torchlight. She might have picked one up if she hadn't heard the swish of wood against wood – a drawer opening or maybe a window. But there was nothing up here – not a scrap of furniture and all of the windows this high in the house were sealed.

At first when she passed it, she didn't realise something wasn't right. Then it came to her and she retraced her steps until, there she was. A woman. On the wall. She wasn't faded or patched or in need of restoration. In the thin, flat beam of light, the figure glowed distinctly. Linda tried to recollect this painting but she was sure she hadn't seen it before. She must have passed here a dozen times since she'd arrived. On her first day she spent a couple of hours up here, squinting at the murals that had saved the house from demolition, trying to make them out. In the main they were faded and sketchy – a mass of images that didn't mean much to her. Just scenes from the bible, clusters of flowers, painted wooden panels and sketched heraldic symbols. One of the pictures was of Samson and Delilah – Linda remembered that story from school, but, as far as she could see, the rest was just flaking paint. What few figures there were, were unrealistic.

Not this one.

She stepped backwards to try to take it in.

Then the woman smiled.

Linda screamed. She dropped the torch and fumbled to pick it up as she backed away, stumbling over her slippers. When she finally managed to direct the beam, the woman's expression was serene. Friendly, almost. She moved again, reaching out calmly. Linda's eyes widened. The top of the woman's index finger was missing. And she was injured too. Well not injured exactly. But in the low light Linda could see her skin was blotchy and not because she was in need of restoration. The poor thing was covered in bruises. 'God,' she whispered. 'What did he do to you?'

Partly veiled, the image slowly moved its head to one side.

'Can you speak?'

She shook her head, sadly.

'Are you…' Linda hesitated, reluctant to say the words. 'Lady Alice?'

Linda waited. She knew what it felt like, to want to be seen. Just as you were. For someone to understand. She stared, slowly taking in the image, the bruises and the woman's sad eyes.

'So you're here? Your body is here?'

Another nod.

'He hurt you? And the bastard got away with it.'

Slowly the image put her hands together as if she was

about to pray. 'You jumped. Or did you? Did he push you? Is that what it is?'

The bruise on Linda's shoulder began to burn. Jim had rained down blows on her. Almost since the beginning. As soon as they were away. She'd stopped going out. She'd stopped everything, cowering in the flat, waiting for him to come home. To see if he was in a good mood or not. It was fifty-fifty. Less than that at the end. A kind of torture.

The woman raised the bloodied remains of her finger to her lips.

'I won't tell anyone,' Linda promised. But that wasn't it. The figure it seemed, was waiting for something. Linda hesitated. She hadn't told a soul. But, well.

'He used to call me Piggy,' she started. She'd always felt too ashamed to admit it. But, then, Jim had never chopped a piece of her off.

'He beat me too. He enjoyed it. I remember thinking that at least I was giving him pleasure. Making him feel like a big man.' Once she'd started she found she couldn't stop the stream of words. 'He said I couldn't cook and he was right. Not even toast.' Tears began to flow. She felt them drip off her chin. 'He made me do things. He tore my clothes. He hit me. He hurt me. He used to scream "How can you be so ugly?" He was right about that. Other women are so beautiful. But me – I'm nothing, really. I'm just ordinary.'

The woman shook her head. She smiled once more. And Linda smiled back.

Linda didn't go back to the kitchen. Instead she sat on the floor. The cold stone seeped through her dressing gown but she kept her eyes on the wall. She wondered who the man had been. She wondered if Lady Alice had ever struck back. And for the first time she felt like she belonged somewhere. 'Did they bury you?' she whispered under her breath, wondering where, if he'd got his way, Jim would have buried her. 'Never again,' she said, as if she was making a promise.

Hours later, she woke on the floor. The grilles were creaking as the heating came on. Her nose was still bright from the cold night-time air. Dawn lit the window. Linda got up. She touched the wall lightly and smiled again.

Around ten, Mark let himself into the kitchen. He clutched a box from Greggs in his hand. 'I think we got off on the wrong foot yesterday. I brought you these. Yum yums. I thought ... with tea?'

Linda smiled. He was trying. But then she realised he was waiting for her to put on the kettle.

'It's over there,' she directed him.

Mark manfully flicked the switch. He fussed looking for mugs and getting hold of teabags. Linda put a pint of milk on the table next to the doughnuts.

'My Mum would kill me,' Mark babbled. 'For what I said yesterday. I don't know what I was thinking. Probably not thinking at all, right? I'm sorry.'

Linda shrugged. The conservator would never see the ghost of Kinneil – she wouldn't reveal herself to someone like him. Everyone had heard of her, but how many people had actually seen Lady Alice? Had Jean lied all those years ago about the woman flying off the top of the roof? Or was it only her? Linda bit into a yum yum.

'You like doughnuts, don't you? I mean, you look as if you like doughnuts,' Mark said.

Linda stopped chewing.

'I mean, who doesn't like doughnuts? Oh God,' his cheeks coloured.

Slowly, she put down the yum yum. The small mirror on the mantelpiece reflected her double chin and a fleck of icing on her lip. 'I don't have to make excuses for what I am,' Linda said.

'Sorry,' he mumbled. 'Sorry.'

She drew herself up. 'You'd better get to work. I'll see you up.'

They climbed the old stone steps.

'Nice morning for it,' Mark said. He was trying to change the subject. 'This stone spiral and the old staircase on the other side, they're tremendous works of engineering and design. They had no machines in those days you know – everything was cut by hand. It's astonishing if you think about it.'

'Yes', she said, 'astonishing'. She walked ahead of him, only half-listening to his prattle as he talked about woodcarvings and layers of paint. The truth was, she was just the caretaker. She didn't have the right accent. Or the right friends. Or enough qualifications. She wasn't rich. Or famous. Her life was normal. Boring. Fair enough. But why did he have to be so rude?

Mark stopped in his tracks and she glanced at him over her shoulder.

'This wasn't here yesterday,' he said. 'I thought you were supposed to stop people breaking in.'

Linda turned. Mark's head was cocked as he took in the figure on the wall

'It's easy enough to get off,' he said. 'But the trustees will have to be told.'

'Don't you like it?'

'What do you mean?'

'It's Lady Alice Lilbourne.'

She'd taken the pencil from Mark's toolbox last night, sketched the figure of Alice in the exact spot she'd appeared, shading in her bruises – which, she'd realised as she drew them, mirrored her own. The marks of his fingers on the shoulders, etched into the soft skin at the top of her arms. The long, dark bruises where he'd kicked her in the stomach.

'You did this?' said Mark raising his voice. 'Are you mad? You can't go doodling all over the walls! This is a listed building!'

'But the other murals don't show what really happened,' she said. 'Not the things that matter.'

A single tear leaked out and ran down her cheek. Mark looked taken aback.

He felt in his pocket for a handkerchief but only came up with a scrap of toilet roll.

'Look it's just... I mean you can't just...' He sighed and shook his head. She waved away his offer of a tissue.

'I'm not going to cry,' she said, brushing the tear with the palm of her hand. She had cried enough.

'Right,' said Mark, 'why don't you go downstairs and make another cuppa and I'll start taking it off. Least said, soonest mended, eh?'

She watched his hand fingering the mobile phone in his trouser pocket.

'Yes,' she said. 'More tea.'

It took him entirely unawares when she picked up the bread knife. It was still where she'd left it the previous night, at the foot of the wall, next to where she'd fallen asleep. She couldn't let him tell the trustees. They'd make her leave Kinneil, wouldn't they? An animal sound came out of her mouth, just like the woman in the wall the night before. Mark turned and his eyes widened with panic but he was far too slow to stop her. The knife pierced his woollen sweater, right between his ribs. Biology was one of the exams Linda had done well in. They'd had to dissect a frog.

The conservator fell to his knees. He made a gurgling

sound. It was quieter than when you saw it on television and there wasn't all that much blood. She'd thought that before. For a big man, Jim had been quiet at the end too. They hadn't found him and they wouldn't find this one either. There were places at Kinneil you could hide a body. Mark had said it himself – no one would ever be allowed to dig up the Roman part of the grounds. Or there was the old quarry, just on the other side of the house. She'd find a way. And the mural would help her. She had time – no one was coming till next week. Not till Mrs Pleitch's day on the rota.

Mark looked peaceful now and Linda sat next to him for what seemed like a long time. She felt the house breathe in and out. Somewhere far off, the old plaster shifted. 'You're not welcome here,' she said. 'That's the thing.' Then she smiled. Kinneil House was home now. She'd look after the old place and the old place would look after her.

Kinnaird Head Lighthouse

Stevenson's Candle
Stuart MacBride

He pulled on the handbrake and sat there with the engine running. Frowned out at the collections of white-and-beige buildings while the DJ yammered over the tail end of a bland song.

'*...Mark Almond and Gene Pitney there, number one for a third week running. Amazing, right?*'

Three single-storey blocky buildings made an open box around his Ford Cortina – North, East, and South – the stones around their doors, windows, floor, and flat roofs were picked out in a sickly shade of butterscotch.

Ten to five and the sinking sun swathed the courtyard in blue and grey shadows. The sky an angry mask of bruised clouds. Not yet dark enough to hide the way the white blockwork was stained in places. Patchy. Peeling.

Well that would have to change. The manual *clearly* stated that all buildings had to be maintained in perfect condition.

'*We're in full World Cup Fever mode here at Broch FM, so stay tuned for in-depth analysis of our boys' stunning three–two win in the qualifier against Cyprus last week. See next year? See 1990? That's the year Scotland takes the World Cup home, I guarantee it!*'

The only building not in need of a damn good lick of paint was the huge ancient structure on the left. A lump of white stone, four stories tall, with battlements at the top of its sugar-cube squareness. And growing out of the roof: the lighthouse tower itself. Dark and looming.

Completely unacceptable.

A spatter of rain hissed against the windscreen.

'And don't forget, it's the night of the big storm, so batten down those hatches, cuddle up with a loved one, and get ready to rock with Dire Straits' "Money For Nothing". Aw, yeah!'

He turned the key, killing the Cortina's engine, shutting off the song before it got past the first couple of notes.

Straightened his tie.

Did the same with his name badge, checking it in the rearview mirror. 'SUPERINTENDENT I. BLACKWELL'

He made eye contact with himself, voice firm. 'You're a superintendent now, Ian. Act like it.' A nod, then he climbed out of the car. Cold air gripped his throat, made his arms prickle beneath the new suit and shirt. Breath fogging for a moment before the wind stole it away.

February in Fraserburgh, he had to be mad.

Ian pulled the big leather suitcase from the back seat. Tucked his clipboard under one arm.

Turned.

The National Lighthouse Board flag snapped and writhed on its halyard, as specified in the manual. Good. At least they could do *something* right here.

Wind whipped at his trouser legs. Ruffled the lapels of his suit.

Back straight, he marched straight across the courtyard to the flat-roofed building that made up the eastern edge of the square. Two beige doors. Ian hammered on the right-hand one. The one marked 'FIRST ASSISTANT LIGHTHOUSE KEEPER'.

It was opened by a woman with thin wrists and sunken cheeks, a pallor and a *smell* about her. Sour and green. As if she'd been sick recently. She pulled on what almost passed for a smile and held out a hand. It was clutching a handkerchief.

He didn't shake it. Instead he put his suitcase down and checked the clipboard. 'Mrs ... Fulton, is it? Where's your husband?' Ian turned and jabbed a hand at the dark tower. 'Any *why* is that light not on?'

'It... He...' Her handkerchief fluttered to her nose and back again. 'It's this bug. He's been sick and...' a blush, voice lowering, 'always on the toilet. We've all had it, it's terrible, I can barely—'

'I don't care if he's on his deathbed: there's a major storm coming! Where's the Second Assistant Keeper?'

'It's his day off and—'

'Unacceptable. Two people have to be on duty at *all* times.'

'But the Occasional Keeper is—'

'I'll deal with your husband later!'

Ian picked up his suitcase, turned, and hurried across to the bulky lump of ancient castle. A pair of half-width doors marked the entrance, painted the same butter-scotch-beige.

He wrenched one side open and squeezed inside, then through the second pair of too-thin doors and into the stairwell. Slammed the doors closed behind him. And stared. Up.

The spiral staircase wound round and round disappearing into the heights, coiling like a snail's shell. The chain hanging down the middle of the spiral was still. Silent.

Idiots!

He dumped his suitcase, gritted his teeth, and hammering up the stairs, one hand on the mahogany railing. 'WHAT THE BLOODY HELL IS GOING ON HERE?'

Around and up. And up.

Past the dark-brown smell of cooking mince.

Up.

'GET THIS LIGHT WORKING!'

Up.

A ladder at the top of the stairs ended at a grey trap-door in the ceiling, its brass handrail polished and gleaming. Which was all well and good, but no bloody use if the light wasn't on.

Ian surged up it, threw the trapdoor open and clambered into the light room.

A greasy smell. A whiff of the unwashed – rancid and oniony.

A collection of cogs and machinery filled a glass-fronted case in the middle of the room, crowding him out to the edge. Above that, a row of bearings. And above *them*, a big metal platform with the lenses and prisms on it – arrayed on heavy metal brackets, all focused around a central pillar where a wide-shouldered man in overalls was hunched over, fiddling with something.

'YOU! GET THIS LIGHT ON!'

There was a pause. A sniff. And then the man turned.

Grey hair swept back from his head like a Teddy Boy's, a moustache the same colour, a craggy face that looked more disappointed than angry. His voice was a fist full of broken knuckles, the accent broad but unplaceable. 'What do you think I'm *trying* to do?' He returned to whatever he'd been fiddling with and light bloomed in his hands. It bounced back from the refractors, getting brighter with every pass through the glass until the whole room glowed.

A grunt and a nod, then he stepped off the central platform and climbed down to the light room floor. His quiff brushed the walkway above their heads. Tall and imposing. He held a greasy rag in one hand, and with a flick of the wrist he lobbed its contents towards Ian.

What Ian caught was hot enough to hiss against his skin, passing it from hand to hand like a baked potato. A lightbulb.

The man opened the glass doors containing the machinery, hooked his foot under a metal bar and popped it upwards. Something inside gave a loud metallic clank. Then another one as the platform above their head swung into life, rotating on its bearings.

Clank. Clank. Clank.

'There we go.' He wiped his hands on the cloth and closed the glazed doors again. 'No need to get our knickers in a twist.'

'Knickers...?' Ian pulled himself up to his full height. 'I want your name and rank. *Now.*'

The mechanism clanked. *Clank. Clank. Clank.*

And finally the big man took a step closer, face set. Voice little more than a growl. 'William Erskine. Occasional Lighthouse Keeper.'

'I see.' Ian made a note on his clipboard. 'Well, Mr Erskine, let me explain to you how this works. In order of importance it goes Commissioners; Superintendents – that's me; Principal Lighthouse Keepers; First Assistant Lighthouse Keepers; Second Assistant Lighthouse Keepers; and not quite, but *almost* scraping the bottom of the keel: there's you.'

The moustache bristled.

'The only people less important than you are the Supernumeraries. And as soon as they've completed their training, they outrank you. As I do. So you will show me the proper respect. Are we clear?'

'Oh I think we're perfectly clear.'

'Good. And why are you out of uniform?'

Erskine looked down at his oil-stained overalls. 'Because I'm fixing the lamp.'

'I see. Well, it's fixed now, so I expect you to dress appropriately for the remainder of your shift. That is all.'

The big lump didn't say anything, just stood there, put well and truly in his place.

Ian nodded. Then climbed backwards down the ladder and onto the landing below.

If you let these people get away with laxity and slovenliness where would it end? Disaster, that's where.

Well not on Ian Blackwell's watch.

He set off down the stairs.

Paused on the next landing. That smell of cooking mince oozed out from behind a door marked 'OCCASIONAL KEEPER'.

Did Erskine think he was an idiot?

He was meant to *stay* in the light room for the duration of his shift – it said so in the manual. All four hours. In the light room. No popping down for an evening meal!

Ian shoved the door open, marching into a large white room with brown lino on the floor topped by a nasty brown-and-orange rug. Old mahogany wardrobe. Old leather armchair. A record player so old it was built into its own sideboard. A single bed in the corner facing a big boxy TV and a white electric cooker.

A small, stocky man stood in front of it, stirring away

at a pot, whistling something tuneless to himself. His big baggy Arran jumper had probably been white once, but the years had turned it a depressing yellow-grey. The room's lights reflected in his polished scalp.

Ian put on his best official voice. 'And who the hell are you supposed to be?'

The man didn't stop stirring. 'Me? You can call us, Big Arthur.' Big Arthur turned and shared a smile. One tooth missing on the top. Face cragged as a cliff, nose a swollen red orb, eyes sagging and moist. A cigarette poked out the side of his mouth, his gunmetal moustache and beard stained a sickly yellow-brown around it. Tattoos covered both hands, more visible where the jumper's neck sagged around its owner's. 'You the new boy?'

'I am the new *Superintendent*.'

'Aye? Good for you.' More stirring. 'Mince, tatties, and skirlie all right for your tea?'

A bell rang out in the light room.

Ian stiffened. 'Mrs Fulton can prepare something.'

'Suit yourself, but see me? When I know someone's got a bad dose of the galloping squits? I'm not eating anything they touch.' Big Arthur went back to his whistling.

He probably had a point.

The Fulton woman didn't look particularly hygienic. And besides—

That broken-fist growl sounded behind Ian. 'Going to move over a bit?'

He span on his heel. 'Mr Erskine: you're supposed to be watching that light!'

The big man didn't move. 'How's tea coming, Arthur?'

'Tatties need another minute.'

'Mr Erskine, I must insist—'

'You', he stepped in, crowding Ian, 'told me I had to put on my uniform, remember? Well, I've just wound the chain up and now I'm here to change.'

'I see. Well, in that case...' Ian shuffled out of the way, letting him past. 'And would you mind telling me what this *gentleman* is doing in your quarters?'

'Big Arthur? He's making mince and tatties.' Erskine padded across the room and opened the old mahogany wardrobe that sat at the end of the bed. Kicked off his shoes and removed his overalls – revealing a string vest, blue pants, and red socks. His back was covered in nautical tattoos, black, dark blue, faded blue, all visible through the gaps in the string vest.

'You are *not* allowed visitors, Mr Erskine. This is a lighthouse, not a social club!'

He pulled on a white shirt that was too small for him, the cuffs not long enough to cover his wrists. 'The Principal Lighthouse Keeper retired last week. The First Assistant's been welded to the bog all day. The Second's visiting his dying mother in Peterhead Hospital.' Erskine pulled on the standard issue dark blue trousers. Tucked the shirt in. 'You want to know who's running this place tonight? Me and Big Arthur.'

Ian stared at the little man stirring the mince. 'Is he even *qualified*?'

Big Arthur shrugged. 'Every twenty-five to thirty minutes, you wind up the chain till it goes *ding*. That raises the weight. The weight slowly sinks back down again, powering a clockwork mechanism that makes the prisms and lenses rotate once every thirty seconds. Which gives the lighthouse its signature character of fifteen seconds.' Another missing-tooth smile. 'Not exactly rocket science, is it?'

'I can assure you there's more to operating a lighthouse than winding a handle!'

Erskine tied a tie around his neck. 'Big Arthur used to work in the fish. There's not an engine or mechanism he can't fix. Good man in a crisis too.'

'Well, no point panicking, is there?' Big Arthur scooped potatoes out of a pot and dumped them in a bowl. 'September, 1972, I was on the *Long Mary*, out of Buckie, chasing haddock across Forties.' He added a slosh of milk. 'Wee Eric Kerr was on his first trip; hawser snapped and cut him clean in two. Everything above the elbows went one way, everything below went the other.' A knob of butter joined the milk. 'All his insides turned into outsides. Lungs, liver, kidneys, guts... All over the deck.' A potato masher appeared from a drawer and Big Arthur stabbed away at his potatoes for a bit, frowning. 'Course everyone panics. We're one day out from port and now we've got to go right back again. We were on a lovely run of haddies too, seemed a shame to waste it.' He pulled a plate from the oven and dolloped a scoop of mash onto it. 'So I says, "Pack him in ice and let's get back to fishing." Wasn't like he was going anywhere, was it? Dead's dead and fish are fish.' A ladleful of mince joined the potatoes. Thick and dark and flecked with nuggets of carrot. Followed by a small mound of pale gritty mush.

Big Arthur held the plate out to Ian. 'You ever seen a dead body, Mr Superintendent? There's cutlery in the drawer.'

'I...'

'Course he has.' Erskine fastened his uniform jacket – a heavy double-breasted navy thing with brass buttons and sleeves that didn't fit. Too short, like the shirt. The trousers were the same, showing off two inches of those red socks. As if his uniform had been made for someone smaller. 'My first was Old Robbie Smith. Forklift truck tipped over on him: didn't kill him right off though, he lay there screaming for what, half an hour? Something like that. Screaming and screaming.' A peaked cap with a white crown, black band and black visor – the NLB crest set proudly in the middle – went on Erskine's head. 'I was all for getting a sledgehammer and putting the poor sod out of his misery, but they wouldn't let me. So we just stood there and listened to him scream and scream. Then he wasn't screaming any more and they stuck a tarpaulin over him; been dead twenty minutes by the time the ambulance finally turned up. I was fourteen.' A small laugh. 'Funny how the first one stays with you.'

Hilarious.

Ian swallowed. Looked down at the plate of food in his hand.

Perhaps not.

He placed it on top of the television. 'Mr...? Arthur. The National Lighthouse Board thanks you for your assistance, but now that I'm here, you're free to return to your home. We can't have unqualified individuals manning the facility, it's a massive violation of the regulations. Mr Erskine and I will take it from here.'

'Aye, but wouldn't it be—'

'*Thank you.*'

A fresh burst of rain rattled the window.

Wind moaned across the glass.

The little man pursed his lips. Looked over Ian's shoulder at Erskine. Raised an eyebrow. Then nodded. 'Fair enough.' He turned the cooker off and grabbed a stained donkey jacket from the armchair by the bed. Stuck out a hand for Erskine to shake. 'See you later, Willie.'

'Aye.'

And he was gone, leaving his pots and pans behind him.

Ian checked the clipboard again. 'Mr Erskine, I shall relieve you at twenty hundred hours. I expect you to remain at your post until then.'

The big man didn't say anything, just picked the plate off the television and walked out of his quarters. His footsteps thumped up the stairs, marking time with the *clank, clank, clank*, of the turntable mechanism.

A small act of rebellion, but an acceptable one in the circumstances.

Mrs Fulton's husband was grey. He'd put on his uniform: all ironed and polished, shoes like black mirrors. Standing to attention in the living room. Sweat making his face shine.

The Principal Lighthouse Keeper's cottage formed the south edge of the courtyard, nearly twice the size of the one this shivering grey man lived in. The benefits of rank.

Its furniture had been installed sometime in the seventies, along with the horrible wallpaper, carpet, and furniture. Perhaps it was a mistake forbidding the keepers to decorate their own cottages? But the rules were the rules.

Ian checked the proffered paperwork. Wind: south-westerly, fifteen knots. Visibility: poor. Temperature: falling. 'You're very fortunate I'm here, Mr Fulton. Very fortunate indeed.'

'Yes, sir. Thank you, sir.' He had the same sour-green smell as his wife.

'As it is, I shall not be entering a complaint against you. But if you ever leave this facility in the care of a civilian again, I'll see you thrown out of the service. Are we clear?'

His Adam's apple bobbed. 'Yes, sir.'

'I'm not a monster, Mr Fulton, but *standards* must be maintained. Now, you are dismissed. Return to your sickbed and be ready for duty tomorrow morning.'

'Thank you, sir.' He turned smartly on his heel and marched out of the cottage, closing the door behind him. Through the living room window he was clearly visible – caught in the glow of the station's lights – slumping, running a hand across his face. The wind made a grab for his peaked cap, but he snatched it down again and staggered back to his cottage. Where he would no doubt tell his wife that the new Superintendent was hard, but fair. A man to look up to. A man to emulate.

Ian nodded. Then went to unpack.

The cottage's chimney moaned. The windows whistled. The front door groaning as the wind prised its fingers into the building, looking for weaknesses to exploit. Beaten back by the coal glowing away in the fireplace.

Ian checked the clock on the mantelpiece – an old-fashioned brass affair. Nineteen forty-five. Soon be time for him to take over the running of Kinnaird Head. His bowels prickled in anticipation. Fifteen minutes. Just enough time to run through the manual again.

But how hard could it be? Erskine's friend, Big Arthur, was right: as long as you kept the chain wound up the rest would take care of itself.

As long as nothing went wrong.

Which it...

Ian frowned out through the window. The lighthouse beams swept across the sky, fore and aft, almost solid things in the rain. But there was another source of illumination, moving across the buildings. Then a car appeared – boxy and pointy at the same time. A Vauxhall Astra. White, with a blue dome light fixed to the roof and a thistle crest on the driver's door – 'GRAMPIAN POLICE' curled around it.

The patrol car parked right outside the cottage, and there, caught in the glow from the station's lights was a woman. White shirt, black tie, black tunic. She poked at the dashboard a couple of times, then slammed the palm of her hand down on it repeatedly, what looked like a telephone handset pressed to her ear.

She sagged back in her seat and screamed something at the car's roof. Before clambering out into the rain. A bowler hat clenched down with one hand, boxy skirt stretched tight, black gloves, black handbag.

A gust of wind thumped her back against the car and she struggled against it, launching herself across to his cottage door and hammering on the wood.

He dropped the manual on the table and pulled on the Principal Keeper's uniform jacket – buttoning it as he marched into the hall. Stepped through the inner door, closed it behind him, and opened one side of the outer set.

She stumbled into the airlock, bringing the wind's roar with her. Then turned and shoved the half-door shut again. Stood there, pressed close against him in the small space, exuding the sharp raw-coal scent of carbolic soap. 'Argh... It's a hurricane out there!'

Ian shook his head. 'Actually, it's not a hurricane until we hit twelve on the Beaufort Scale. The last reading put this at force ten, so it's just a storm. These distinctions are important.'

She raised an eyebrow. 'Any chance we could step into the property, sir? Only this is a little cramped.'

'Yes. Of course. Sorry.' He backed through into the hall. Gestured her into the living room.

'Ooh...' She made straight for the fire, standing close

enough that steam rose from the shoulders of her uniform. 'Have you seen any strange individuals, sir? Anyone suspicious?' She turned. Just below the hem of her rigid skirt, the thick black tights were torn. The skin beneath speckled with little red dots.

Suspicious? Well, William Erskine was definitely that. As was his tattooed little friend. But suspicious enough to merit police interest?

'I shall require more information than that. Specifics.'

A nod. 'This would be someone recently escaped from police custody, sir. Someone it would be ... unwise for a member of the public to approach.'

'Someone dangerous.'

She smiled at him. 'Is that a yes?'

'I only arrived here three hours ago, and to be quite frank, everyone I've met is strange.' Ian checked the time again. Nineteen fifty. He picked up the Principal Keeper's peaked cap, tucked it under his arm. 'I'm afraid I have to be going, Miss...?'

'WPC Miller. Valerie to my friends.'

'I see. Well, Miss Miller, I need to relieve Mr Erskine from duty.' He waved a hand at the living room window, indicating the courtyard and the buildings beyond. 'You are, of course, welcome to question the staff, but I would advise caution. The wind-speed is over fifty knots, that's nearly sixty miles per hour. Don't stray out onto the cliffs – the National Lighthouse Board can't be responsible for your safety.'

Her smile got brighter. 'Then I shall do my best not to die.'

Ian cranked the handle, tendons and muscles heating up his arm and across his back. Until the mechanism dinged at him. All set again.

The ratchet clanked. *Clank. Clank. Clank.*

To some the constant clatter would be an annoyance, but not to him. It was a sound that meant all was well. The clockwork mechanism was working: the turntable was turning. The lighthouse was functioning.

Clank. Clank. Clank.

The only other noise came from the two small wooden doors on opposite sides of the light room, leading outside. They roared. Their edges howling as the wind stampeded in from the north-west, whipping the sea into a frenzy, hammering raindrops into the wood like a million frozen nails. It was a shame the only windows were above his head. A full three hundred and sixty degree panorama of glass – it would be magnificent to stand there, on the walkway and look upon the storm's majesty.

But that would mean stopping the turntable and stalling the light. Destroying its sole purpose for being here.

And that would not do.

So, instead, he settled into the wooden chair beneath the ladder. Looked up through the mesh walkway at the lenses and prisms as they rotated around the lightbulb. A smooth and perfectly timed dance, never speeding up or slowing down. Constant and beautiful.

He allowed himself a sip of strong coffee to celebrate. His first ever shift manning a lighthouse. And in full dress uniform too. Yes, it wasn't technically *his*, but it was a reasonable fit and much more in keeping with the occasion than his own suit.

Ian sighed. Stared up at the rotating lenses again.

How could anyone not love this?

Then another noise joined the clanking, howling, and hammering, souring his utopia. .

'*HELLO?*' It came from downstairs, muffled by the

trapdoor. *'IS ANYONE THERE?'* A woman's voice, screeching like a fishwife.

Of *course* there was someone here. It was a manned lighthouse station, how could there not be?

He sighed, put his mug down, and sidled around the mechanics. Hauled the trapdoor open.

The WPC, Miss Miller, stared up at him from the bottom of the ladder. Her uniform dripped onto the red and beige floor. Nose, cheeks, and ears a burning shade of scarlet. 'It's horrible out there!'

'I am well aware of the weather, thank you. What are you still doing here?'

She took off her bowler hat and wiped the water from her face. 'Gah...'

'It's been over an hour, surely that's more than enough time to—'

'Wind's so strong I could barely *stand up* on the way over here. Thought I was going to have to crawl.' She shivered. 'Mrs Fulton insisted I stay for tea while my tunic dried. Don't know why she bothered: completely soaked through again. It's like wading through a cold bath.'

'This is a restricted area, Miss Miller, and I have a very important job to—'

'Mr Erskine.'

Ian pulled his chin in. 'What about him?'

'Where is he? You said you were relieving him. I'll need to speak to him.'

Oh for goodness sake. Ian pointed down the stairs. 'Next floor down. Door marked "Occasional Keeper", but don't keep him long – his shift starts in two and a half hours and I want him rested.'

A grin. 'Thanks.' Then she was off, squelching her way down the spiral staircase.

The sound of knocking echoed up from the floor below.

'*Mr Erskine? Mr Erskine, it's the police, can you come to the door please?*'

Clank. Clank. Clank.

More knocking.

'*Mr Erskine? Hello?*'

The knocking turned into banging.

'MR ERSKINE! THIS IS THE POLICE! OPEN UP!'

Clank. Clank. Clank.

WPC Miller appeared at the bottom of the ladder again. 'The door wasn't locked. He's not there and his bed's not been slept in.'

Damn. 'You'd better come up.'

She climbed through the trapdoor, into the light room. Stared at the clockwork cabinet and the revolving lenses above it. 'Wow.'

Ian folded his arms. 'This person you're looking for, they're dangerous?'

'Alex Doyle. My radio kept cutting out because of the storm, but from what I can tell he's killed at least four people. They were moving him to a secure psychiatric facility when he escaped.'

'And why us? Why are you searching Kinnaird Head?'

Her forehead creased. 'We're not. Not *specifically*. There was a sighting of him in Fraserburgh, so we're working our way through the town. It's...' She turned and stared at the little wooden door leading out onto the external walkway as the wind rattled the thing on its hinges. 'Is it safe up here?'

'This lighthouse was built by Robert Stevenson, it's stood here since 1824 – a candle in the darkness, lighting the mariner's way, saving his life. The castle it's built into was constructed in 1570. I hardly think it's going to blow down tonight.'

'Alex Doyle has … it's not really multiple personality disorder, he *becomes* other people. Genuinely believes he's them. But there can't be two of him, so whoever the original person is, they have to go.'

'He kills them, then he becomes them.'

'Something like that. Sometimes he doesn't even know he's *not* them.'

Ian raised an eyebrow and stared at her. Utter nonsense, of course. How could a man not know who he really was? It was preposterous. Of *course* he would know.

There was a thump somewhere below. Then the sound of heavy boots on the spiral stairs. Getting closer.

Erskine.

Erskine. With his uniform that looked as if it was made for someone else. Erskine watching an old man getting crushed to death when he was fourteen. Erskine who—

His face appeared at the bottom of the ladder. 'Blowing an absolute *hoolie* out there.'

Ian stared down at him. 'Where have you been? The police want to talk to you.'

A shrug. He'd changed out of his uniform into a sou'wester and thick yellow oilskin jacket, both slick and shiny from the rain. Wellington boots leaving puddles on the stairs. 'North-westerly, force twelve.'

WPC Miller turned to stare at the rattling wooden door. 'That's a hurricane. I was out in a hurricane…'

'Wind speed?'

Erskine unbuttoned his oilskin. 'Ninety-three knots and rising.'

She swallowed and stepped forwards, until she was looking down at him. 'Mr Erskine, have you seen anyone about on your travels? Anyone strange or suspicious?'

He laughed. Then shook his head. 'Anyone out in that

isn't strange, they're suicidal. Got slates flying off roofs all over. Couple of fishing sheds that way,' he hooked a thumb over his shoulder, 'peeled apart like oranges. You'd have to be insane.'

'Insane. Yes.' She pulled out her notebook. Frowned at him. 'Have we met before?'

'No.'

'That's...' Another frown. 'I can't quite place your accent, Mr Erskine, are you local?'

'Me? Born and bred in the Broch!' Another laugh. 'I pick up other people's accents, have done since I was a wee lad. Put me in a room with a Geordie, or a Paddy, even a Yank, and I'll be sounding like them in five minutes flat. Can't help it. They call it a whore's ear.' He shrugged. 'There's worse things.' Then turned. 'I'm putting the kettle on, if anyone wants a brew.' Disappearing back downstairs.

As soon as he was gone, Ian pointed, keeping his voice low. 'Him. What if it's him?'

'Your Occasional Keeper? How could it be him? You *know* who he is. Alex Doyle only escaped this morning.'

'I don't know him from Adam! He was here when I arrived, he told me he was the Occasional Keeper. He could be *anyone*.'

She smiled. Then placed a hand on his arm and squeezed. 'Don't worry, you're perfectly safe. It can't be him – Alex Doyle escaped with his best friend, George Banks. They were inseparable in prison, he wouldn't just abandon him.'

'But he had a friend! Big Arthur: short, sturdy looking. Bald, with a beard. Tattoos on his hands and this bit of his chest.' Ian patted his collarbones. 'They kept telling me about all the dead bodies they'd seen.'

'I see.' She bit her bottom lip. Shifted the handbag

hanging over her shoulder. 'Is there anyone here who *can* identify Mr Erskine? Someone who's worked with him before?'

'Yes.' Ian shuffled his way around the light room to the pale-cream phone mounted to the wall and pressed the button for the First Assistant Keeper's cottage. Held the handset to his ear and listened to the silence. No buzzing. No tone. He used a finger to flick the hook up and down a half-dozen times. Still nothing. 'It's not working.'

'Probably the storm. Bet there's telephone poles down all over the north-east.'

'No, you don't understand, this isn't an external line. It connects the lighthouse to the three cottages and the engine room, it's all internal. It *has* to work!' A lumpy grey telephone sat next to it: a proper one with a rotary dial. He grabbed the handset. No dial tone. Nothing but silence. Ian hung up. Tightened his hands into fists. 'It's him. Erskine. He's done something. He's cut us off.'

She peered down through the trapdoor again. 'Let's not jump to any conclusions.'

Ian glanced at the mechanism whirring away in its glass-fronted cabinet. According to the manual, fully wound-up the chain would run the turntable for thirty minutes.

Yes, but he couldn't just *leave* it.

What if Erskine decided to sabotage something else? What if he cut the power? The light would go out. There was the back-up paraffin lamp, but that would... How did you light it? How did you keep it lit? What if it didn't work? What if a ship was wrecked because Kinnaird Head was in darkness?

No. Not on Ian Blackwell's watch.

Deep breath. Then he stepped onto the ladder. 'Let's go.'

They crept along, following the winding spiral downwards. One full turn to the Occasional Keeper's quarters.

Ian peered around the open door.

No sign of Erskine, but a large metal kettle steamed away on the old electric cooker, juddering as it boiled. He stepped inside and shut off the ring. 'Must be downstairs.'

They descended a turn and a half. A door led off the stairwell into a tiny corridor.

WPC Miller stepped forwards, but Ian put out a hand and stopped her. 'Just want to check something.' He hurried down the spiral stairs' last half turn to the ground floor, where the paired narrow doors led out into the storm.

The bottom loop of the chain hung in the middle of the space, but it wasn't the only thing that descended from above. A thick bunch of cables made a black line down the walls, disappearing into the bulky collection of metal boxes right in front of him. Two cables were snipped clean through, the copper wire within gleaming at their core. One would be the intercom line. The other the phone.

Erskine...

Ian backed away. Looked up.

WPC Miller was hanging over the handrail, staring down at him. 'What?'

'I was right: he's sabotaged the wiring.'

Well, enough was enough. Ian ran up to the landing, two steps at a time. Pushed past the woman and into the small corridor. Three doors. Straight ahead: flushing toilet, no sink. Left: a storeroom with raw stone walls. Right: 'PARAFFIN ROOM'.

Ian shoved the door open.

The paraffin room was huge. Two storeys high with a balcony jutting out of the right-hand wall, facing a double-height arched window – the glass turned into a mirror by the darkness outside, rattled by rain. Wind howling outside the lighthouse walls like a starving wolf. A hot-candles-and-petrol stench filled the air in here, probably coming from the four man-sized tanks in the far corner. Paraffin.

No Erskine.

So he wasn't—

Wind screamed and roared, buffeting Ian forward. Then a slamming noise from the stairwell. He turned, but the WPC had gone.

Her voice: *'Mr Erskine?'*

That broken-knuckle rasp: *'Fit like, Quine?'*

Ian turned and bellowed it out. 'MR ERSKINE! I DEMAND YOU GET IN HERE THIS INSTANT!'

'Oh for God's sake, what's the wee fanny after now?'

Fanny? How *dare* he!

Thirty seconds later, Erskine sloped into the paraffin room – still dressed in his oilskin, Teddy-Boy quiff plastered flat by the rain. 'What now?'

Ian pulled his shoulders back. 'Why did you do it?'

A pause. Then Erskine raised an eyebrow. 'I'm getting tired of being barked at, *Superintendent*.'

The WPC appeared in the doorway behind Erskine. 'Someone's cut the phone cables. Intercom too.'

'And you think it's *me*?' He shook his head. 'Why? Why would I cut the phone line?'

Ian slammed a hand down on the work bench. 'Because you're not William Erskine, you're *Alex Doyle*!'

'Who on earth is Alex Doyle?'

WPC Miller put a hand on the big man's arm. 'Alex Doyle escaped from police custody earlier today. He's …

he's very confused and he needs our help.' She even gave him a smile. 'He might hurt someone, or himself, if we don't help him.'

Erskine / Doyle curled his lip at her. 'What's that got to do with me?'

'Superintendent Blackwell thinks—'

'It's you, isn't it, Erskine? You assume other people's identities, you kill them and you take their place. It's not just your ears that belong to a whore, your whole personality does too!'

'Me?' He shook off the woman and stepped forward. 'I've worked here for nine years, you jumped-up wee shite! You want someone who's not who he says? What about you? Eh?'

'Preposterous. I've never—'

'You turned up this afternoon, throwing your weight around, with nothing but a name badge for ID. And now look at you!' He jabbed a hand forward. 'That's the Principal Keeper's uniform. You've not *earned* that, you can barely work the sodding chain! You've never done a light-room shift in your life.'

'I AM A SUPERINTENDENT AND YOU WILL RESPECT ME!'

WPC Miller's mouth fell open. 'Oh my God...'

'Oh don't tell me you *believe* him? He's clearly delusional!'

'I'll "delusional" you.' Erskine grabbed a hammer from the workbench. 'If you're really a superintendent, when was the Commissioners' last inspection? Come on, Blackwell, if that's your real name.'

A hammer. Exactly the kind of weapon one would expect of the lower ranks.

The woman walked forwards, staring up at the balcony. 'Is that...?'

Ian snatched a hand axe from the wall. 'You'll put that down. *Now*!'

She pointed. 'How did...?'

'For God's sake, woman, *concentrate*. You need to arrest Erskine, before he hurts someone.'

No response.

He followed the line of her finger, up to the balcony where... 'Oh no.'

The First Assistant Keeper, Mr Fulton, was up there, slumped back against a stack of equipment. Face dark and swollen, eyes wide and bloodshot, mouth open, tongue thick and purple where it protruded. Dead. Definitely Dead.

Erskine stared. 'Robert?' Then snarled. Coming at Ian with hammer held high. 'You!'

'Oh no you don't!' Backing off, axe ready. 'You killed him, Erskine. You cut the phone lines and you killed him.'

WPC Miller held up her hands. 'All right, that's enough! Both of you, put the weapons down.'

'You heard her, Erskine. Drop the hammer. It's over.'

'You drop the axe!'

'I'm not the one who—'

Erskine lunged, the hammer's dark head whistling through the air in a flat arc, slamming into Ian's shoulder. Driving him down to his knees as fire burst through the bones and muscle, burning its way across his chest and down his arm. Forcing a scream from his mouth. Left arm hanging limp and heavy.

The hammer flashed up again, then down.

Ian kicked out, propelling himself backwards across the dark-red linoleum. Just fast enough – a dark blur whipped past his left cheek. Then the pop of something internal breaking as the hammer's head smashed into his chest instead of his head. Throwing wood on the inferno.

'GRAAAAAAAAAAAGH!' He lashed out with the axe. Its blade flashed across Erskine's arm, ripping through his oilskin jacket and out the other side.

Erskine curled away as bright red spilled down the yellow material. Teeth gritted.

Then back again, hammer whistling.

No time to move. No space to duck.

This was it, he was going to—

WPC Miller thumped into Erskine, knocking the hammer wide, sending him sprawling on his side. Grappling with him for the hammer.

Time to put a stop to this.

The axe sang in Ian's hand as it glinted up, then down again, burying its head deep into Erskine's thigh. So deep the blade jammed itself in the bone. Wedged there as Ian tried to work the axe free.

A scream.

Erskine's elbow snapped out, catching WPC Miller in the face, snapping her head back. Then another roar as Ian finally pulled the axe free. Blood pulsed from the thick gash in Erskine's leg.

Erskine swung the hammer. Missed. He scrambled backwards and hauled himself up the wall. Stood there, bright red running down his slashed arm, more staining his trouser leg. 'You're insane!' Then he turned and hobbled from the room, leaving a scarlet trail behind him.

Ian rolled over onto his side.

His chest and shoulder burst into flame again – everything numb from the elbow down.

After him.

Get up and get after him!

Downstairs, a door banged open, then another one and the wind's roar intensified. The Paraffin Room whoomping like a giant heart as the storm broke its way into the lighthouse.

A deep breath got him over onto his front, legs curled, forcing himself up, cheeks hot and wet with tears. One more push and he was on his feet, left arm dangling at his side throbbing with flame.

WPC Miller coughed out a spatter of blood. Struggled to her knees, one hand clutched over her nose and mouth. Dark red dripping between her fingers. 'Arrgh...'

'Stay here.' He stooped and picked the axe from the floor, then staggered out, after Erskine.

The front doors were open, debris swirling in the spiral stairwell, like stepping into a tornado. Only there was worse outside.

He couldn't grab the handrail, not with a broken shoulder, not without letting go of the axe. So he slumped sideways against the wall and stumbled down the stairs.

'Wait!'

He turned and there was WPC Miller, white shirt stained dark pink.

'I told you to stay there! It's too dangerous.'

She followed him down to the ground floor. 'I'm a *police* officer!'

'Women!' Ian forced his way into the airlock, against the wind, rain battering his face and chest.

Stepping outside was like being punched by a giant fist. Bullets of frigid rain strafed his skin, stinging and screeching their way down to his bones. Shoving him against the ancient castle walls.

There – over on the other side of the square. Erskine. Dragging one leg. Disappearing through the gap between the washhouse and the engine room.

Well, if he thought he could get away, he was wrong.

Ian ducked his head and lunged into the wind, leaning

forward so far he was at forty-five degrees, every step a battle. 'AAAAAARGH!' Tears streamed back from his eyes. Rain nailed itself into his face and hands. Fighting. Struggling. Forcing... Until he reached the relative shelter of the Assistant Keepers' cottages.

He shoved his way along the wall, past the washhouse. Then out into the gap between it and the engine room.

The stillness was like a warm hug – the north-westerly blocked by the engine room's bulk. He hurried on, stopping at the end of the short alleyway.

Erskine had made it all the way down the path, to where an eight-foot-high chainlink fence sealed off the lighthouse grounds from the thin strip of grass that lay between it and the cliffs. He was just visible at the furthest reach of the station's lights, struggling with the gate. He limped sideways out onto the grass, the fingers of his good hand laced through the fence's wire.

He was going south, towards the fish houses and Fraserburgh Harbour. Clinging on for his life, back hunched against the raging wind. Oilskin flapping like a dying bird.

The lighthouse beam swept through the storm, swallowed by the night.

WPC Miller thumped against the wall, opposite Ian, face contorted against the rain. Having to yell, just to be heard. 'WE HAVE TO STOP HIM!'

'IT'S TOO DANGEROUS!'

'HE'S INJURED, HE COULD DIE!'

'IT HAS TO BE OVER A HUNDRED KNOTS OUT THERE!'

She tugged at her tunic, and shook her head. 'I'M A POLICE OFFICER, I CAN'T JUST—'

He punched her. Once in the stomach – she folded

over, eyes wide – once on the jaw. Driving her to the rain-drenched concrete. Not the first time he'd hit a woman, but the first time there was a noble reason for it. 'IT'S FOR YOUR OWN GOOD, YOU'D DIE OUT THERE!' It was time. 'IF ANYTHING HAPPENS TO ME, I NEED YOU TO WIND THE MECHANISM EVERY HALF HOUR! KEEP THE LIGHT TURNING! LIVES DEPEND ON IT!'

Then Ian stepped out from the alley's safe embrace.

The hurricane ripped the air from his lungs. Nearly shoved him off his feet. He curled into it, head down. Pressing on. Axe held out in front of him. Staggering and lurching along the path to the gate.

A gust drove him to his knees. Threatened to rip him from the earth.

At *least* a hundred knots. Probably a lot more.

And William Erskine was getting away.

No.

Ian struggled back up into a crouch, leaning into the wind, shuffling crab-like to the gate. Through it.

The storm tore at his back. Pressing him on and down.

Should grab hold of the fence, but that would mean letting go of the axe.

Can't let go of the axe. Erskine had the hammer.

Move.

One foot in front of the other, the wind shoving and jostling, its fingers tearing at his jacket and trousers. Rain clattering against his clothes and skin. But he kept going.

Getting closer to Erskine with every lunging step.

The old man looked back over his shoulder, eyes squinted against the rain. He snarled. Turned. Staggered backwards. Raised his hammer.

Ian pushed himself up, axe ready. Teeth bared. A bellow

of rage torn from his mouth and swallowed by the hurricane.

And he was flying. Feet no longer connected to the earth. One with the rain, twirling and flailing, swept up with Erskine – tumbling and screaming, dark skies then grass, flipping around and around caught in the air's crushing grip.

Past an ancient stone tower and out into space...

His first ever dead body was the next-door neighbour, killed in a car crash. Mr Kennedy kept to himself, mostly. No one really knew what he looked like, except for Ian: the little boy who mowed the lawn. So the police asked his parents to bring him down to the mortuary and identify the body. He was eleven years old. Standing in a room full of the dead, to say he knew whose mangled remains lay on the stainless-steel table.

Erskine was right, you never forgot.

The roar of the waves.

The howl of the wind.

The unforgiving rocks, rushing up like—

Valerie stares, one hand holding her aching jaw, as Superintendent Blackwell is hurled away into the darkness. William Erskine is visible for a fraction longer, his bright yellow oilskin tossed by the storm and then gone.

Oh God...

She covers her eyes and sits there, huddled against the wall. Jacket and skirt heavy with rain. Hair plastered to her head.

Then crawls back to the lighthouse, hugging the ground as the wind pummels her. Shoves the doors shut and collapses against them. Outside, the hurricane roars. Denied its final victim.

* * *

Thin white clouds skate across the pale-blue sky, sunrise making the white buildings glow orange and gold as Valerie steps out of the lighthouse into the courtyard.

A chunk of corrugated iron lies up against the washhouse, like some child has built a makeshift fort. Leaves and litter piled in the corners.

She hurples around the corner, back aching, shoulders tight from a night spent winding the chain and its weight up from the lighthouse's depths. Once every half hour. Keeping the light turning until the sun came up and the storm died down.

At least the patrol car hasn't blown away. The Astra's still parked where...

Oh sodding hell.

A chunk of slate sits on the back seat, surrounded by a sea of shattered safety glass. That means a form to fill in. Probably several.

She opens the driver's door and groans her way into the seat. Slumps as the ancient padding sinks, closing around her bum, back, and thighs. Stares at the steering wheel. What is it with police officers and picking holes in the vinyl? Thing looks like moths have been at it.

Valerie lifts the Bakelite telephone handset off its dashboard hook and presses the button with her thumb.

The words come out with a decided lisp: 'DE3/2 to control, come in, over.' Her mouth aches with the effort. Probably got a bruise the size of Bernard Manning by now. God knows her face stings when she prods at it.

So she digs her fingernails into one of the steering wheel's holes instead, making it bigger.

'DE3/2 to control, are you receiving me, over?'

A hard teuchter accent thumps out of the earpiece. *'Val, that you? Where the hell have you been? Got half of Grampian Police out looking for you!'*

'Oh, thank God: you're there. Had to take shelter, last night. We had a hurricane…'

'*Val? You sound—*'

'I got elbowed in the face and punched in the jaw.' She shifts the rearview mirror so she's framed in the middle. Yup: massive bruise. And two black eyes too. Lovely. 'Listen I've got a dead body at Kinnaird Head lighthouse. Think it's the First Assistant Keeper. Strangled.'

'*Strangled? Right… Give us a second, I'll get the duty inspector—*'

'I think it was Alex Doyle. I think he and his mate George were impersonating keepers and superintendents up here. Can you do a PNC check for me on one Ian Blackwell and William Erskine? One of them's got to be—'

'*Really?*' A sigh. '*God save us from women police constables, you're a sweetly pretty lot, but talk about dizzy.*'

'I'm serious! Alex Doyle was—'

'*Look, just put PC Roberts on, OK? At least he'll have some sodding clue.*'

'This isn't a joke! Alex Doyle—'

'*Alex Doyle can't have been impersonating a lighthouse keeper, because Alex Doyle is a woman. And so's Georgina Banks. Is it your time of the month or some-thing? That why you're hysterical?*'

Valerie takes the handset away from her ear and stares at it.

Alex and George are women.

The tinny little voice crackles into the car's interior. '*Stay put and I'll get someone over there for your dead body, assuming there even is one and you haven't made that up as well. Probably be about an hour. Meantime: hot sweet tea's meant to be good for hysteria. Get someone to make you one, eh?*'

They were women.

What a stupid mistake to make.

She hangs up.

Wipes a hand across her eyes.

Can't afford to make stupid mistakes like that. Not now.

Valerie climbs back out into the gusty morning. Walks around to the boot of the patrol car and pops it open. Of course Georgina 'George' Banks is a woman. Look at her, lying there amongst the traffic cones and warning triangles and all the other gubbins. Throat open like a scarlet grin. The woman lying next to her doesn't look any better, neck bent back at an unnatural angle, eyes open and lifeless. Hands cuffed behind her back.

Ah well.

Valerie fetches a container of paraffin from lighthouse and drenches the patrol car's interior with it.

Being a WPC was fun, but it's time for a change. And she knows *just* the thing.

Searching the Principal Lighthouse Keeper's cottage turns up a rule book and a clipboard. A man's blue suit hangs in the wardrobe, complete with name badge: 'SUPERINTENDENT I. BLACKWELL'.

Isobel Blackwell steps out of the Principal Keeper's cottage and wanders across the courtyard to her nice new Ford Cortina. Throws her suitcase in the boot and jumps in behind the wheel, cranks up the lovely meaty engine and pulls up next to the paraffin-soaked patrol car. Takes out a box of matches and strikes one, drops it back into the packet and tosses them in through the Astra's window.

A glance in the rearview mirror as she pulls out through the lighthouse gates shows white smoke streaming out, followed by a whoomp of orange flames.

Perfect.

She turns the radio on and Dire Straits belt out of the speakers: 'Money for Nothing'.

That's the thing about finding something you love. Do it and you'll never work another day in your life. And Isobel truly loves what she does.

Crookston Castle

History Lesson
Gordon Brown

I haven't seen my sanctuary for thirty years. The castle
– dark, solid, timeless – is embedded into the small rise
above me. A shadow of its former self, but still a place
of strength. Of quiet power.

Its dank reek floats to me on an ice-cold wind born
in the Arctic and I can see myself inside, sitting on cold
rock, thighs at my chest, arms wrapped around my legs
– rocking. My head buried in my knees. Face wet with
tears. Twelve years old. Scared.

The memories are strong. Their roots, like the castle's
foundations, deep.

Not that this was a bad place for me. It was just a
place I went when bad things happened. A cold, shaded
room in its bowels providing a place of safety. Somewhere
beyond the reach of others. A place to reflect on what
I was feeling safe from.

I consider walking up to the castle. Standing beside
it. Touching it once more. My past meeting my present.
I shiver. The wind is pulling at my coat – an expensive
fashion statement that has more form than function on
this dreich, bitter January day in Glasgow. But that's not
why I'm shivering.

Although the castle was the one place in my childhood world where I felt secure, it was also where I felt most alone. Lost. Knowing that leaving its thick walls would return me to a father who would raise his fists. No solace existed beyond its walls. I'd sit, buried in ancient stone, praying for another future. For a better tomorrow.

I shake these old feelings, turn and walk to the hire car. It takes me a few seconds to realise that I'm scuffing my shoes across the pavement. A schoolboy's walk: looking down, shoulders hunched against the world. The flashback has turned me into a kid.

I lift my head, smooth down my suit, straighten my silk tie and look at my Rolex.

I slide into the car, the interior still warm. I fire up the engine and slam my foot on the accelerator, sending the German power plant into a screaming rage, trying to banish the memories.

The sat-nav tells me I'm fifteen minutes from my destination. I inhale the fresh-out-of-the-wrapper scent of the car as I speed through streets that still look familiar.

I've not been back to Glasgow since the day my father was imprisoned. When my mum, a broken woman, took the God-given opportunity to hand back the keys of our council house and move us to live with her sister in London.

Now my father is dead. Three days ago. A call from my uncle. Cancer of the spine. The phone conversation, the first I knew that he had been ill. My uncle has made all the arrangements. I was in Australia when he called. I should have jumped on the first flight out. I didn't. I finished up my business and timed the flight to land in Glasgow this morning.

I slide the car between the gates of Linn Crematorium – a utilitarian, modernist creation that tends to the dead of southern Glasgow. Ahead of me, the driveway splits into two. A small sign tells me that there are four funerals due today. My father's is in the smaller chapel. I have less than ten minutes until it starts.

The car park next to the crematorium is quiet. Three cars. I wait a few more minutes before getting out and walking to the main door. A small huddle of people are hiding from the wind. I join them.

A bald man nods at me. Then, one of the others, an older man who smells of beer, steps forward and asks how I know the deceased. When I tell him I'm the son, his face creases. 'Jamie?' he says. I nod. He wants to talk more but, before he can, the hearse rolls up, trailed by a limousine. He steps away from me in deference to the arriving coffin.

I view the approaching cars. I should have been sitting in the rear one with my uncle. Instead, I told him my flight got in too late and I would make my own way there. A lie.

The cars stop and the passenger door of the limo opens. A sombre man, dressed in black, exits from the passenger door to help my uncle out. My uncle emerges.

He walks up to me. 'Jamie.'

I reply. 'Hi.'

'Sad day.'

I can't tell if he means sad that my father is dead or sad that I've shown up.

'It is.' My words sound like a question.

After bearing the coffin, I zone out from the funeral service. Standing and sitting when required. Mouthing to the hymns. Eyes anywhere but on the coffin. I'm grateful when it's lowered into the basement.

The order of service has a picture of my father on the front. A shot from the sole family holiday we had. A week in Ullapool. The photo is black and white. My father is wearing the crumpled bunnet he always wore. The head shot hints at the car crash that was his teeth. He would spend hours, mouth open, close to the electric three-bar fire in our living room, trying to gain relief from toothache. For all his reputation as the local hard man, he was scared shitless of the dentist. I haven't looked on his face in twenty-five years.

After the minister says his last words my uncle asks if I want to stand at the entrance and thank the mourners. I decline and leave to indulge in a cigarette.

There's cold tea and stale sandwiches to be had back at my uncle's house. I intend to go but I'll not stay long – I'm on the last flight back to London tonight. When I told my uncle of my plans he was vocal. Vicious almost.

'*Why the fuck are you coming at all?*'

Because a son should be at his father's funeral? Or, to make sure the bastard is dead?

Deep down, another part of me just wanted to come back to Glasgow. To see the place again. To confront the past.

As I light a cigarette I notice the next batch of mourners are beginning to gather, their hearse and other cars hanging back, waiting for us to go.

I draw the first cloud into my lungs. I've no thoughts on giving up on the habit. I enjoy it too much. I had a moment when I heard about my father's cancer. The moment passed.

As I watch the last dribble of my father's mourners leave, I scan the new crowd, which is far larger than our pathetic effort.

My uncle walks up to me. 'Do you have my address?'

I nod. He leaves.

The bald man, from the small huddle, is looking at me. Light stubble ranges across his shaved head. He strokes a small goatee and throws me a smile. I freeze into a store window dummy. Rock still. My eyes on that smile.

My stomach cramps a little. The feeling from the castle rising again.

The man walks over to me. 'Hi, Jamie.' The voice older, deeper, but still familiar.

'Donnie?' I whisper.

'I'll see ye back at y'r uncle's.'

He leaves and I'm thrown back to a hot classroom a lifetime ago. Mr McFarlane, our History teacher, is standing at the front of the class. Behind him, written on the blackboard, are two words – Crookston Castle.

My castle.

Mr McFarlane is talking to a kid called Donnie Elder. 'Ok Donald, give me one good reason why I shouldn't give you the belt?' Donnie has just been caught reading a copy of *Playboy*.

Donnie is sitting at the back of the classroom and I have to turn around to see what's going down. The class is lapping this up – revelling in it. Donnie isn't fazed. He's the resident nutter in my school. Mr McFarlane is holding the magazine. Donnie reaches out to grab it. Mr McFarlane pulls it away.

Donnie smiles as he speaks, 'Because I'll tell my da' whit ye did and he'll come and find ye and kick y'r teeth in.'

I remember the look in Mr McFarlane's eyes. Fear. It's hard to hide. But he's long enough in the tooth to find a way of handling the situation. 'Right, Donald, I'll see you about this – after class.'

Mr McFarlane spins away from the confrontation and

points to the blackboard. 'Now, who can tell me about Crookston Castle?'

My hand is so high in the air that I'm out of my chair. Waving it like an idiot. Mr McFarlane points to me. 'Jamie?'

I stand up. 'Well, the castle was built by Robert de Croc who was a knight...'

It's as far as I get. From behind Mr McFarlane, Donnie, emboldened by our teacher's capitulation, shouts out, 'Jamie Duncan thinks Crookston Castle wis built by Robert's *Cock.*'

A wave of laughter washes across the classroom. Me the beach to its tsunami. Anger builds in me. I know so much about the castle. I fight the laughter. 'I didn't say cock,' is my indignant response. 'I said *Croc.*'

Donnie stands up. Spoiling for the fight. 'Aye – a right croc of shit.'

This brings more laughter. Mr McFarlane should step in. Should shut it down. That's what I thought back then – still think – but the flicker of fear in his eyes tells me that he's pondering a confrontation with Donnie's father. Better to let me take it in the neck and then regain control.

Donnie loves the attention. 'Jamie Duncan uses the ol' lavvy in the castle. He likes tae shit there.'

More laughter. My anger keeps building. Donnie saunters up to me. He's centre stage now – milking it. He goes for a killer end-line. Smile as wide as the Clyde Tunnel. 'Hey Jamie, dae ye play with y'rsel' when y'r in the castle?'

Donnie now has a grin that could be seen from Ben Lomond. I want to lash out. To stop this. He's taking my moment away and he knows it. I step forward. I lean in. 'Fuck you.'

Donnie's smile vanishes. The classroom laughter dies. Donnie's face turns to stone. 'Whit did ye say?' Tone low. Hard.

The reality of the moment washes over me. I'm fronting up Donnie Elder.

His eyes lock on mine. 'Wanna kickin', Jamie? Eh?'

I don't want a kicking.

He moves in. 'So, whit ye gonna dae now?'

There's no answer to that and he knows it. Mr McFarlane begins to move. To intervene.

Donnie grabs my hair. Pulling my head down. That's when it happens. Pee flows into my trousers, down my legs, onto the floor.

Donnie jumps back, shouting. 'He's pissed himsel'.'

'Excuse me.' The voice snaps me back from the past. I look up. Donnie has gone. A man is standing in front of me. 'The service is about to start. Are you going in?' he says.

The new mourners have vanished. I'm on my own. I shake my head and shuffle towards my car.

I slide back into luxury and, as I drive, I'm thinking about Donnie. Why the hell was he there?

My uncle lives a few streets from the castle and I park outside his house. I sit. Engine running. Mind churning.

Getting out I see a man at a window. The man rubs his bald head. He smiles. I bleep the car and turn away. I'm not going into the house. Not a chance.

I have hours to kill. I think about walking past my old house but I'm drawn back to the castle. I tread the streets I used to play and cry in and discover that a new estate has been built on the road that sits below my sanctuary.

I wonder if the castle will have changed in all this

time. I almost laugh at myself. To Crookston Castle thirty years is a flea bite on a scabby dog. I cross the road, climb the path to the fence that surrounds the fortress and walk into the grounds.

I stop to examine the ruin but I'm distracted. I'm unable to fathom Donnie's presence at the funeral and questions are whirling in my head. Our families weren't friends. Although what my father called my *fucking pathetic whining about his bullying* meant he knew who Donnie was.

Ducking through a small, metal-gated door and under the slot where the portcullis would once have sat, I begin to climb stone stairs.

It could have been yesterday – the last time I was here. I'm on remote as I enter the roofless banqueting hall. I pause when I reach the bottom of the spiral staircase in the far corner. To my left is a small nook. Donnie was right about me sitting in the castle's lavatory. The tiny space I used to squat in has a hole that once emptied waste out through a slot in the outer wall. A small sign, with the single word *Latrine,* now informs visitors about the room's former purpose. Unless someone has scrubbed them off, grey streaks of medieval excrement will still stain the walls outside.

This is where I used to hide. Sometimes for hours. Wind whistling through the toilet gap. Nursing a beating or anticipating one. On the day I wet myself at school, I sat there for so long, piss freezing on my legs, that when I went home, my mum thought I had hypothermia.

My father warmed me up by leathering me.

I climb past the latrine, circling up the staircase. As I enter the old laird's bedchamber, I look at the fireplace. Sometimes when it got too cold to sit in the latrine I would retire here.

A plaque on the wall tells of the castle's use, in World War II, as an anti-aircraft observation post. Testimony to the building's continuing impact on history.

I climb to emerge onto the roof. I'm standing at the centre of a concrete-covered square, maybe twenty feet on each side, surrounded by waist-high metal railings. The tower, the last one standing of the castle's original four, has a panoramic view of its surroundings – lording it over Pollok.

I walk to the south side. It takes me a minute, but I finally spot my old house. My bedroom window is visible. When I wasn't up here I could be found kneeling on my bed, elbows on the windowsill, head in hands, staring at the castle.

I'm thinking I should just have driven to the airport, tried for an earlier flight, got the hell away. There aren't any decent memories here. It may have been my place once – but it's providing no succour now.

I grab the metal rail that guards the stairs down. I'm swinging to descend backwards when a voice comes from below. 'Back in y'r castle, Jamie?'

I stop, one foot on the second step down. I look through my legs. I see Donnie Elder standing at the bottom of the stairs. My knees weaken. A Pavlovian response. I hover, immobile, caught between descending into his space or rising back to the roof. Nowhere to run. Trapped.

What the hell is happening? I'm shitting myself. I'm an adult. Not a kid. I should be able handle this. Front up to the man. Yet my stomach is churning, the fear of youth in full flow, my school experiences rushing back. I want to keep descending. I want to overcome the fear and walk right past him. Ninety-three stairs down. That's all it would take. Then I'd be out. Gone.

'Are ye comin' doon?' Donnie shouts.

I can't go down. It's a simple matter of flight or fight and I'm choosing flight.

I step up.

'Ok,' he says. 'I'll come up.'

I look at the railings and think how easy it would be to be thrown over them. I know that irrationality is running the show here. But the irrational is often more potent than the rational. Adrenaline is gushing into my system – screwing up my thinking.

'Fucking stop,' I shout down the hole.

'Whit?' Surprise from Donnie.

'I said stop. Don't come up.' My voice has a tremor. Donnie stops climbing. 'I jist wanna talk.'

'Then do it from down there.'

'Really?' Confusion is writ hard in his voice.

I lean down. 'I'm warning you. Come up here and I'll...' I'm not sure what I'll do. The size of the small hole, where the top of the metal stairs sits, means I could easily kick at Donnie's head as he appears – but something stops me saying more.

Donnie sounds baffled. 'Or y'll dae whit? Fuck, all I wanna dae is talk. Whit's wrang with ye?'

'Just do me a favour and stay there.' I compose myself a little. 'How did you know where I was?'

'I saw ye walk away from the hoose. I followed ye. I knew where ye wir goin' as soon as ye headed this way. Come on doon. Back tae the hoose. I'd like tae talk tae ye.'

'Donnie, say what you have to say from down there.'

Silence. Then he backs off. Dropping down the two stairs he has climbed. 'Ok. Hiv it y'r way. I wis only here tae say I'm sorry aboot y'r da'. He wis a good man.'

'A what?' The words are out before I can stop them.

'He wis a good man.'

Ire replaces fear. I'm staggered at the statement. 'Was he fuck. What would you know? Good? In what way was he good?'

'Y've been away a lang time, Jamie. When wis the last time ye talked tae y'r da'?'

'It's been a while.'

'When?'

I think about my reply, rage boiling in me. Do I really want to have this conversation? Here? Now? With him?

I lean over the stair's guard rail. Donnie is standing below, one foot on the first step, staring back at me. 'What's it to you?' I ask.

Donnie might have been a vicious bastard but he isn't stupid. He senses my confusion. His reply is quiet. 'I'm only askin'.'

'If you really want to know, it was at my mum's funeral,' I say. 'He came up to me. Sixteen years old I was. Told me that I'd needed to make my own way in the world now. That was all he said. Then the officers escorting him on his compassionate leave took him away. I haven't seen him since.'

'So, ye hivnae talked tae him in how lang? Twenty-five years. Longer?'

A gust of wind pulls at me. 'What's it to you? Why are you here? Why were you at the funeral?'

He ignores the questions. 'Ye used tae love this place. Y'r hidey hole. A nut on the place if I remember right.' Then he smiles. 'I wis a bit of an arsehole back then.'

The confession catches me cold. Is he here to say sorry? After all this time, is that why he came to the funeral? To see me? To apologise?

'An arsehole.' I answer. 'An *arsehole*. You were more than that. You picked on me all the fucking time.'

Donnie laughs. 'Ye wir such a fuckin' wimp. Say boo and ye pissed y'rsel. We wir kids. Kids dae that shit.'

'Is that your excuse?'

Donnie stretches his arms above him. As if he's bored with the conversation. 'It wis school. Fuckin' years ago.'

I'm struggling here. Struggling with his lack of empathy. 'You made my life a misery. Day after day. A misery.'

Donnie thinks about this. 'Whit? A misery? Did I fuck. Maybe I hid a go at ye once in a while. Nae mair than that, though. I didnae know ye that well.'

I have one of those moments when you don't know what to say next. The moments you stutter – wondering where to start with a reply.

Donnie fills the gap in the conversation. 'Jist kid's stuff,' he says.

I'm flattened by the statement. *Kid's stuff*. The day that I wet myself my father, belt in hand, screamed at me about being a coward. Told me I needed to be a man.

'Kid's stuff?' I whisper.

'Whit did ye say?' Donnie asks.

'Kid's stuff.' Louder.

'Aye, whit else wis it?' Donnie sounds thoughtful. 'It's that lang ago I cannae remember much aboot it.' He pauses. 'But I dae remember the day ye wet y'rsel'.' He laughs.

I want to drop down the hole. Feet first. *Stamp* him into the ground.

He's unaware of my rage. 'Ye know,' he says, 'Graham talked a lot aboot ye.'

That takes the wind from my sail. The casual use by Donnie of my father's name sounds alien. Wrong. But it eases my anger a little. 'When did you talk to my father about me?'

'In Bar L.'

'Prison?'

'Aye, I did some time.' He says it as if everyone goes to prison now and again. 'Y'r da' wis on a second stretch. We wir in the same hall.'

I didn't know my father had done a second spell behind bars. 'And you two became friends?' There's sarcasm in my voice.

'Once he knew I had known ye – well, he kinda took to me.'

'You didn't *know* me. You just *abused me*.'

Donnie ignores the dig. 'We spent a lot of time together. Me and y'r da'. He wis a good mate.' Donnie begins to pace the floor. 'When we wir both oot o' prison we kept in touch. Mostly o'er pints of lager. Him, me and sometimes y'r uncle. Y'r uncle wis always on at y'r da' tae get in touch with ye'. Y'r da' telt him tae leave it. Said y'd come back when ye wir ready. Graham wis right proud of ye.'

'Proud of me?' I'm struggling to hang on to the arc of this conversation.

'Aye,' Donnie continues. 'He kept an eye on ye from a distance. When ye bought the transport business in London he splashed oot for a round for the entire pub. He wis always tellin' people how well y'd done.'

The transport business had been a big deal. The one that made me. I'd been in the newspapers. I'd even had an interview on BBC Radio 4. But it had been touch and go. I'd sunk every penny I had into the deal and still came up short. I was twenty-four hours from going belly up, from losing everything, when my advisors told me they had found a new investor.

'He knew about that?' I said.

'Ye wir his only son.' Donnie seemed to think that explained everything.

'He used to beat me,' I blurted out.

Donnie took the comment in his stride. 'Aye, so did my ol' man. Kind of the norm back then.'

I'm taken aback. I've never told anyone about the beatings. I expected more of a reaction. I try and re-inforce my statement. 'No, I mean he *really* beat me.'

'Whit, like a pit-ye-in-hospital-type beatin'?'

'No.' I hesitate before finishing the sentence. 'But it was still bad.'

Donnie stops pacing and swings his backside onto the lower stair. 'So, it wisnae *that* bad. I had a few broken bones to explain away when I wis wee. Look, can ye come doon noo? I'm fuckin' freezing here.'

I ignore the request. The beatings were bad. The belt across my back. Mum dragging my father off. They *were* bad.

Donnie says something but it's lost to the wind. He's talking to the floor.

I lean down. 'What did you say?'

He looks up. 'Y've done well, Jamie. Dragged y'rself oot of this place. I never did. I should hiv left lang ago. I've a boy. He's twelve next week. I love him tae bits but he worries me. I can see too much of me in him. Nae enough of ye.' He stops talking. His eyes are else-where – then he pulls back up the smile. 'Dae ye know they laid siege tae this place? Even dragged yon big cannon from Edinburgh Castle o'er once. Ye know the one that fires at one o'clock? They blew half this fuckin' place away with it.'

Donnie's history lesson is wrong. It was a cannon called Mons Meg, not the one o'clock gun, but it makes me think this could be a siege. Him down there. Me with the high ground. Me the defender, him the attacker. Only that's not the way it feels. The conversation is unsettling me. Making me think differently about things that I've long tried to bury. Donnie's casual indifference to what he did to me is forcing me onto the offensive. *I'm* the attacker, not him. I'm assaulting my past as he forces a new perspective on me. Him defending what happened back then.

I need to know more.

'How well did you really know my father?'

'Well enough tae be invited tae his funeral.'

I issue a dismissive grunt. 'Aye, well that says it all. How many were there. Seven? Pitiful.'

'Did y'r uncle nae tell ye aboot y'r da's request?'

'What request?' Another blast of wind rips across the tower. I wrap my coat tighter.

'Y'r ol' man made it clear he only wanted family and his five best mates there. I'm proud tae hiv been one of them. Shit, it would've been mobbed otherwise. Did ye think that wis all the people y'r da' knew?'

I did.

Donnie stands up again, rubbing at his goatee. 'Y'r da' kept the clippin' from the *Daily Record* aboot y'r transport deal in his wallet.'

'He was a bastard to me.' I'm shouting.

Donnie shrugs. 'Aye, he had issues all right. But they sorted him oot second time in Bar L. Ye won't know, but y'r da' wasnae right in the head.'

This is too much information for me to process. 'Seriously?'

'Aye, mental health issues. It also made him angry. IED is the name for it noo. Intermittent Explosive Disorder.' He pronounces the three words with care.

'Took years for them tae sort it oot. But when they did, he wis a new man.'

'My father was ill when I was a kid?' I'm shocked.

'Who knew aboot that sort of stuff back then?' Donnie is rubbing his hands together for warmth. 'Jamie, come doon. Come back tae the hoose. I've asked my boy tae come roond. I'd like ye tae meet him.'

I'm confused. 'You want *me* to meet your son?'

'Aye. I'd like for ye tae hiv a wee talk with him. Ye know? Show him how well y've done. That sort of thing.'

I sit down. My back to the stairs. Trying to get a grip on what's happening. Donnie Elder is asking *me* for a favour?

I lean my spinning head backwards. The sun is dipping. The sky heavy with cloud.

'Jamie?' Donnie shouts up.

'Can you leave,' I say. 'I need to think.'

'I've got mair I can tell ye aboot y'r da'.'

'Can you go. Please.'

'Come on back tae y'r uncle's and we can chat. Meet my boy. I'd like ye tae talk tae him.'

It's the last thing I want at the moment. I tell him so. 'I don't think so.'

I hear a footstep ring out on the metal stair. 'Fuck ye Jamie. I'm no askin' much. Ye owe it tae y'r uncle. He arranged y'r da's funeral. Nae help from ye.'

'Why would I help? I'm not even sure why I'm here. My father was a bastard.'

'So y'v said – but I telt ye y'r da' wis sick. Ye really need tae talk tae y'r uncle. There's mair tae this than ye know.'

I stand up as Donnie's head rises through the gap. Invading my space. I look down on him. 'What are you going to do Donnie, drag me back?'

Donnie stops climbing. 'Fuck. Ye think y've got it all figured oot. Don't ye?'

'What's to figure? Ok so my father was sick. He still hit me. He still fucked off and never got in touch.'

'I telt ye – he kept an eye on ye'

'Sure, and did he boast about me in the pub – take some of the credit? Did he tell everyone I was a chip off the old block? I bet he did.'

Donnie shakes his head. 'So, y'r not comin' back tae the hoose?'

'No.'

'Ok.' He raises his hand and points at me. 'Ye need tae know somethin' Jamie Duncan. Y'r da' made us promise not tae tell ye till he wis gone – and if y'r not comin' back tae the hoose I need tae be the one tae tell ye.'

I've no idea what Donnie is talking about. 'Tell me what?'

Donnie raises up another step and rests his arms on the roof. 'Y'r uncle wis gonna tell ye. Back at the hoose. When ye wir doin' y'r deal, the transport one, ye got a last-minute pile of cash. Didn't ye? An anonymous investor, eh?'

'How do you know that?'

'Fuck. Did ye no ask where the money came from?'

I had asked, but my advisors told me the investor didn't want to be identified. I hadn't looked a gift horse in the mouth. I was so desperate I had taken the cash, no questions.

'Well, Jamie Duncan,' Donnie says. 'Jist so ye know. And ye fuckin' *need* tae know.' He pauses, as if the words are an effort. Then he spits it out. 'It wis y'r da' that gave ye the money.'

'What?' I stagger back.

'Ye heard me.'

'No chance. It was a hundred grand. Where would my father get a hundred grand?'

'Where dae ye think?'

Donnie leaves the question hanging. The wind, promising rain, is building strength. Rain is never far away in Glasgow.

I dismiss what Donnie has just said. 'Bollocks. The only way my father would get a hundred grand would be to steal it.'

Donnie raises his eyes. 'And?'

My confusion is deepening. My surety vanishing.

'I helped him get it,' says Donnie. 'One last job. A jewellers in the Argyll Arcade. Risky as fuck. Y'r uncle helped. But if we'd been caught y'r da' wis starin' at ten years. Third time round they would hiv thrown the cell keys away. It took balls tae dae that job. Real balls. And he did it all for ye. He knew ye wir close tae goin' bust.'

I'm lost for words, again.

Donnie starts to descend. 'So think on it, Jamie. Y'r a big success now and I know ye hate y'r da'. But ye didn't know y'r da'. Not really. I'll be with y'r uncle at the hoose – if ye can be arsed.'

He vanishes. I'm rooted to the spot. Dumbfounded.

After a few seconds, I walk to the edge of the roof. Donnie emerges below. He doesn't look back as he departs.

I hear the whine of a jet engine above me but the thought of my flight back to London is a distant thing. I chew Donnie's words over. IED. A good man. Proud of me. The cash.

What else is there that I don't know?

I cross to the other side of the roof and seek out my old house again. I roll back thirty years. A twelve year old, head in hands, staring at his castle, wondering when the pain would stop. This was my *special* place – my sanctuary when my family home was a sixties-built torture chamber. This castle has stood here since medieval times, built by a knight of the realm, gifted to the country; but back then it belonged to me. It *was* bad back then and a few minutes' conversation with a thug like Donnie can't re-write history.

I feel the first spots of rain from the approaching storm.

With a last glance at my old house, I climb below. When I reach the banqueting hall, the rain is teeming down. I stand, waiting for it to ease a little, thinking. I'd been happy to see the small pitiable huddle at the funeral. It reinforced my beliefs – told me that my father had died unloved. Unlovable. If I'm honest, it even made me feel better about coming. Now Donnie has thrown in a time bomb by telling me, if he's being straight, that my father had changed. Without me knowing anything about it my father had helped me. Being there when I needed him. Invisible. Trying to make up for what went before. Being a dad.

I step out into the rain, my head reeling as I exit the castle. I look up at the ancient building, water streaming in my eyes, wondering how many other dramas have been played out within its walls, appreciating that Donnie Elder had been trying his best to put a dressing on my battle wound.

I need time to think.

To reflect.

But not in this place.

Crossraguel Abbey

Come Friendly Bombs
Louise Welsh

Craxton spent the last months of the war in Paris, praying for a bomb to blow Notre-Dame Cathedral to smithereens. His plane had been shot down somewhere near Lorraine and he arrived in Paris after a sodden, mud-soaked journey that sloughed the skin from his feet and rattled his nerves as hard as the crash landing had rattled his bones. It would not have been beyond Craxton's abilities to reach the coast and cross the channel home, but he found refuge with a friend from his Sorbonne days, and even when his fractured collarbone was mended, fear and the city held him.

Jules Renard had never been a close friend, but he was the most likely of Craxton's Parisian acquaintances to collaborate with the occupiers, while remaining disloyal to all but his own interests. The war was turning, the presence of an injured British airman risky, but excellent insurance against post-war reprisals, should the allies win.

'You are a sight for bleeding eyes,' Jules whispered when Craxton hailed him softly from the shadowed alleyway opposite his mother's building. Jules had been returning from some excursion, a greasy paper parcel clutched in his hand. He scanned the street and then shushed Craxton inside. Some accident had stiffened Jules' left hip and turned his neat walk into a lurch since Craxton had last seen him, but he was still light on his feet. The Frenchman led the way, up the marble staircase with its wrought iron banister, past the door to his mother's large apartment and into a tiny attic room at the top of the building. He was a short man, dark with sallow skin and a creased brow that made him look somewhere in his late thirties, though he was not yet twenty-five. He set his parcel on a table, closed the door softly behind them and turned the latch.

The small space stank of sweat and cabbage. Craxton took in the unmade bed, the clothes tumbled on the floor, the empty bottles and curling, out-of-date newspapers. Mme Renard had been a fussy housekeeper with a penchant for wax polish and antimacassars. It was hard to imagine her living in squalor.

'Where's your mother?'

Jules turned his back and looked out through the small window, towards the cathedral spires.

'The war took her.'

'I'm sorry.'

'She should have died sooner.'

Craxton's collarbone was pulsing. He lowered himself onto the edge of the unmade bed. An image of the smashed plane flitted through his mind. The flight engineer's face had been broken by the impact, his brains leaking ... he must not think of it.

Jules turned away from the view of the city and picked up the parcel. Something seeped from its paper wrapping onto his fingers. He made a face and rubbed them on the hem of his jumper.

'You must be hungry.'

Craxton had survived on raw eggs stolen from henhouses in the dead of night. At first he had supplemented his diet with foraged berries and mushrooms, but his knowledge of botany was poor and a morning bent double in a ditch, wondering if he was fatally poisoned, had dissuaded him.

'Starving.'

Jules was unwrapping the parcel in a tiny kitchenette housed in an alcove. 'You look like death.'

'Everyone looks bad, except for the Germans, and some of them don't look so good.'

It was not entirely true. Jules had none of the pallor of the Parisians Craxton had seen. They were ghost-thin, so drained of colour they almost melted into their surroundings. Jules' face was fleshier than he remembered, his lips fuller. Craxton wondered if he had made a mistake in trusting the Frenchman.

The sound of a knife blade striking against a chopping board jerked Craxton upright. He realised he had been nodding asleep. There was a hiss of gas, followed by the pop and whoosh of a flame as Jules lit a small primus stove. Something sizzled.

Craxton had barely escaped the cockpit before it caught fire. The flames had spread quickly, lighting the night, offering him a last view of the smashed Lancaster even as they consumed it. The tail gunner's screams had ripped the world apart.

Jules said, 'I saved this onion for a special occasion. Open the window, will you please? We don't want anyone to scent us out.'

Craxton limped to the window and lifted the sash. The air outside was cool, the sky darkening; Notre-Dame's outline stark against the oncoming dusk. He thought of his father's farm in Ayrshire and Crossraguel Abbey where he had walked as a boy. People said it was haunted by the ghosts of dead monks, but he had never felt their presence.

He said, 'Does no one know you're here?'

Jules moved the onion around the skillet. 'They know I'm here. I try to be useful, without drawing too much attention to myself.' He paused his task and walked two fingers along a weaving, air-born path. 'It's like walking a tightrope. One miscalculation and...' He tumbled his fingers downwards, like a man falling to his death.

'Sorry for making things more difficult.'

Jules shrugged. 'Remember what Professor Bernard used to tell us? *During the course of construction, you will encounter many difficulties. The test lies not in designing the perfect building, but in solving the problems presented by its construction.* I have taken that as my motto for survival. I concentrate on finding solutions.' He grinned and lifted the contents of the stained package in both hands, as if offering it up as a sacrifice. 'This is the solution to our hunger.'

A large and bloody heart flopped in the Frenchman's hands; ventricles gleaming like jewels, veins and arteries dangling.

Craxton felt his gorge rise. 'What is that?'

Jules raised his eyebrows. 'A pig's heart.'

Craxton's father kept pigs on the farm. As a boy it had been his job to feed them. He had liked to watch them eat, amused by their seeking snouts and wet, snorting enjoyment.

'It must have been some size of beast.'

Jules was busy with his knife again, separating meat from gristle.

'It was.'

He flung the sliced heart into the pan and the room filled with the scent of burning flesh.

Craxton dreamt of Crossraguel that night, as he had every night since the plane crash. He was crossing the cloisters with his dog at his heels. It was dusk, the gloaming ghosting in. The dog let out a low growl and hunkered down. Craxton followed her gaze and saw a man standing in the shadows. A bolt of excitement set the hairs on his arm alive. The dog growled again and the man took a step towards him.

He was sitting on the edge of the bed drawing, when Jules returned from whatever had kept him out all night. The Frenchman looked tired, but his cheeks were still plump; like a child's ready for pinching. He lifted a paper package, blotted with blood, in the air and gave a triumphant grin. 'I brought breakfast.'

Craxton set his pencil on the bedclothes, surprised to find that he was hungry. 'Another heart?'

Jules grin grew wider. 'No, this time it is *filet.*'

The two men ate facing each other across the small table. The filet was fresh, its flavour strong. It took all of Craxton's willpower to eat slowly. He felt Jules watching him and said, 'I thought meat would be in short supply.'

The Frenchman chewed and swallowed. 'It is, but when someone kills a pig, they share it.'

'I'm surprised there are still pigs left in Paris to kill.'

'More than you would think.' Jules nodded to the paper bag Craxton had been drawing on. 'What are you designing?'

Colour rose to Craxton's cheeks. 'A cathedral. I planned it in my head on the walk to Paris. It helped to keep me going.' He looked towards the view of Notre-Dame, a vision of buttresses in the morning light. 'A replacement should that one be hit.'

It was Jules' turn to flush. 'No one will bomb the cathedral.'

'You think God will keep it safe?'

Jules put his knife and fork down. 'God has forgotten Paris. The Luftwaffe and the Royal Air Force use Notre-Dame as a landmark to guide their way. I've heard they do the same with St Paul's and Cologne.'

It was true. Frankie, the navigator, had ringed the cathedrals on the aerial map before each of their missions. Craxton was not sure if Frankie had been dead, or only unconscious, after the crash. Either way he was ashes now, like the rest of the bomber's crew.

Craxton rubbed his eyes. 'There will be a lot of work for architects, when the war is over.'

Jules looked at him. 'There is a lot of work for us now, but not of the architectural kind. Let's wait until you are stronger.'

Craxton spent a fortnight confined to the attic, letting his bones knit. Jules' mother's flat had been requisitioned by Nazi officers. He heard them in the rooms below, their voices growing blurred at the edges, the patterns of their footsteps more fitful as the days passed.

Jules slept by day and slipped from the building with the dark. Craxton slept between the same musky sheets at night, dreaming of Crossraguel; the dog at his heels growling, the man stepping from the shadows. He passed his days in drawing. Paper was in short supply and so he used the wrappings from the packages of meat Jules smuggled home each dawn. At first the bloodstains bothered him. They raised the spectre of the flight engineer's ruined skull. The sound his blood had made as it dripped onto the controls. Craxton trained himself to think of the stains as difficult topography, the *problems presented by construction*, of which Professor Bernard had warned them.

Craxton's designs were clean-lined: airy buildings to replace the Paris and London landmarks he hoped would be bombed. In addition to Notre-Dame Cathedral these included St Paul's, the Houses of Parliament, the Louvre, the Arc de Triomphe, Tower Bridge and Buckingham Palace. A new world rose in his mind's eye and stretched across the soiled scraps of paper. He imagined walking city streets flanked by his own constructions.

Each night was punctuated by the booming of actual bombs. Some exploded close enough to shake the apartment block, toppling the empty bottles lined along Jules' mantelpiece and fluttering the pages of half-read books. One raid shattered the attic window. Shards of glass rained on the bed, like one of the sudden hailstorms of Craxton's Ayrshire childhood. He cowered beneath the covers, fearing for his life and hoping the cathedral would take a direct hit. But the streets around him remained defiantly standing, Notre-Dame barely marked.

When the sounds of the bombing grew too great, or the tail gunner's screams echoed too loud in his head; or the sight of the engineer's leaking brains became too sharp; he would draw Crossraguel. The memory of the abbey calmed him. It was the place where he had first fallen in love with buildings.

Craxton had been ten years old, exploring the ruins with his dog Meg, when he had his epiphany and realised that the abbey had not simply grown there like potatoes in soil, or been erected to an age-old pattern like the dry-stane dykes that edged the fields. Someone long ago had planned Crossraguel's design. An individual had dictated how the tower would stand in the land, the way the cloisters would be at the centre of the structure. Craxton had not yet known the word *architect*, but he knew he wanted to be the man who put buildings onto the landscape. He wanted every traveller, every passer-by and inhabitant of a district to see his work. He did not yet know the word *landmark*, but he knew that once his buildings were erected, he wanted it to be impossible to imagine their site without them.

Craxton had only been qualified for three years when the war started. He had not yet won a big commission, but had faith that his time would come. He had imagined his future as he flew the Lancaster Bomber over darkened countrysides, a full load in the plane's belly, heading for enemy territory. The war would leave whole districts, whole cities, flattened. When it was over, there would be opportunities for men who managed to stay alive.

Jules' face was bruised when he returned that morning, his lip split and bloody. A long, bulky package protruded from the pocket of his raincoat. Craxton jumped from his seat and helped Jules inside. The Frenchman's breath was ragged, his eyes wide. There was a pitcher of dusty water by the bed. Craxton settled Jules in a chair, poured some into a glass and handed it to him.

'What happened?'

The glass trembled in Jules' hand. 'They almost caught me.'

There was no need to ask who. Craxton said, 'What were you doing? Are you with the Resistance?'

Jules had taken the package from his pocket and placed it on his knee when he sat down, now he passed it to Craxton. The architect winced at the warm softness of it. Whatever cut of meat Jules had brought home this time, the beast was not long dead. He could almost feel its pulse beating through the paper wrapping.

His voice sounded small. 'What is it?'

Jules nodded at the bloody parcel. 'Unwrap it.' Craxton hesitated. Jules repeated, 'Unwrap it.'

The wrapping was heavy with blood. Craxton began to unpeel the sodden paper. Dread numbed his fingers and made his movements clumsy. The shape of the object was familiar. He knew what it was, but could not comprehend the possibility of it and so when he drew back the final layer and saw the human arm, its bloody stump and bone, the shock was as strong as if he had not already guessed.

He flung it from him, ran to the window and vomited onto the sloping roof tiles below. Jules was between him and the door, still sitting at the table. His lip was swelling, his words muffled.

'You didn't guess?'

The horror of it hit Craxton again, along with the memory of the meals they had shared since his arrival, the heart, *filet*, kidneys, liver and rump steak; the brains. He leaned out of the window retching.

'All of it?'

'Where else would it come from? I thought you knew.'

'You said it was pig meat.'

'It is.' The Frenchman started to laugh. 'Prime pork.'

Jules picked the arm off the floor and wiped the dust from it with the discarded wrapping. A glimmer of early morning sunshine reached through the shattered window turning the hairs on the arm golden.

Craxton grabbed his drawings. 'I would never have … if I had known I wouldn't…'

Jules carried the arm to the tiny kitchenette and got busy with his cleaver.

'You knew. You're an intelligent man, a farmer's son, for God's sake. Deep down, you knew.'

'You told me it was pig meat and I believed you.'

Doubt niggled him. The meat had been reminiscent of pork, but it held a hint of corruption that added depth to its flavour. Craxton was disgusted to find his saliva glands responding to the memory.

Boots sounded in the lobby below. Jules paused his

cleaver. His eyes met Craxton's and he raised a finger to his bruised lips.

'Shhh.' He reached into a drawer, took out a knife and passed it to Craxton. His voice was a whisper. 'I thought I'd lost him. We may have a problem to solve.'

Jules moved to the door. He undid the latch and crouched with the cleaver poised. The footsteps were outside, on the landing. Craxton's collarbone ached. He stood frozen, in the middle of the attic, his knife blade pointing towards the door. The doorknob turned. Jules passed the cleaver from one hand to another, as if warming its handle. Craxton could hear his own breath, travelling through his mouth and nose, down into his chest and then out again. The door slowly opened.

The Nazi was dressed in a greatcoat, his preposterous metal helmet on his head, a Luger in his hand. He saw Craxton and said something dark and bitter in his own language, moving towards him, the gun pointed at Craxton's head.

Jules lurched from behind the door and felled the German with a chop to his knees. The Luger flew from the man's hand and skated beneath the bed, but the greatcoat was thick, the cleaver designed for domestic cuts of meat. Jules' strike did not draw blood. The Nazi let out a cry and scrabbled for the door, but Craxton was on him. He sank his knife into the man's jugular. Jules closed and bolted the door as warm blood geysered from the German's neck, splashing Craxton's face, drenching his clothes. The room smelt like a charnel house. The memory came to Craxton of his father bleeding a pig in one of the barns, the sound of blood dripping into the aluminium bucket, ready to be made into black pudding. He was surprised to discover that he was hungry.

* * *

The farm kitchen was bright. The smell of fried bacon scented the room. Craxton knew his parents were bemused by his refusal to eat meat, but they were so relieved to have their son home after months of not knowing if he was alive or dead, they accepted this new eccentricity. His mother thought it something to do with the men incinerated by the plane crash, the smell they must have made. She wondered if they should avoid eating meat in his presence. But Craxton's father was resolute. The war was over, their boy safe home in Scotland. The sooner everything got back to normal, the better. The lad had always enjoyed his food. Eventually he would come round.

Craxton's mother gave him a worried smile. 'Are your eggs alright, son?'

Craxton looked at the fried eggs glistening on his plate, soft yolks waiting to be released.

'Aye, fine. They're good.'

'They're fresh today. I collected them myself.'

The eggs were always fresh. A couple of days ago Craxton had discovered a spot of blood in one of the yolks, the vestige of an unformed embryo. Since then he had found them hard to stomach. He sank his fork into the yellow centre and watched its contents slide across the plate.

Craxton's father had been up at 5am and had already done a good day's work. He forked a rasher of bacon into mouth. His lips opened and closed as he chewed, giving glimpses of his sharp teeth, the churning meat.

'I had a chat with Davie Hewatt yesterday. He says they've got a stonemason coming to Crossraguel.'

Davie Hewatt oversaw Ayrshire's monuments and historic buildings. Craxton stared at his plate. The ruined eggs. He had not yet been to the abbey, though he still visited it at night in his dreams.

His father shovelled another rasher into his mouth and took a slurp of tea.

'The place has been neglected since the war. Davie said they could do with an architect to oversee some renovations. He wondered if you'd be interested.'

Craxton's father glanced at his mother and Craxton knew they had already discussed the proposal, maybe even prompted the invitation themselves. Davie Hewatt and his father were in the same lodge. He would have heard of his return and be keen to help.

His mother topped up his tea. 'It's a good chance, son. It'll help you get back on your feet. You always liked the abbey.'

Craxton spread a slice of toast with a thin layer of marmalade and forced himself to take a bite.

'I'll go and see him today.'

'Good idea, strike while the iron's hot.' Craxton's father kept his voice casual, but relief beaconed from his eyes. 'The stonemason's a Dutch lad, around your age.'

Craxton stared at his toast, willing himself to take another bite.

'Are there no stonemasons in Ayrshire?'

His father shrugged. 'They've got their hands full, trying to repair bomb damage in the cities. Clydebank pays better than Kirkoswald. Davie said this Dutch lad had a hard war. He needs a bit of peace and quiet. You'll maybe get on.'

Craxton took a small bite of toast and forced himself to chew and swallow. The sweet-sharp taste of the marmalade reminded him of sweetmeats and he almost gagged. He tried to smile.

'Aye, maybe we will.'

* * *

The grass around Crossraguel was longer than it had been, the stonework marred by encroaching moss, but otherwise it was just as Craxton remembered. The abbey reared out of the lush Ayrshire countryside, a skeleton complex of ruined walls and fractured buildings. It had stood on the same site for over seven hundred years, indifferent to the wars that had thundered across Europe. The abbey had remained untouched as his plane tumbled to earth. It was unaffected by the first Nazi he stabbed, or the bloodiness that had followed.

Craxton walked through the archway, past the gate-house. He was early and had the abbey to himself. He crossed the long grass to the abbot's house, a square three-storey tower. Two of the tower's walls had fallen away, revealing its interior. Craxton traced the line of the staircase up to the abbot's bedroom with his eyes, marvelling at how nimble the monks must have been, to run up and down it. As a boy he had imagined the abbot as a big man sitting up in bed, the monks serving him like harried ants. The memory made him smile.

Craxton turned towards the cloister. The sound of men's voices carried across the abbey towards him. Craxton swore under his breath. He had a sudden urge to run away.

'Here's the boy.'

Davie Hewatt's voice was loudly jocular. He was a squat man, short but powerfully made, with a face reddened by days outdoors and nights spent in various Ayrshire howffs. He strode across the grass and slapped Craxton on the back.

'Welcome home.' Real emotion glimmered in his eyes.

Hewatt's companion was a thin young man, neatly dressed in dark blue overalls. He stood back, careful not to interrupt the homecoming. A breeze ruffled his blond hair.

Hewatt shook his head. 'We thought you were done for.'

I am. Craxton wanted to tell him. *Done for and bound for Hell.* He shook Hewatt's hand and returned his smile. 'It takes more than a few bombs to get rid of an Ayrshire man.' His eyes met the stranger's and Craxton knew he was not fooled.

'Good lad.' Hewatt slapped Craxton's back again. He turned to the stranger. 'This is Jimmy Craxton, a talented, young architect who knows Crossraguel like the back of his hand. He'll oversee the renovations.'

The Dutchman held out his hand. 'My name is Daan. I am pleased to meet you.'

The sun came out from behind a cloud. The abbey walls gleamed. The blond hairs on the Dutchman's arm glinted gold.

'Jimmy...?' A note of concern sounded in Hewatt's voice. 'Are you okay?'

Craxton realised he was staring. 'Sorry.' He forced a laugh and shook Daan's hand. 'It's strange being back here after so long. I'm looking forward to working with you.'

Craxton's first task was to review the stonework. He would have preferred to reacquaint himself with the abbey on his own, but now that Daan was there, it made sense to use him as a second pair of eyes. They started at the heart of the abbey, in the cloister, deciding what needed to be repointed. The men were formal with each other, each one taking notes in his own notebook. It started to spit with rain. They continued their inspection, but the sky darkened and they were suddenly pelted with hailstones. They ran together, skin stinging from the assault, to the shelter of the choir.

Craxton sank onto a stone bench set into the wall. The hail had reminded him of Paris, the bomb blast shattering the attic window. He wiped a hand across his face and took a flask of tea his mother had given him that morning from his bag. He poured a cup and offered it to Daan.

'Thanks.' The Dutchman took a sip and winced.

Craxton filled the lid of the flask and drank, the atmosphere of the attic was still on him: the blood. He looked at the Dutchman. 'You prefer coffee?'

Daan shrugged. 'I've grown used to tea.'

The complacency in his voice irritated Craxton. 'We're lucky to get it.'

Daan gave him a weak smile. 'I don't mean to be ungrateful. It's good to drink something warm.'

There was something unfortunately Germanic about the stonemason's fair hair, his neat good looks, Craxton thought.

Daan reached out and traced one of the mason's marks etched into the hand-carved stone blocks that formed the wall. 'My father gave me my mark when I finished my apprenticeship. He said it would help me get paid if each stone I carved was signed. It wasn't until he died that I realised the marks carry a message to the future.' Daan kissed his fingers and touched them to the mason's mark again. 'All stonemasons are brothers. All masons.' He turned away from the wall. His eyes met Craxton's. 'Your father's invited me to his lodge. He told me Robert Burns used to drink there.'

Craxton had joined the freemasons before the war with the intention of pleasing his father and furthering his career, but despite his father's encouragement, he had not visited the lodge since his return. He wondered if the invitation to Daan had been intended to pull him in too.

'Rabbie Burns took his drink wherever he could get it, his women too, by all accounts.'

Daan started to inspect the stones inside the choir.

'Do you have a girlfriend?'

The question was unexpected. Craxton took another sip of tea.

'No, I was always too deep in my books for girls when I was younger, then the war came along.'

The stonemason jotted something in his notebook.

'A lot of people found romance during the war.'

Craxton thought romance a strange word for the fumblings and swift release his RAF friends had boasted of. He looked away. 'I didn't.'

The Dutchman's eyes met his. 'No, me neither.'

That night Craxton dreamt of Paris, of blood and bone and stinking guts. The window shattered inwards and the tail gunner screamed.

He woke to his father's hand on his shoulder, his mother standing in the bedroom doorway.

'Are you okay son?'

He had never seen his father look frightened before.

'Aye Dad, fine.' The bedclothes were drenched in sweat. 'Just a bad dream.'

His father stretched out an arm and for a moment it seemed he might touch the tears on Craxton's face, but he pulled his hand away.

'You're a good lad, Jimmy. Try and get some sleep.'

Craxton's father ushered his mother from the room and closed the door. The slice of light that had stretched in from the hallway shrank and died, leaving Craxton alone in the dark.

Craxton's life took on a new rhythm. Each morning he went to Crossraguel. He returned to the farmhouse in the late afternoon and worked until bedtime on his plans, drawing the abbey in detail, outlining and costing the renovations. He worked late and read long into the night, delaying sleep until exhaustion pulled him under. Now that he was at the abbey every day, he no longer dreamt of it. Instead he woke each night from *Grand Guignol* nightmares set in Paris.

Daan took a bite of his sandwich. 'You look unwell.'

They were sitting on the lawn at the centre of the cloisters, eating their packed lunches. Craxton had grown used to the Dutchman's forthrightness. He rubbed an apple against the sleeve of his shirt, polishing its skin.

'I'm fine.'

The stonemason was lodging with the Hewatts. Davie's wife Maureen was delighting in feeding him. He lifted the lid of his sandwich and showed Craxton the slab of spam at its centre.

'Perhaps if you ate meat you'd feel better.'

The sight of the pink meat, the sudden piggy-ness of it twisted Craxton's guts. He only just managed to reach the long grass before spewing up the contents of his stomach.

The Dutchman followed him. 'I'm sorry. That was stupid of me.' He passed Craxton a handkerchief. 'Your father's worried about you. He thought perhaps if we talked... You were in France during the occupation, I was in Holland...'

Craxton raised the handkerchief to his lips. 'I can't talk about it.'

Daan nodded. 'I understand. We all saw things... did things...' He stepped closer to Craxton. 'I have bad dreams. Some nights I come down here and walk around the abbey. It calms me. Perhaps you should try it.'

Craxton met his gaze. The Dutchman's eyes were the same blue as the Firth of Clyde on a sunny day.

'I don't think so.'

He folded the soiled cotton square and shoved it into his pocket.

That night when he woke soaked in sweat, the memory of blood in his mouth, Craxton thought of the abbey. He wondered if the Dutchman was there, walking the ruins, and felt an urge to pull on his clothes and follow him. He huddled beneath the covers and tried to sleep, but he was still awake when the dawn crept in.

From then on, when Craxton woke in the night, screams and laughter in his head, he felt the pull of the abbey. He held out until the full moon. The bedroom curtains were open a crack, a sliver of light stretched across the counterpane, like a path. He thought of calling his mother and asking her to strap him to the bed until morning, like a mariner lashed to the mast in a storm, but the moment passed. Craxton dressed quickly and left the house by the back door, careful not to make a sound. The old sheepdog growled as he crossed the yard. He shushed it and walked his bicycle to the road so it would not crunch against the gravel.

Moonlight lit the way. It was a windless night and the hedgerows and trees were still, as if they had been wrought out of metal. Craxton pedalled past darkened cottages into the open countryside, towards the abbey. An owl screeched. He was less than ten miles from Alloway Kirkyard where Rabbie Burns' Tam o'Shanter had encountered the witches. Craxton's heart beat faster, but he had set his course and did not turn back.

Crossraguel Abbey was a ruined silhouette. Craxton got off his bike and wheeled it beneath the arch of the main gate into the grounds. A farm cat, out on the kill, crossed the South Court. It stopped to give him a knowing look. Craxton ignored it and walked across the dew-drenched grass. The dome of the ancient doocot was outlined against the sky, like a giant beehive. He turned his back on it and entered the cloisters. It was darker inside the shelter of the walls. Craxton paused, letting his eyes adjust. The bike ride had not quite blown away the memory of his nightmare. The remnants of blood and tearing flesh still clung to him. He rubbed a hand over his face, wondering why he had come to Crossraguel in the dead of night.

Something moved in the darkness of the passageway that led to the East Range. Daan stepped from the shadows, his blond hair bright in the moonlight. They stood still, regarding each other, and then the stonemason walked across the grass. The hairs on Craxton's arms rose, alive with electricity.

Daan said, 'I wondered if you would come here tonight.'

The Dutchman was close enough for Craxton to smell the scent of the carbolic soap he used and beneath that the scent of his body, his flesh and blood.

Daan reached out a hand and touched Craxton's face. 'I have nightmares too.'

Craxton caught the stonemason's wrist. 'Perhaps we can help each other get rid of our bad dreams.'

Daan's face was close, his eyes blue. He whispered, 'Perhaps.'

Craxton shovelled bacon and black pudding into his mouth. His mother had made no comment when he asked for a full breakfast, but he could feel her eyes on him, her smile.

His father slurped his tea. 'Maureen Hewatt was round early. She said thon Dutch boy wasn't in his bed this morning.'

Craxton's mother was frying potato scones on the range. She turned from her task.

'Poor Mo's been over-fretful since they got the news about their Tommy. The Dutch lad's been a blessing. Someone to look after and take her mind off the fact that her son is never coming home.'

Craxton spoke with his mouth full of bacon and blood sausage.

'I'm afraid Mrs Hewatt will need to find a new pet.'

His father looked up from his breakfast. 'Is something wrong with Daan? He was meant to be coming to the lodge tonight.'

His mother slid the potato scones onto a plate and brought them to the table.

'Maureen will be beside herself. What happened, Jimmy?'

Craxton helped himself to another rasher of bacon.

'The peace and quiet did its work. He decided to go back to Holland. Daan's a good stonemason. He's more use in a city, fixing bomb damage, than repointing stones at Crossraguel.'

His mother poured herself a cup of tea.

'Maureen will be sad to see him go, all the same.'

Craxton slathered butter on a slice of toast.

'Is there any more black pudding?'

His mother got to her feet and went to the range.

'He might have waited to say goodbye, after all she's done for him.'

Craxton bit into his toast. 'I think he was worried about upsetting her.'

The black pudding spat and sizzled as his mother dropped it into the fat.

'It's a cowardly way to go about things. He could have said thank you before he went.'

His father shook his head. 'Maureen said he left all his gear in his room.'

'I know. Daan asked me to pack it up and send it on to him.'

Craxton's mother's voice was sharp. 'You should have told him to do it himself.'

She set another slice of black pudding on Craxton's plate.

'It's not Jimmy's fault, love. He didn't know the boy would leave like that.' His father finished his tea and got to his feet, ready to resume work. 'To tell you the truth, I'm glad he's gone. There was something not quite right about that lad. I couldn't put my finger on it, but I never felt easy about him and Jimmy working alone together, up at Crossraguel.'

'I'll not be there for much longer either.' Craxton wiped the remnants of his toast across his plate, soaking up the last of the meat juices. 'I've decided to head to London. Daan's right. This is a chance to help build a new world. Who knows, if I play my cards right I might get the chance to build something really good.'

His father set his cap on his head. His jaw bunched the way it did when he was disappointed.

'I thought you'd stay longer. After all you went through.'

Craxton's mother went to her husband and put her arm through his.

'Ach Jim, you knew Ayrshire was never going to be big enough for our boy. Be proud of him.'

His father put an arm around her and squeezed.

'I am proud. I just like knowing he's safe. '

Craxton pushed his plate away. He smiled at his parents.

'Don't worry. I'll come home for visits.'

Ayrshire was not small he thought to himself. Not small at all. It was a fertile region full of fields, ditches, hidden coves and forests. It was a place where a man could lose himself, a place where a man could easily be lost.

St Peter's Seminary, Cardross

The Twa Corbies of Cardross
Craig Robertson

As I was walking all alane,
I heard twa corbies makin a mane;
The tane unto the ither say,
'Whar sall we gang and dine the-day?'

I'm Black, he's Stout. Simple names for simple lives. We work together, best we can. Two sets of eyes can see opportunities in double quick time, take advantage before some other thief can step in and steal your pitch. If he goes hungry then so do I. We're a team, Stout and me. A team.

'Where are we going to eat today, Mr Black?' he asks me.

'If you want to fly to one of the cities then how about the Witchery?' I reply. 'Or maybe the Rogano? I've heard the fish at Ondine is the best there is.'

'Too rich for my blood,' Mr Stout says. 'Far too rich. I'm a country bird at heart, a bird of simple tastes, you know that. Besides, my purse is as empty as my belly. Our pickings will have to come as free as the air. What's fresh on the wind today, Mr Black?'

Stout knew I was joking. The best tables weren't for the likes of us. Old Stouty and I aren't welcome, you see. Our faces don't fit. Not even close. It's not just that the people don't want us. It's that they barely notice we exist.

They don't see us as we fade into the grey of the sky and the thick of the clouds. We fly in the shadows and pick at their pockets, trip at their feet. We were here before them and will still be here when they are long gone. We see everything and are seen only by the few. We're in the woods and the concrete, we're in the rafters and the gloom, we're deep in the blood of the place.

The truth is we eat anything, Mr Stout and me. That's how desperately we live our lives. It might be the spoils of the fields or whatever we can salvage from the leftovers of those better provided for. We'd eat each other if we had to. It's all fair game when you're hungry.

You've never known real hunger unless your belly has been properly empty. Empty like the wind or a broken promise, empty like a past forgotten or a future that will never be. Proper hunger drives you like the devil.

What was fresh on the wind? Well now, there was a question indeed.

> In ahint yon auld fail dyke,
> I wot there lies a new slain knight;
> And nane do ken that he lies there,
> But his hawk, his hound an his lady fair.
>
> His hound is tae the huntin gane,
> His hawk tae fetch the wild-fowl hame,
> His lady's tain anither mate,
> So we may mak oor dinner swate.

The place in the woods near Cardross is riddled with corridors and cells, chapels and concrete arches. It's a derelict house open to all, weather and visitors alike, a dark maze of ruin and stagnant pools, of secluded and secondary thoughts. The tourists might venture there for a thrill or a dare but rarely after lights out, not after the safe company of others has gone home for the night. Then it becomes home to the likes of us and those who would do us harm. In the deep dark, the place in the woods is for dangerous travellers.

They used to call it St Peter's. They came here, young men all bright and shiny, seeking to learn how best to serve their shepherd. Priests of the citadel, children of the altar, dressed in black smocks from to neck to toe.

One day, the button bright boys left forever and others arrived. Bags of bones with cheeks of flint, eyes dulled and skin grey, these new recruits were not like those who went before. This army served other gods who treated them badly.

Stout and me, we watched them build it, this concrete palace, and we watched it crumble. Years it took as the wind and the rain ate it, chunk by chunk till the woods and the rhododendron swallowed it up, claiming it for their own. No matter how hard you looked, you couldn't tell where nature stopped and the building started. It's like that now, at one with the Kilmahew woods and those of us who live in them.

At the edges, its ownership is blurred but at its centre it remains the sanctuary of the boy priests. This was where they came to pray to their god and, of a night or a winter's morning, you can hear them still, young voices carrying on the wind.

It's dark and wet down there, guarded by a smashed granite altar, as blind as those who will not see. The sanctuary is a cold bed on a November morning, bitter in the shadows where the sun can't touch. No place for a soldier boy far from home. No place for the dead to lie out of sight and mind.

I've had sense of the slain warrior and tell this to Stout. His ears prick immediately and I see him sniff the same chance as me. When your prospects are as bleak as ours then you learn to seize the few that come your way.

'No one knows he's there, Blacky? You're sure?' Stout is a cautious sort until he's certain all the odds are on his side. His side and mine, of course.

I reassure him. 'No one knows he's there except those who left him that way.'

'And who's that?' Stouty's black eyes narrow meanly. He's not much for morality, not being able to afford such a luxury, but he's keen on practicalities. Stout knows what's important and what's not.

'His dog, his friend and his woman. The dog is a brown and grey mutt, a nasty looking mongrel with a scratch across one eye. The friend is tall and dark, word is he's a sly guy with an eye for the prize. One worth the watching he is.'

'And the woman?'

'Fair of face by all accounts. A looker. The kind that young soldiers pine for when they're far from home.'

Stouty nodded, satisfied with my report. 'And where are they now?'

'Off for fresh pastures and fresh meat,' I told him. 'They left the poor soul before he was cold, left while his last breath still clouded the air in front of him. It's thought he took a tumble in the dark, from rotting beam or plundered stair, or took a step across fresh air. He fell unseen, lay undiscovered, left by one and left by the other. The hawk-eyed pal slipped into the night, he and the woman claiming oblivion to the soldier's plight. It's said she's already taken another lover and I'd wager, at such speed, it's most likely the erstwhile friend is the beneficiary.'

'So, the fallen soldier is all ours then.'

'All ours, Stouty boy. As long as we're nimble and quick.'

'Which we are, Blacky. Which we are. We'll eat well this morning.'

You'll notice that Stout didn't ask if the soldier's friend or his woman, or even his nasty dog, had caused him to be lying dead in the shadows. Facts like that aren't important to the likes of Stouty and me. You can't eat facts just like you can't chew on morals or line your stomach with the thin meat between right and wrong. Only those who are already fat can choose to care about such fine details.

For us, it's all about the feed. A body doesn't eat, a body doesn't survive. If we don't make the most of what scraps we're offered then we'll end up as dead as the corpse of St Peter's. That's not an option we fancy so we do what it takes. Black and Stout, survivors both.

We catch the smell on the wind long before we get there. Our senses are full of it. We can taste it, hear it, soon to see and touch it. The sweet reek of death is a familiar refrain to those who live in these woods, a dawn chorus and a midnight dirge. It's the song we all sing, eventually.

To Stout and me, it can only be good news. If someone else is dead then it's not us. The smell of it this day enflames our blood, excites us like a chase and so we sing on the wing.

'We'll eat today, Blacky boy. We'll eat like princes.'

'Like kings, Mr Stout.'

'Like emperors!'

Ye'll sit on his white hause-bane,
And I'll pike oot his bonny blue een;
Wi ae lock o his gowden hair
We'll theek oor nest whan it grows bare.

We slow as we near St Peter's, no time this to ruin everything with carelessness. From the air it is a sight, a concrete monolith, rearing up unexpectedly from the woods, battered, pillaged and weather-wrecked. It's the grey amid the greens.

Even in its prime it was a magnificent but ugly beast, a citadel of cement, pebble-dashed and brutal. It's still a shock to find it there, now smothered in legend and neglect.

We take a perch on high, Stout and me. We are quiet and watchful, ears alert, hearing only the breathing of the dead and the hush of the morning wind. Stout looks north while I scour south. Back to back we turn, studying east and west. Nothing but the cold stone and the weeds that choke the walls, nothing but the silence and the eager whispering of ghosts. Nothing but the body of the stricken soldier.

He lies in the sanctuary, on its shallow pool of dormant rain and rippling reflections. We edge closer, seeing that he is indeed not much more than a boy, freckles on a face as ashen as death's pale horse. His golden hair grows dark at the ends where it is damp with the dawn's dew, his lips as blue as his eyes. His clothes are shades of brown, disguise for the desert and the poppy fields.

He is a picture, this soldier boy blue.

Will you wake him? Oh no, not I. For if I do he will surely cry.

For a moment, a weak but beautiful moment, I imagine

that Stout and I feel for the soldier. We mourn his loss and his pain, we rage at his loss and at the cruel world that makes it so. In truth, of course, we do not. We are glad of his death and because of that we must be glad of his pain.

We're sure he's in St Peter's because he's one of them. An explorer. We've heard them called urbexers, Mr Stout and me. They are the people who followed the addicts who followed the priests. They come alone or sometimes in twos or threes, slipping in unseen and searching St Peter's from top to toe just for the thrill of it.

They do it in the cities too, finding their way into man-made places they shouldn't, just because they're told they can't. They see Keep Out and they read Come On In. They go under cover of night and concealment, their whereabouts unknown and their safety compromised. They are vulnerable as they sneak into the abandoned and the derelict, the tall and the tunnels, getting their kicks where they dare, out of sight and out of mind. Yet one misstep, one fatal fateful turn and they've explored their last. This soldier boy has dared and lost.

Yet as we sidle closer still, we learn another truth. He did not lose, rather he has been defeated, slain most royally. The boy's skull is cracked asunder, the victim of several savage blows. No accident this, he a hero fallen on the wrong battlefield. We look at each other, Stout and me, and shrug our surprise into disregard. We have not time or care for such distinctions when faced with such a repast.

We work quickly, a quality of excellence borne out of practice and necessity. He holds and I take. I hold and he rakes. Not an inch of cotton or a square piece of skin goes unexamined for the treasure it might hold. Everything makes a pretty price when you know where to sell it to. There's cash, both coin of the realm and folding money, and there's plastic that artful alchemists can turn into gold. Close your eyes, soldier boy. Best you don't see how ugly this world is.

Stout plucks them out, those bonny blue eyes. I do for the heart and the liver while Stouty comes back for the lungs. It's a bountiful harvest. We strip him bare and have it away with his boots and even his hair. A man's DNA is as good as money in the bank, a nest egg for a rainy day in a land where the clouds come to tea and never leave.

When we've had our fill of our bloody feast, we sit sated for as long as we dare. Stout and me, patting our full bellies like pigs from the trough. The boy has been picked clean and is at peace with nature. He and the weeds and the rhododendrons will become one, melding into the bones of the old place like he was born to it. We can do no more and to tarry will only leave us vulnerable.

So, when Stout looks at me with one gimlet eye and the other closed in thought, I begin to worry. He is debating, I can see that, but can't for the sorry life of me imagine what troubles him.

'Blacky, this poor wretch has served us well. Perhaps it is only right that we do him some favour in return.'

I look at the fallen hero and wonder what favour can be done for him now. Stripped to the bones and with less life than the ground he lies on, he seems beyond help. I look at Stout too and think he might have taken leave of his senses or been struck by some dangerous attack of conscience. Still, he is a canny crow is Mr Stout so I give him the courtesy of explaining

'Help him how, Stouty?'

'We find the rogue that has caved in his skull with such brutal blows. Resourceful fellows like ourselves, should be no trouble at all. We can become detectives.'

'Detectives?'

'Are you a parrot or a crow?' Stout cackles. 'Yes, detectives. We shall find the killer of the soldier boy. You and me.'

'Stouty?' I knock gently on his head to make sure he's in. 'Are you feeling okay? Detecting is not our game. We owe this boy nothing other than perhaps a vote of thanks for a fine meal. That gratitude surely doesn't extend to putting ourselves at risk for the sake of others.'

Stout throws back his head and laughs till the old seminary rings with the sound.

'Hee. Blacky boy. Your face! Do you really think I'd come over all sentimental for this bag of bones? Find the soldier's killer we will, but for us, not for him. It's an opportunity, Blacky. Can you not smell it?'

I say of course when I really mean no but Stouty sees through my poor charade immediately. He laughs to himself and takes to the wind.

'Come on, Blacky. Time to take our leave and give the soldier boy the peace of the ages. And time for you to use the senses you were born with. Think, Mr Black. Think!'

We scurry and scamper and make ourselves scarce, seeking the shadows and counting our wares. My head is full of Stout's words and I know from his mocking that the answer is within my reach. Find the boy's killer. Find him for us. Find the boy's killer. Find him for us. Find the killer. Find a body. A body for us! Eat, eat and eat!

I look up to see Stout has been watching me, seeing the wheels tumble in my mind and the safe door spring open. Jackpot. He screeches and hoots and nearly falls over in his delight.

'He gets it. He gets it. Mr Black, your senses are intact. Are you with me?'

'I am, Mr Stout. I am. Whoever has killed our sweet knight will likely kill again. We find him, follow him and bide our time. When the murderer does what murderers do then you and I will be there. We will dine like princes.'

'Like kings, Mr Black.'

'Like emperors!'

*　*　*

Mony a one for him makes mane,
But nane sall ken whar he is gane;
Oer his white banes, whan they are bare,
The wind sall blaw for evermair.

Shadows are useful places for those who know how to use them, and St Peter's is punctured with them. For Stout and me they're a natural home. You can see a lot when no one knows you're looking. And they can't know you're looking when they don't know you're there.

We are patient creatures, particularly when our hunger has been fed. So, we sit and wait and watch from the safe distance of anonymity. The battered old building breathes in and out, and its ghosts and its residents wander by and by, rushing here and brushing by each other there. They are either unaware of the soldier's death or just don't care. Their world spins on regardless.

I see the woman first and nudge Stout, who immediately recognises her for who she is. Red-eyed and pale, she walks unsteadily, eyes darting left and right. She's scared, this one. Rabbit running, twitching and ready to bolt. She steals across the bridge of sighs and she's inside.

The explorers love this place. It was built for the baby priests, and God knows their father's house has many rooms. All exposed to nature wild. They come here and think it theirs but it can never be. It's ours, Stout and me and the wind and rain.

Will she turn left towards the sanctuary and her slain soldier blue? Stouty and I hold our breaths, nodding knowingly at each other as she hesitates on the pass. We sense her anguish and see a hand go up as she uses the back of it to wipe at her eyes.

'Crocodile tears?' asks Stout.

'Guilty conscience?' asks I.

She makes right, away from her beau, picking her way across strewn debris and up one of the unmasked concrete staircases, climbing to where our friend the wind howls and swirls, to where the grey greets the blue. Stout and I are just about to follow her when we see him. The sly mate. The sometime pal. He's walking in the shadows like an untold lie, wearing them like a cloak or a comfort blanket. We can sense something of ourselves in him.

'He's our man,' Stout whispers to me.

'No doubt about it,' I say. 'I can smell it on him.'

'He reeks of it. After him, Blacky boy. But we'd best tread carefully, this one knows the walkways and the stairwells and the short cuts. He's slippy.'

'Slippy is our middle name, Mr Stout. We invented this game.'

'That we did, Mr Black. And this could be our richest winnings yet.'

So, we followed him, Stout and me. Watched him flit from chapel to cell to cloister, along cobbled path and by floating concrete slabs, eyes darting left and right as he steals down walkways, slips by painted walls and hides in the shade that's always there if you know where to look. He is armed with a camera, the weapon of choice of the explorers. They take nothing but photographs, leave nothing but footprints.

This knave is different though. He's taken a life and left his friend behind to rot like the building he lies in. We offer him our contempt for his action and our gratitude for his offering.

He makes for the rear of the place, stepping over missing floorboards and broken stone, ducking under falling beams. Past pillar after pillar swathed in graffiti, painted offerings to the gods, the goths and the gallus.

He walks and she walks. Together yet separate, they stalk the halls of the place in the woods, one following the other following the one before. They circle each other these explorers, like water going down a drain.

These two were there the night before, losing the soldier boy in the dark of the ruins, losing him to the abyss. Now they return. One to search for their missing wheel, the other drawn back to the scene of the crime. We are Stout and Black, Detectives Incorporated, and now the play is upon us.

'A crime of passion, that's what it is, Mr Black. A murderous ménage. This hawk-eyed villain has butchered his friend in order to steal his lady fair.'

'Fair is foul and foul is fair, Mr Stout, but this wretch breaks all rules of comradeship.'

'Trust is paramount for partners in such endeavours, Blacky old boy.'

'One falls, all fall,' I tell him.

The sly guy walks down the spiral stair, stepping vigilantly on charred wood and passing by untrustworthy walls. He is bound for the sanctuary, bound for our once blue-eyed boy. Stout and Black are on his tail.

We see him slow his tread. We see him stop. We see what he sees, the soldier slain lying in the sanctuary's gathered rain. Me to Stout and Stout to me, glances fast and glances keen. The time is now, the game afoot, just rewards for hot pursuit.

The knave advances upon his one-time friend, the blue boy broken at his feet, picked clean by Stouty and me. He lets loose a scream on seeing skin and bone where the bonny blue eyes once shone so bright. The cry rings through the citadel, echoing off the concrete, off history, waking ghosts of priests to be and addicts at the altar of redemption.

'Too late for conscience,' Stout whispers to me.

'Too late for regret.'

As we watch, the knave falls to his knees, scooping up the bones of the boy blue and cradling them to his own. He hugs him tight, wailing as he does so.

'Conscience.'

'Regret.'

He peels the soldier from his breast, gazing upon him with a look we cannot fathom, a tenderness beyond our expectation. Then he swoops down, like from the heavens, and kisses the soldier on the lips. He seals his being to the other's with a passion unforeseen and lingering. Stout and I are on our backs, our expectations overthrown.

'Lovers,' Stouty screeches. 'Lovers!'

From the darkness comes the lady fair, like a storm

from the east, quick and sudden to trap the unwary. Her step is swift from the shadow, her footsteps ringing on the cement but not heard above the man's grief.

'Fair is foul and foul is fair,' I shriek.

She strikes. Hard and fast. A swishing blow of metal rod that produces the crack of bone and then another. The thumps and whacks rain down like vengeance, the old place chanting in time to the clouts, its echoes and intonations of violent mourning.

The skull leaks life and still she strikes, crushing it with fervour. In seconds, there is one more ghost in the sanctuary, one more soul lost and found. In a flash, Stouty and me see just how the soldier boy met his own untimely death.

'Her not him,' Stout crows. 'Her not him. And them not her. A ménage but not as we thought. They the lovers and *she* the spurned. She the murderer of the soldier boy.'

'Hell hath no fury, Mr Stout. This sister scorned, this fair foul ladykiller.'

We dance, Mr Stout and me. Circling each other with little hops of delight, the prospect of the feast driving us to a frenzy. Such a banquet of enchantments, a basket of charms laid out so royally that we must squawk and sing our appreciation.

She hears us, the lady fair, but pays us no heed. Her senses drown in blood and only revenge has her ear. She stands and shakes, shocked to find the metal in her hand and drops it with a clang that can be heard across the sanctuary and the seminary and the woods and the village beyond. The only thing louder is the silence which follows.

At length, her legs buckle and she falls to the side of

the poor soul she dispatched into the darkest night. She lifts his head and holds him in her lap, her hands stroking his hair, matted thick with the burgundy-red of his blood. She takes sacrament, her lips wet with his life, shining like rubies, in grace and disgrace.

She kisses him. His blood on her lips. Her lips to the lips that kissed the soldier boy. A last farewell. Ae fond kiss and then they sever.

As she stands again, eyes red and wet, she lingers over the body of the blue boy. And spits upon his soul.

She turns and slinks away, picking over the corpse of the place, the wood and the weeds and the bones of stone, the rubble and the ruin, until she again climbs the spiral stair towards the skies.

'She flees, Mr Black.'

'Like a thief in the night, Mr Stout.'

We care not for the morality of her absconding from the scene, having no time or want for unnecessary extravagancies but we are keen to follow her every move given that she is such a generous provider of food for the needy.

Up through the main block, along narrow walkways and up staircases, she rises through the building like a prayer. Up and up until only the heavens are above her, wind hammering at her from all sides as it rushes through where glass once barred the way. She treads with care over flooring gapped like a beggar's teeth, boards wet and warped and rotten to boot. At last, she stands on the concrete collar from which she can see all the way to the sanctuary below.

We see what she sees, the broken bodies lying in the rain. The forbidden lovers, limb over limb, sleeping on their gory bed of stone.

She sways upon the wind, a gentle wavering on the edge and for a moment, a brief but beautiful moment, we think she is going to take her own life, that she will fall from grace until she crashes on the concrete floor way below.

The lady shares not our romantic whim and resists any temptation to such caprice. With a final look down at the star-crossed pair cast into perdition, she turns to take her leave.

I look at Stout and Stout looks at me. Two sets of eyes can see opportunities before they even occur.

'For the fallen knights, Mr Black.'

'For us, Mr Stout.'

'Forever.'

We have at her, plunging from our perch in the shadows, raining down with shriek and holler, catching the lady unaware and on the spin, her balance lost like her mind. She moves from our assault but that is her undoing and she grasps at air but finds that air cannot be grasped. Her scream is loud but short.

Her body finds sanctuary but sanctuary proves no refuge. The noise it makes would sicken most but Stouty and me are made of sterner stuff.

We do not wallow but instead we rise. We take to the wing and soar on high, we swoop and climb, we glide and sing our happy song as we stare down on the place in the woods. From our spot in the heavens, we can see to the heart of it, where nature has carved a hole through man's design, to the place of altar and sanctuary and sacrifice.

'We shall dine like princes for ever more, Mr Black.'

'Like kings, Mr Stout.'

'Like emperors.'

The Twa Corbies

As I was walking all alane,
I heard twa corbies makin a mane;
The tane unto the ither say,
'Whar sall we gang and dine the-day?'

'In ahint yon auld fail dyke,
I wot there lies a new slain knight;
And nane do ken that he lies there,
But his hawk, his hound an his lady fair.

'His hound is tae the huntin gane,
His hawk tae fetch the wild-fowl hame,
His lady's tain anither mate,
So we may mak oor dinner swate.

'Ye'll sit on his white hause-bane,
And I'll pike oot his bonny blue een;
Wi ae lock o his gowden hair
We'll theek oor nest whan it grows bare.

'Mony a one for him makes mane,
But nane sall ken whar he is gane;
Oer his white banes, whan they are bare,
The wind sall blaw for evermair.'

Anonymous Scots Ballad, first published in
print by Sir Walter Scott in 1802 in
The Minstrelsy of the Scottish Border

Edinburgh Castle

Nemo Me Impune Lacessit
Denise Mina

God, they were tired. Long-term tired. Give-up tired. Jake's loud singing was drawing the eyes of everyone in the street to them.

'The cas-TLE! Cas-TLE! Casss-TLE!'

Audrey wasn't enforcing his rigid behavioural programme properly any more. It wasn't changing anything. She had even stopped forcing his medication into him. She was so tired.

Jake was eleven and didn't sleep. He skulked around the house at night. He stood at the end of their bed for hours, staring at them. They had installed CCTV in their room and saw him do it. One morning they found a hammer at the end of the bed. When they watched the recording back they saw him practise-swing it at Audrey's head and laugh to himself. They installed pressure alarms on Jake's bed after that to wake them when he got up. Audrey knew it was coming to a head. She could feel it. They all could.

At the top of the hill a man in full Braveheart costume crossed in front of them, looking down at Jake's loud singing. He had a blue Saltire flag painted on his face. Jake saw it and changed his shriek to 'Blue-LOO-LOO-LOO.'

He sang in soprano. As they approached the Royal Mile his voice was increasingly amplified by the high tenements.

Trailing behind Jake were six-year-old Simon and seven-year-old Hannah. His little brother and sister kept their hands deep in their pockets, their heads down. Audrey and Pete followed up the rear, both shamefaced and thinking the same thing: they should have kept Jake on his medication. The pills made him fat and tearful, he wet the bed more than usual and that made it hard for them to go away anywhere. Audrey had to corner him and pinch his nose to make him open his mouth. She had to force him to take them. She didn't know if she could manage his behavioural problems any more.

Years ago, when Jake had tried to drown Simon in a paddling pool and laughed when they told him off, Audrey's mum had said: 'He hasn't got behavioural problems, he's just a vicious little arsehole.'

Audrey had sobbed at that. Her mum cuddled her and cried with her and said 'no, sweetheart, look, he'll grow out of it. If someone doesn't kill him first. Ha ha. Have you considered exorcism?'

Audrey stayed away from her mum now. Jake didn't need any more negativity around him. He got enough of that at school. He'd killed the class gerbil, he hurt other children if he was left alone with them. Play dates and parties always ended unceremoniously. Only Audrey saw how isolated Jake was, how vulnerable. He was desperate for friends. He didn't care what age they were. He was always wandering off when they were shopping, following children or adults. He seemed terribly alone and it would only get worse. She knew that.

At the end of the road Jake saw the castle, threw his head back and ululated, 'CASTLULULULULULUL!'

Their last faint hope was that Jake would grow out of it. He had been on different types of medication, seen psychologists, psychiatrists, ministers, been on behavioural boot camps. When he beat the neighbour's dog to death with a brick two years ago, social work moved him to a different school. They wanted him to go to a residential facility. Pete was keen but Audrey couldn't send him away. Their last and only hope was that he would grow out of it.

'CASTLULULULUUUUUU!' Jake's eyes were protruding. He was shaking. He was going to blow.

It was a busy street. Everyone was looking at Jake. His body was rigid, his blue hoodie was drawn tight around his intensely red face. Tourists were watching him, not judging, just interested in the mad singing boy. They had no idea how bad things were about to get.

Hannah put her arm out to stop her little brother from walking into Jake's clawing radius. She grabbed Simon's green hood, pulled him back down the hill to a safe zone. She looked imploringly back to her parents.

Audrey hurried over and knelt down in front of Jake. He looked feral, eleven but small. His eyes were wide and blank. He couldn't see her. She leaned in, filling his field of vision with her face, and held him firmly by the shoulders.

'Jake, I need you to calm down.'

'CALM! CALMLULULULUL!' He ululated in her face. Spit flecked her eyelids.

'I need you to take a deep breath and caaaalm yourself down.'

Audrey moved her hands to his upper arms and held

him tight, ready for a secure hold if he went for her. 'Breathe in and out, in and out. Do it with me.' She breathed deeply, setting an example.

Sudden as a cat spotting a mouse, Jake focused on her face. 'I fucking hate you, Mummy.'

'That's it, breathe in.'

'I hate you.'

'And out.'

'I'll bite you again.' He looked at the scar he had gnawed on her chin.

Audrey was very, very angry but she blinked it back. Jake was being provocative to get a strong reaction. She would only have to act calm for a short while because it was Pete's turn to drag him back to the hotel and guard him while he had a tantrum in a stimulation-free environment.

'You're too excited.' She spoke in a flat voice. 'You've let yourself get too excited.'

He glanced at the castle again and suddenly realised what 'too excited' meant. He was going to be removed, denied the castle and the cake and the baked potato lunch. She steeled herself as Jake's body tensed, he bared his teeth and bent his knees, ready to spring.

The shadow of Pete fell over them, hands out, in position to apply the hold they had been taught to use on him. Jake's eyes flicked to his father and he flinched, knew his physical attack on his mother was foiled.

'When you're asleep...' Jake growled. He saw the spark of alarm in her eyes and smiled.

This morning in the hotel Audrey had swung her feet over the side of the bed, stepping onto a jagged glass ashtray discarded on the floor. She hadn't told Pete. It was terrifying. It was an escalation.

'I'll do it,' he snarled.

Something snapped inside of her, a cold wash over her heart. Eleven years of soul-grinding humiliation, of shame and blame, of confrontations about Jake's behaviour. And tiredness. Everyone thought it was her fault. Maybe it was her fault. She had done her best. Her best was enough for Hannah and Simon but it wasn't nearly enough for Jake. She couldn't do this any more.

'Right,' she said, 'We're going home.'

Jake glanced desperately up to the castle. 'To the hotel?'

'No. To Surrey. Remember Helen, the social worker? She'll meet us there.'

'Why Helen, Mummy?'

He was too old to call her that. It sounded facetious and strengthened her resolve.

'You need help.' She squeezed his upper arms hard. 'And I've tried but I can't seem to help you. I'm finished.'

Never confront him, Pete had said, nursing a bloody cut on his forehead. Audrey didn't care any more. She shut her eyes, expecting him to start clawing at her, at her eyes, at her lips.

But Jake didn't. He looked at her, expressionless, unblinking, and spoke in an unfamiliar voice, 'I'm finished too.'

It was a normal voice, not strangled or grating. Not the voice that made strangers in the street want to slap him. 'I'm finished too, Mum.'

'You've finished what?' she whispered.

'This behaviour. It's finished.' He looked at the castle battlements then back at her. He held her eye.

Pete hadn't heard this. When he spoke his voice sounded high and frightened, 'We popping back to the hotel for a time out, Jakey?'

Audrey released her grip slowly but Jake didn't move.

Hannah and Simon backed away. But Jake didn't go for anyone. Uncertain, Audrey stepped away.

Jake smiled up at her, a warm smile, and his eyebrows tented in a question. He looked up the winding lane to the castle and back at her for permission.

Reckless with exhaustion, Audrey raised an arm to the castle. He trotted away along the pavement.

Hannah and Simon watched their brother run off by himself. Hannah chewed her cuff. She did that when she was scared. Little Simon was baffled by the lack of drama and looked anxiously to his father for reassurance. Pete ruffled Simon's hair and watched Jake walk calmly away. He looked at Audrey. She shrugged that she didn't know what was going on either.

'He said he was finished with his 'behaviour'.'

'What, the ululating?' asked Pete.

They watched him walk away, dazed by the change in his mood.

'I don't know what he meant.'

Jake glanced back, saw they weren't twenty feet behind – he had been warned about staying a safe distance to the group – and stopped. He waited. Audrey couldn't believe it.

'Okay,' said Pete, tentative but hopeful. 'It's a castle. There probably isn't that much he can break.' He swung Simon onto his shoulders. 'Come on then. Let's just see how it goes.'

Audrey was cautious but she was desperate enough to hope.

It was an extraordinary hour.

They took in the views of the hills from the wide esplanade leading up to the castle. They queued for cartons of juice from a van. They had to wait because a man in front of them had ordered an elaborate coffee but Jake didn't go crazy. He didn't get frustrated with the lady serving or throw all the food out of the baskets at the front of the van.

They walked together. Jake didn't run or shout. He didn't walk ahead of the group or pester his siblings. He didn't demand Simon's place on his dad's shoulders. He was calm, even cheerful sometimes. He kept trying to get Simon to pull his green hoodie up like him and pull it tight around his face. Eventually Simon did and they laughed together because they both looked bonkers. Usually any concession to a demand by Jake just prompted him to make more and more and more demands but he didn't do that this time. He just touched his little brother fondly on the hood and let him alone.

It was exposed on the castle forecourt. A bitter wind picked up and the sky darkened as they approached the entrance. A little wooden bridge over a twenty foot sheer drop led to the Portcullis Gate. They were standing near one of the official guides to the castle, an older man wearing the red anorak uniform, with a walkie-talkie clipped to his shoulder. Pete asked him who the statues were on either side of the Portcullis Gate. The Guide explained that they were William Wallace and someone else. Audrey wasn't listening. She was watching Jake. He was listening to the man, reacting appropriately, nodding to show he understood. It was remarkable. Apparently he could behave when he wanted to. She was delighted and furious in equal parts.

Pete snapped pictures on his phone and the Guide offered to take a family photo. They gathered dutifully and the Guide took it and gave the phone back to Pete. He showed it to Audrey. They all looked surprised, except Jake. He was in front of the rest of them, smiling straight to the camera.

Pushing their luck, Pete asked what the Latin inscription over the Portcullis Gate meant. '*Nemo me impune lacessit*', said the Guide, 'means "Cross me and Suffer".' He giggled, a high pitched and contagious laugh, 'Oh! It's not very friendly, is it?' He laughed again.

Simon caught Jake's eye and they laughed together. Audrey couldn't remember that happening, not since Simon was a baby. He knew better than to catch Jake's eye now.

Pete was happy and excited. 'Okay gang, let's go and see this castle!'

Audrey watched him lead the boys up a steep cobbled lane. Hannah hung back with her mother. She was unsure of New Jake, less willing to trust. She chewed her cuff, keeping her watchful eyes on Jake.

Audrey took Hannah's free hand, 'Okay, honey?'

Hannah smiled up at her mum but her eyes were scared.

'What is it, sweetie?'

'What's—' She glanced at Jake and stopped. Hannah didn't talk much. The school had highlighted her 'virtual selective muteness' as a cause for concern. Audrey filled in for her, a habit the school had warned her against. 'What is happening with Jake?'

'Hmmm.'

'I think he's trying to be good.'

Hannah gave her mother a sceptical look. Audrey nodded, 'I know but look how happy Daddy is. We'll see. Let's try to have fun while we can, okay?'

Hannah nodded, keeping her reservations to herself. She had been through so much, suffered because of Jake's behaviour. She was so brave about it. Audrey said, 'You're lovely, Hannah, d'you know that?'

Delighted, Hannah blushed at her shoes and squeezed her mum's hand.

Before Jake got really bad a family counsellor told Audrey and Pete that they simply weren't giving Jake enough positive reinforcement for good behaviour. She was wrong; they did it all the time. They complimented him for anything that wasn't spiteful or vile. He never responded to compliments the way Hannah and Simon did. He didn't really seem to care what they thought.

Wind buffeted them in the steep-walled lane. They stepped out of the blustery current, into an exposed yard and a battlement wall where a cannon overlooked the city. It fired at one o'clock every day. Simon and Jake ran over to it.

Magnificent views looked out over the north of the city across to a glittering strip of sea.

A different Guide in the familiar red anorak was giving the history of the western defences to a Chinese tour group. Pete and Audrey and the three kids loitered nearby, listening in.

The castle was being besieged by Jacobites, announced the Guide. Some of the soldiers inside were sympathetic to the rebel cause and conspired to let in the besieging army. But they were caught. They were hung from these very walls by their own coats, left to rot there as a warning to others.

The tour group took turns looking over the wall, cooing, gasping, giggling with fright. Simon and Jake and Pete looked over the edge. Simon screamed. Jake laughed at him and Simon took it in good part. Audrey looked over and felt her stomach jolt at the sixty foot vertiginous drop to jagged black cliffs below.

Hannah stayed well back, giggled into her cuff and shook her head when Audrey pretended she would make her look.

When they were safely twenty feet away Simon did a little leap sideways towards the wall, pretending he was jumping over, showing off to Jake. Jake threw his head back and laughed. Simon was delighted at his brother's approval. He loved Jake so much but it had never been safe to show it before.

They walked on, Simon pretending to jump over every wall they came to. He wore the joke out, he was only little, but Jake was kind about it and grinned when prompted.

They stopped for a cake and the boys sat together. Jake pretended his ginger cake was jumping off the battlements. Simon was thrilled that Jake was copying him. He was so happy he actually glowed. With their hoodies over their heads, one blue, one green, they looked like mismatched twins. Only Hannah held back.

When they had finished their cakes, Jake asked to see some dungeons. They walked up to an exhibition about prisoners of war. Napoleonic prisoners had been held in these very vaults, the sign said. They were held here for years. Hammocks were strung up high on the walls and plaster models of prison loaves were nailed to wooden plates. The kids wandered around, touching things and looking, and Pete and Audrey finally got a minute to speak.

'What is he doing?' Audrey whispered.

'I don't know,' beamed Pete.

They watched the kids clamber onto a high bench.

Simon and Jake pretended to eat the plaster loaf. It was chipped and worn but they were miming eating it as if it was delicious. Hannah sat apart from them, still watchful, but softening.

'Maybe he *has* just grown out of it?' said Pete.

The boys were getting down and Jake put his arms around little Simon's chest and swung him easily to the floor. He tried to help Hannah too but she yanked her arm away and wouldn't let him touch her.

Audrey hummed noncommittally. Something felt wrong. Growing out of behavioural problems was gradual, she knew that. It would be fitful, would come and go, if it happened. She should tell Pete about the ashtray by the bed this morning but it would spoil his day. She'd tell him later.

Crown Square was the highest point in the castle, a small courtyard with buildings on each side. It was busy, the clock was creeping towards lunchtime. Tourists thronged in groups, talking loudly in many languages, queuing impatiently for the tea room and the toilets.

They had promised the kids a baked potato for lunch, their favourite, but they had just had a cake so they needed to wait for an hour or so. The least busy door led to the National War Memorial.

Pete led them up the circular steps to the open entrance.

It was a beautiful building. It had been a church, a munitions store and a barracks, but its insides had been scooped out and it was refurbished as a secular chapel. Across from the entrance was an apse with a steel shrine containing an honour roll of all those who had died in conflicts since 1914. High windows of fine stained glass gave the place a sombre, whispery atmosphere. The kids liked it because there was lots to see. They all walked down to the left, to the western transept and found the memorial to noncombatants. The kids were guessing at Latin translations to the regimental insignia. They were all calm and whispering appropriately. It was how Audrey had always hoped it could be.

She nodded to the Latin motto the kids were struggling with.

'What does it really say?' She whispered to Pete, who had a little Latin.

'Hmmm. "If... you like... pina colada...".' He smothered a smile.

'Interesting.' Audrey cupped her chin, playing the part of the interviewer, 'And this second line here, what does that say?'

'Ah, something about enjoyment and rain. Just let me conjugate the verb "to capture".'

They giggled, muffling their laughter, leaning into one another, snorting. Their foreheads touched, just briefly, but it felt like a kiss. They hadn't laughed together for such a long time. Audrey and Pete looked at each other, here in this unexpected pocket of calm. He mouthed, 'You're gorgeous, Audie' and she smiled and slapped his arm playfully. She looked up for the cause of all their worries.

Jake was gone.

Simon and Hannah were together, she chewing her cuff, he with his green hoodie pulled up and tight around his face, tracing names carved into marble with his finger. The War Memorial was crammed with people.

'Jake!' Audrey's voice reverberated around the silent stone room. Every face turned to look at her, none of them Jake.

Pete grabbed Hannah and Simon by the shoulders and ploughed his way through the crowd to the door. Audrey followed in his wake.

From the top of the stairs they could see the entire courtyard, see the alleys and doors. Even at a gallop he couldn't have gone far.

'STAY HERE!' Audrey shouted at Pete and the kids.

She ran diagonally across the courtyard, past David's Tower and up to a wide battlement with a low wall.

No Jake.

A pack of French schoolchildren milled around her chatting, checking phones, waiting for someone. She ran over the wall and scanned back towards the Portcullis Gate.

No Jake.

Getting her bearings, she realised that there were lots of places to hide over at the other side of the castle. Loos and cafes and doorways. She bolted downhill, running over the lawn at the back of the War Memorial, scanning the thinning crowds for Jake's blue hooded head. Nothing.

Down through a narrow lane, she elbowed her way through a tight group of Korean women. She could hear them calling indignant reproaches after her as she ran, back to the cafe where they had eaten their cakes. She kept thinking *I am going to find him. I am going to find him.* She ran the phrases over and over in her head like a mantra, as if she could will it true.

Down by the cannon where the Jacobite soldiers were hung. No sign.

In the cafe, no sign.

She sprinted down into another courtyard. No sign.

She checked all the toilets she passed, holding open the doors of the gents' and shouting 'Jake?' but nothing.

Then she saw a Guide with his walkie-talkie crackling on his shoulder. She ran over to him.

'Help me!' She was out of breath, sounded rude. 'Sorry, I've lost my son.'

He nodded calmly, as if this happened all the time, and held his walkie-talkie up to his mouth. 'What's he wearing?'

'Blue hoodie top. Cotton, pale blue. Hood up, pulled tight around his face. He's eleven. He's lost.'

The Guide put out a call to all of his colleagues, giving them her description of Jake and the last place he was seen.

Audrey caught her breath and looked around. Walking towards her, trotting down through the narrow lane, was Pete. He was alone.

'THE KIDS?!'

'I saw Jake! On the corner! I left the kids with a Guide and ran but he disappeared. He's still here!'

'Was he alone?'

'I don't know. I caught a glimpse of his hood and turned to tell the Guide to watch the kids. I ran to the corner where he was but he was gone.'

The Guide who had put out the call for Jake reassured her that no one could leave the castle without passing two gates. If any child came that way they would stop them. They had CCTV everywhere as well. It would be all right.

He sounded so confident that Audrey covered her face and cried with relief. Peter held her shoulders. 'Come on. We'll find him.'

Audrey was out of breath. She put her head between her knees and caught up with herself. A lady from the cafe brought her a glass of water. She thanked her and drank it. Her throat was terribly dry.

Finally she said, 'Let's go back. He might appear again.' She wanted to see Hannah and Simon. She wanted to hold them.

Pete kept his arm around her shoulders as they walked back up the steep path. They were in the narrow, crowded alleyway when they heard the scream. Bare and animal, it was a cry of visceral panic. They ran back down.

The crowd in front of the cannon were arranged around a blonde woman. She was standing back from the wall, hands wide at her sides, her mouth open in shock. The Guide reached her and the woman screamed again, quieter this time, and pointed a shaking finger to the wall. The Guide went over and looked down. He staggered back. He stood still for a moment.

Moving very slowly, he lifted his hand across his chest and reached up to his walkie-talkie. He muttered something and then his head dropped to his chest.

Audrey broke away from Pete and ran to the edge, shoving through the startled crowd to look.

Jake. Broken on the cliffs below. She couldn't scream. She couldn't breathe. She couldn't move. Finished. He was finished.

Pete was there. He looked and saw it too. Far down on a cliff ledge lay a tiny body. It was face down, the blue hood turning red, redness creeping through the blue was the only movement. Legs bent in wrong ways. Inaccessible from above and below.

Audrey staggered backwards and curled over her knees. She vomited acid chunks of cake.

The Guide had moved everyone back from the wall when a sudden flurry of movement heralded the arrival of more red anoraks and other men in black fleeces. The air crackled with radio messages, to and fro, fast voices.

Pete was sitting on the ground, head dropped, hands resting on his knees. He looked drunk.

'I'll get Han and Si...' Audrey backed away on rubber legs.

She turned and walked blind. *No,* she thought now. *No. No. Nonononononono. No.*

The tourists in Crown Square were oblivious to the tragedy unfolding below them. They moved in audio guide trances, slow, lazy, diffident. Audrey barged straight through them. She turned the corner to the National War Memorial and climbed the steps. When she saw the Guide's face she knew he had heard. He was shocked. He stood to attention when he saw her.

He touched her shoulder, tilted his head, searched her face for eye contact. Audrey shook her head at the ground. 'Can't,' she hissed. 'I can't.'

He understood. She couldn't feel this now. He stood straight, shoulders back and spoke very clearly. 'What can I do for you?'

'My other children. Boy and girl. Here. Who are they with?'

He searched her face again. 'With me. Their brother came and got them.'

He had misunderstood.

She took a breath and said it again: 'My daughter and son were left with a Guide while we looked for the boy in the blue hoodie.'

He nodded. 'They were left with me, ma'am. The wee laddie in the blue top with the hood all tied up tight, that wee fella's came up and said they were to go with him. Ten minutes ago.'

She couldn't process that but the man was certain. 'He was just himself, I made sure of that. The call just came that you couldn't find him and a minute later his

Dad spotted him and ran after him. Then he came back and said his Daddy said to bring the wee ones. They all went down that way.' He pointed to David's Tower, 'I'm a father myself. I thought you'd be over the moon. He was bringing them to you.'

Audrey ran as fast as she could down to Pete, to the crowd, to the shocked guides and the men in black who were lowering a thick black rope over the wall.

A stretcher and paramedic in a harness were preparing to go over. An ambulance was rumbling up the hill towards them.

'He came back,' she said quietly. Pete looked up from the ground. 'After you ran. He came back and said you'd sent him for Hannah and Simon. They left with him...'

The police sealed the castle. No one was allowed to leave. The ambulance parked on the forecourt of the cafe, the doors propped open.

At first the other tourists were sympathetic. They thought it was a terrorist attack. They became angry when they realised it was about careless parenting and lost children. Tour organisers approached the cops and made their cases angrily: they had a flight to catch, a restaurant booking, tickets for other attractions. But no one was allowed to leave.

The guides were kind. Chairs from the cafe appeared for Pete and Audrey. There was still no sign of Simon and Hannah. They asked them what sort of kids they were? Sensible? Nervous? Naughty? A complete search of the castle grounds was organised. The police were led by the guides to all the sneaky corners and hidden places.

Audrey and Pete sat side by side on chairs, upright, watching the black rope snaking over the wall. They couldn't tell the police or the guides what might have happened. What could have happened. Who they were dealing with.

Men formed a tight circle around the rope and a pulley was fitted. They watched the rope tug and tighten. Jake was coming up.

Audrey stood up, legs so stiff with terror that she nearly fell over. Pete had to catch her.

They stood, watching the men crank the pulley, lifting the basket stretcher up to the battlement walls. The stretcher was for an adult. The slack little body barely half filled it. He was strapped in tight with neon yellow belts, turning pink from all the blood. He had a tiny neck brace on, his face covered in bloody cotton wool with a hole in the middle for the oxygen mask. His chest wasn't moving.

Audrey could tell from thirty feet away.

So could Pete.

The blue hoodie was too long.

Her knees buckled. It wasn't Jake in the stretcher. It was Simon with Jake's top on. Pete didn't catch her this time. She slipped slowly down to the ground as the red stretcher was placed into the ambulance. A shocked quiet fell over the crowd, as if they were all praying in their many languages, to their many gods.

Suddenly the police walkie-talkies crackled to life in a chorus: '*A girl matching Hannah's description has been found in David's Tower. She's been strangled with her own coat. Don't tell the parents yet*'.

Too late. They could see Audrey and Pete had already heard.

Pete sank down next to Audrey on the ground. Crowds shrank away from the couple as if their sorrows were a stain, as if they were contagious.

In the silence Audrey could hear the wind, the rumble of the ambulance engine, Pete breathing, short despairing puffs.

A voice behind her, familiar, loud, pleased.

'I'm finished, Mummy.'

Mousa Broch

The Return
Ann Cleeves

It might seem strange after all that has happened, but Shetland is my escape and my place of sanctuary. It's still where I run to at times of stress. People say that a city's the place to hide, but I feel anonymous in the islands, lost among the tourists, the birdwatchers, the history nuts. I go in the autumn when the gales send spindrift onto the cliffs and the rain blows across the islands like breaking waves on a shore. With my hat pulled low over my forehead who would know me?

Or I'll travel up on the ferry in mid-winter when it's packed with folk returning for the fire festival of Up Helly Aa. Then the ship's bar is full of half-remembered faces, and if people think they recognise me, they imagine that I'm a distant relative or someone they might have been to school with, not the person splashed all over the front page of the newspapers one summer ten years before.

At Up Helly Aa itself, I mingle with the crowds on the busy pavements. Once the street lights are switched off everyone is hidden. I'm one middle-aged woman among many watching the guizers carrying the flaming torches before the magnificent Viking galley is set alight.

It's as if I'm a ghost. I *am* dead after all. At least that is what everyone thinks.

Shetland attracts the wealthy middle-aged. They come for the history or the knitting, and for the sense of safety that such a remote community gives. For the puffins and the ponies, the ganzies and the bonnets. Among these visitors, I can hide in plain sight. Women of a certain age are often overlooked. I wasn't brought here by puffins though. I despise sentimentality in all its forms. I was brought here by passion; by a certain academic rigour that demanded that I see for myself the places about which I was reading. I was first brought here by a story.

I came across Elizabeth Blunt's work when I was doing post-doctoral research at Durham. My specialism was Norse mythology. Modern poetry meant little to me and although I knew Blunt's name, I'd never read her. My niece gave me a copy of her first anthology one Christmas. Harriet is my older brother's child and was the closest thing I had to a daughter. She's bright, clear-eyed and clear-headed, but more socially gifted than I am. Fear makes *me* awkward and aggressive. In Durham I had the reputation of intimidating undergraduates, of being something of a bully. In fact, the younger students, with their confidence and energy, terrified me. They seemed to glow with health and privilege. Even then, when I was in my thirties, I had the mousiness, the grey dowdiness of middle-age.

Harriet glows too. She was an undergraduate when she gave me the gift of Blunt's book. It was a birthday present. I read it almost immediately out of politeness, because I knew Harriet would be waiting for a response. It was the voice of the poet that first pulled me in. Blunt seduced me as a lover would; I felt that she understood me. She sensed my insecurities and small vanities. From the very first stanza there was the thrill of recognition. I phoned Harriet. 'I loved it!'

'Ah,' Harriet said. 'I knew that you would. Blunt's a visiting prof at my uni and I heard her lecture. You two have a lot in common. She even looks a bit like you.' A couple of days later a slim parcel from Harriet was pushed through my letterbox. Another book by Blunt. Not poetry this time but a collection of short fiction. It was called *Below the Tideline* and one of the stories was set in Shetland.

Intellectually, I could see why the stories were less popular than the poetry. They were rougher, less precise, occasionally misshapen. Perhaps because of that, I loved them even more. There was the same honesty, but they had a mocking humour too. Her characters were often unattractive: ugly, petty, self-deceiving. Occasionally, however, the writing achieved a lyrical beauty that matched the verse. That was the case in the story set in Shetland. It was called 'The Return' and told of a boat trip to the small island of Mousa. It was that tale, set in mid-summer, which took me to the islands. It described a woman travelling to Mousa with the ashes of her violent partner. The man had been a soldier, recently returned from Afghanistan. A Shetlander whose moment of triumph had been his role as Guizer Jahl, the leader of the Up Helly Aa procession. The story had the ferocity and simplicity of a Norse saga.

My first trip took place in mid-summer. When else could it be? It was Harriet's idea: 'Why don't we go to Shetland, see where that story that you love so much is set?' She'd finished her finals and was killing time before going travelling. We took the train to Aberdeen and hardly spoke at all on the journey, both absorbed in our books. I was re-reading Blunt. At one point Harriet looked up. 'Don't you think you might be becoming a little obsessed, Aunt Eleanor?' Then she smiled to show that it was a joke; she was pleased that I was so passionate about her favourite writer.

On the ferry, we paid a little extra to have dinner in the lounge. We were there early and were given a table by the window. The evening sunlight was reflected from the water as we slid out of Aberdeen, and the gulls seemed startlingly white. After the meal, I noticed a woman eating alone. Her short hair was already grey, but her face seemed unlined, almost youthful. She was wearing the obligatory jeans and a green sweater, in a soft wool that was probably cashmere, and a necklace of green glass beads. I, who care nothing about clothes, took in all these details. She didn't look up from her newspaper as I walked past, but she made a deep and lasting impression. Harriet was walking ahead of me and seemed not to notice the woman or my interest in her.

We woke early and were on deck as the ship approached the islands. I couldn't help looking out for the woman I'd seen the night before. When I was a student I made a few clumsy approaches to other women, usually after I'd drunk too much. The few relationships that developed always ended in awkwardness and embarrassment. Later I resigned myself to a single life. Sex, I decided, was much overrated. I valued my independence and my work much more. On the deck that morning, already in full sunlight, I decided it was the romantic nature of the journey that had coloured my reaction to the stranger. In any event, I didn't see her before we left the ship to pick up our hire car and make the drive south.

I'd booked a cottage close to the shore below Sandwick, because it was the closest accommodation I could find to the island of Mousa. Self-catering suits me better than a hotel. I hate the ritual of breakfast in the presence of other people, the interruptions by housekeeping staff when I'm working in my room. It was the last house at the end of a low terrace – tiny, with two small bedrooms, a shower room between, and a larger kitchen. But the view was magnificent. There was a long garden at the front with a bench close to the house. I made coffee and we took it outside. From there, we had our first view of Mousa with its Iron Age broch.

The broch is towards the south end of the island, close to the water. It has double walls with stone steps in between. After all these centuries, it's still possible to climb the steps and look out towards the Shetland mainland. This was where the woman in Blunt's story scattered her lover's ashes. The building is squat and solid, not large or overpowering. It's not a masculine, showing-off kind of structure. Staring at it, squinting in the bright morning sunlight, the building took on a mythical significance, a connection in physical form of all that was important to me. I've never resorted to belief in the supernatural, but that day I experienced an almost religious sense of being human within the landscape. I still remember the taste of the coffee, the smell of salt and seaweed, the sun on my face.

I'd booked a trip to the island, a crossing that replicated the details in the story. The boat would leave for Mousa at eleven thirty in the evening and return in the early hours of the morning. That time was chosen because storm petrels, birds that apparently spend the daylight hours at sea, come in to the island to feed their young at night. There are few other places where they can be seen. We gathered at the jetty a short walk from our cottage. There were people with binoculars and cameras, a family with a reluctant teenager. Despite the late hour, it was still light, that strange half-dusk that Shetlanders call the *simmer dim*. Most of us had boarded the boat when a car rattled down the road to the jetty. It pulled to a halt and a woman jumped out. I recognised the passenger from the ferry the night before and suddenly it seemed that all the events of the day had been leading up to this moment. In her arms, she carried a big bag, a hand-knitted jersey and a coat. She pulled the garments on as soon as she got on board, giving the impression that she was always in a rush and accustomed to doing more than one thing at once.

The boatman helped her aboard. Harriet nudged me and nodded towards the woman.

'Look! It's her!'

'Who?' Of course I was interested, and again, when the answer came, I wasn't as surprised as I should have been.

'It's Elizabeth Blunt. Don't you recognise her from the photo on her book?'

But the edition Harriet had given me had no author photograph, and my attraction to the woman, at least on first seeing her, was nothing to do with her work.

The boatman's assistant cast off the rope and jumped aboard. The engine started and we moved slowly away from the jetty. We were sitting on a slatted wooden bench that ran around the bow, and Blunt squeezed in beside Harriet. I was tense, excited, but too afraid of making a fool of myself to speak. Harriet, though, spoke with the natural ease and curiosity of a small child.

'You *are* Elizabeth Blunt, aren't you? I came to one of your lectures in Bristol.'

The woman seemed amused, almost pleased to be

recognised. Perhaps literary writers aren't celebrities in the popular sense, so this was a novelty for her.

Harriet went on: 'This is my aunt, Eleanor Rushmore. She's probably your greatest fan.'

Blunt leaned forward so she could look past the girl at me. 'Not E J Rushmore? I've read your papers. Fascinating.' And she began to ask questions about my theories and the roots of my ideas. I forgot my nervousness and began to answer her as if she were simply another academic. It helped that Harriet was still sitting between us. If there'd been any physical contact between Blunt and me I'd have been too distracted.

When we arrived at Mousa, the light was opaque, milky. It took my eyes a while to adjust to it. Blunt seemed to know her way. She took my arm in hers, and Harriet followed. The path was too narrow to allow three people to walk together and my niece lingered behind us, allowing a sense of intimacy between we older women. The other passengers had walked ahead, desperate to catch a glimpse of the elusive storm petrel. I asked Blunt how she knew Shetland so well.

'Oh,' she said. 'It's my spiritual home.' Which even then didn't seem very much of an answer.

We came to a dry-stone wall that had collapsed over the years and had gaps to allow easy access to the other side. 'Stop.' Blunt's voice was soft. 'Listen.' I heard other-worldly murmurs and calls from inside the wall. The young petrels calling to the adults, demanding food.

By the time we reached the broch, the adult birds were there, bat-like, swooping towards the walls of the tower. Shadowy. They too looked like ghosts. Blunt led me up the steps between the twin skins of the broch and stood with me at the top, pointing out the flashing beams of the lighthouses, naming them, as if she were reciting one of her poems. We stood there until the boatman called us back for the ride home. By then the sun was already sliding up from the horizon and the sky in the east was pink and grey.

Over the next couple of days, Elizabeth Blunt became part of our lives. As soon as we'd arrived at the jetty at Sandwick she'd driven away, yelling out of the car window that she was in a rush to get back and she'd be in touch. I never expected to see her again; after all, we hadn't exchanged phone numbers and she had no idea where we were staying. Yet the following evening, as I was preparing supper, the door opened and she walked in. No knock. Just the open door letting in a beam of sunshine, and then Blunt, blocking the light once more.

'What a terrific smell! Is there enough for me?'

We sat, crushed around the small table, and ate pasta and drank syrupy red wine. I can't remember what we talked about that night. Not Blunt. Any personal questions were ignored or laughed off. This time Harriet was more engaged in the conversation. I was proud of the way she argued her point of view. She seemed suddenly a grown-up, my equal and not a child. Again, Blunt had to rush away, but this time she made an arrangement to see us the next day.

'I'll call for you at ten and we'll go to Eshaness. You need to see the cliffs.'

She was out of the door before we could answer and there was an assumption that whatever we had planned would be dropped in favour of the trip. She was right, of course. Harriet and I were so excited to be part of the great woman's world that we were only too grateful for the invitation. Harriet, I saw, was as infatuated as I was with our new friend.

The next day, Blunt was late. So late that we'd given up hope of her arriving. When she did come, it was in a taxi. 'You don't mind if we take your car? I'll drive.' No explanation.

She drove north up the Shetland mainland, rather fast, flinging out descriptions of the places we passed. Again, there was nothing personal in the conversation; she could have been a tour guide. She parked at the lighthouse and we got out to walk. She lit a cigarette, suddenly nervous, it seemed. It was still sunny but there was a gusty wind that blew our hair and our clothes. We walked to the edge of the cliff to watch the waves boiling below. I felt a strange giddiness, a mixture of exhilaration and fear.

'I need your help.' It was the last thing I'd been expecting.

'Of course,' I said, much too quickly. Usually I was cautious when people came asking for favours but I would have given this woman anything.

'I need you to go back to Mousa tonight.'

'With you?' I imagined the two of us back in the strange half-light of the summer dusk walking together towards the broch.

'No,' she said slowly. 'That would never work. I need to be here on the mainland. That's why it has to be you.' She turned to me and took both my hands. 'Please don't ask any questions. You'll understand later, I promise'. I saw then that Harriet had been right and there was a physical similarity between us. In an old sweater and wearing no make-up, she could have been my mirror image. 'I've booked a place on the ferry in your name,' she said. 'It's all paid for.'

Of course, I should have asked for an explanation, but that day I saw the strange request almost as a test of my loyalty. And so I went. I was flattered that she'd chosen me to help her. I savoured the idea that she would be in my debt, picturing a relationship that would spread into the future. Intimate dinners and weekends away. Discussions about literature. Perhaps in the end we might become best friends, even lovers. I asked Harriet if she would like to come with me but she shook her head, too easily bored, I imagined, as young people often are, to want to visit the same place twice.

There were fewer passengers that night, perhaps because of the strong breeze and the choppy water. The boatman recognised me and nodded me aboard. I wasn't sure what I was expecting in the broch. Blunt to be there, waiting for me after taking an earlier boat, with a picnic hamper and a bottle of champagne? She seemed the type for a dramatic gesture and I was crazy, my head full of romantic notions. In the end the trip was an anti-climax. I had nothing to do except retrace my steps from the earlier night. The petrels arrived and the other tourists were suitably impressed. I hadn't thought to pack a flask or wear enough clothing, and when the boatman took us back to the mainland I was freezing. The cottage was in darkness as I'd expected. Why would Harriet wait up just to see that I was safely back? It took me a long time to get to sleep. I felt oddly dissatisfied after the anticipation I'd experienced in the morning. Resentful.

I woke late and the place was quiet. I wandered into the kitchen to make coffee. The weather had changed and a misty rain was blowing in from the east. Mousa was entirely hidden from view. I poured coffee for Harriet and knocked at the door of her bedroom. There was no reply and I pushed it open. Her bed was empty, and so was the room. The rucksack in which she'd carried her belongings onto the ferry from Aberdeen was nowhere to be seen. I phoned her mobile but the call went straight to voicemail. The morning already had a weird, dreamlike quality. Now I felt stranded and helpless. I couldn't think what to do except wait in the hope that Harriet would return or get in touch. It occurred to me that Blunt might have arrived while I was still asleep and whisked my niece away on some extravagant adventure, but I couldn't believe that Harriet wouldn't have left a note of explanation. Blunt herself had still not given me a contact number, or any idea where she was staying in Shetland.

I didn't want to worry Harriet's parents – she prided herself on being an independent young woman and would have hated that – but as time crept on the desire for some form of action grew. I felt trapped in the cramped cottage while the fog grew thicker outside. I told myself that Harriet was an adult, that when evening came there'd be the sound of Elizabeth Blunt's car outside and they'd both tumble in, all apologies, laughter and explanations. So I didn't act and when evening came, still there was no news. I longed for someone to talk to, someone who might give sensible advice or reassurance, but I was alone in a strange place, and even in Durham I had few friends. I considered contacting the police but was worried about making a fool of myself. In the end, long after midnight, I went to bed and lay there, wide awake, listening for any sound that might mark Harriet's return.

In the morning, I called Harriet's phone yet again. Still no answer. I dressed, went out to the car, and drove into Lerwick. I couldn't spend another day waiting. Now my anxiety was spliced with anger. How could she run off, leaving me feeling so shit? I parked at the harbour and went into a little café in one of the lanes that led up towards the main street of the town. I'd hardly eaten the day before and suddenly felt hungry. I bought coffee and croissants. There were copies of the local newspaper in a rack by the door. A familiar face stared out at me. My face. I recognised the photo, which had been used on my university ID. I pulled out a paper and took it to a table outside on the pavement, turning my back to the other customers.

Woman wanted for questioning in Davy Mather disappearance.

Davy Mather, it seemed, was a local man, something of a celebrity. He'd been Guizer Jahl at the Up Helly Aa parade a few years before and was a former soldier, decorated after action in Afghanistan. There was a photograph of him, tall, strong and handsome in a Viking kind of way. Immediately I remembered Blunt's story. Had she known this man? What was her connection to him? Mather's wife was mentioned in the newspaper piece. She was called Mary and it seemed she was distraught. 'I know he had his problems – he wasn't the same man when he came back from the army – but I loved him. He just left home four nights ago, and he never came back.' Mather had been seen arguing with a woman who matched my description near the cliffs at Eshaness. A blood-stained knife, wrapped in a scarf, had been found at the base of the broch on Mousa. There was a photo of the scarf. It was blue and green and I knew it at once. Harriet had persuaded me to buy it in Aberdeen while we were killing time waiting for the ferry. I'd looked for it before my first trip to Mousa but hadn't been able to find it.

Lack of sleep dulled my brain for a while. There was the sense of unreality, of living in a nightmare, that had been with me since I discovered that Harriet was missing. And, of course, I couldn't bear to accept that I'd been

taken for a fool. Because although I couldn't work out
the details at that point, it seemed clear even to my
befuddled brain that Blunt and Harriet had set me up.
I've always been a logical woman and, horrifying though
the idea was, I could see no other explanation.

Then the rigour of my academic training took over. I
faced the problem just as I would have done a dense
and apparently unintelligible piece of translation. The
deception had been so well planned and executed that
there was no way I could argue my innocence to the
police. Blunt was a famous woman and she would be
believed. Immediately, I had to move away from the café
where I'd easily be recognised. Then I had to stay away
from the car. My name would be on the hire agreement.
I couldn't go back to the cottage. I was lucky that the
police hadn't turned up there the night before and that
I had plenty of money in my bag. I had to disappear.

I left the café, walking normally, one of those grey,
middle-aged women who blend into the background. In
the Save the Children shop I bought a complete change
of clothes, including a jacket and hat. Harriet would
have told the police what I was wearing and, besides, I
had started to hatch a plan. It wasn't enough to disappear. If Davy Mather had been murdered by Blunt, the
police wouldn't stop looking for his killer. I had to die.

I bought sandwiches and water in the Co-op, then
thought again and went back for a notebook. I had a
pen in my bag. There was a bus about to leave for
Sandwick and I got onto that. The driver took my cash
without looking at my face. I got out at the top of the
bank so I could look down on the cottage. There was a
police car parked outside. My mind was clear now. Icy.
It took me a long time to compose the suicide note. The
wording had to be right; even to save myself I wasn't

prepared to confess to a murder I hadn't committed.

You might be wondering why I decided on this step so swiftly. Because I'm as clear-eyed as Harriet, and I knew that she would do all she could to incriminate me. She'd given me Blunt's book to hook me in. Her relationship with her visiting professor was intense; I'd sensed my niece's infatuation with her over dinner in the cottage. She and Blunt were bright women and they would have left nothing to chance. There must be some reason why we'd gone to Eshaness in *my* car. Besides, what evidence did I have to suggest the famous poet's involvement in the disappearance of Mather? A short story that predicted the death of a lover? The police would have laughed at me. This was the only way to escape suspicion and to give myself the chance of a future.

The fog had cleared and Mousa was visible now from where I sat. I wrote my note:

I can't live with what has happened. Don't bother looking for me.

Then I signed my name. I stayed at my post, hidden behind a dry-stone wall very similar to the one on Mousa, until the light faded. The police car drove away, but I didn't go to the cottage. There might have been an officer left inside. I walked down to the pebble beach, close to the jetty where the Mousa ferry was moored. I took off all my clothes and left them in a tidy pile above the tideline. The note went into the clear plastic bag that had held my sandwiches and was weighed down by a rock. I dressed in my purchases from the charity shop. Eleanor Rushmore was dead.

It was an intellectual challenge to develop a new identity for myself once I got back to the British mainland, but I rather enjoyed it. I won't go into details, they aren't important. Now I'm a freelance proof reader with the name of Amy Sharp. I chose the surname with Blunt in mind and still feel a little superior whenever I sign my name. It was less of a wrench than I expected to leave Norse mythology behind. I'm single – I've never been able to trust anyone since that trip to Shetland – but not lonely.

Harriet and Blunt are still a couple, rather famous, often appearing on the arts pages of national newspapers. I suspect that Harriet worships the older woman as she did when she was a student and that her lover basks in the adoration. Like everyone else, Harriet's parents believe that I'm dead. While the police stopped short of naming me publicly as Mather's murderer, they didn't look for anyone else in connection with his death. Blunt admits to having had flings with men when she was younger, but has never mentioned an unpredictable former soldier called Davy Mather, whose body was discovered close to the Eshaness cliffs, and who was killed with a knife found on the island of Mousa.

Now it's ten years on. I'm making my first summer visit to the islands since the trip with Harriet all that time ago. Nobody takes any notice when I board the NorthLink ferry. I arrive in the self-catering apartment that has become my favourite place to stay and phone the Mousa ferryman to book a trip to the island. I say that I'm an archaeologist and would like a little extra time on the island. Could he take me out early, and I'll return with the other passengers? He agrees. I expect Blunt and Harriet to have flown in the same day. This isn't just a guess on my part. They come to Shetland every year at mid-summer. They celebrate their relationship in this way and make a very public fuss about it.

On Mousa I climb to the top of the broch and wait, lost in thought, until I hear the arrival of the ferry. It's a clear, still night so sound carries. The other passengers are elderly, which suits me very well. Blunt and Harriet are the only people to climb the steps between the double skin of the tower. There's the first beautiful moment when they see me. Whatever else happens I'll cherish that: their horror and astonishment. Harriet recovers first.

'So you *are* still alive. I always wondered.'

Blunt backs towards the edge of the broch. That suits me too.

'Tell me exactly what happened,' I say. 'You owe me that.'

Blunt speaks. She's always been a performer. 'I met Davy at Up Helly Aa. I'd been invited to one of the post-festival parties. He was so strong, so gorgeous. But very soon he got violent and possessive. When I ended the affair, he threatened to go to the press, to the university, to his wife. I told him I didn't care. Then he threatened to kill me. I knew he meant it, and I knew he was capable of it.'

'So you hatched a plan to get rid of him first.' I say.

'That was Harriet.' Blunt throws my niece a fond look. 'She saw how physically close you and I are. I was careful about my relationship with Davy, but if any islanders had seen me with him, they could easily be persuaded that *you* were his lover.'

'You dropped the knife on that trip to the island when we met,' I say, 'but you wanted me to go back so the boatman would remember me. You drove my car to Eshaness, so it would be seen close to where the body would be found.'

Blunt gives a little smile. I walk towards her and put

my hands on her shoulders. How easy it would be to give a sharp push to send her flying over the edge. I'll claim it was an accident and of course Harriet will have to agree. She'll have no choice. I'm Amy Sharp and I have no relationship with either woman. Eleanor Rushmore is dead.

Blunt is no longer smiling. I hesitate for a moment, but I turn and walk away. My phone has recorded the conversation and when I get back to Shetland mainland it will go straight into an envelope addressed to Inspector Jimmy Perez. When I reach the boat, the sun is already climbing once more above the horizon.

Locations

BLOODY
SCOTLAND

Mousa Broch

Maeshowe

The Hermit's Castle

Kinnaird Head
Lighthouse

Stanley Mills

Forth Bridge

St Peter's   Kinneil   Edinburgh Castle
Seminary   House

Crookston Castle
Bothwell Castle

Crossraguel Abbey

Maeshowe
Orkney

Built some 5,000 years ago, Maeshowe is one of Europe's finest chambered tombs – a masterpiece of Neolithic design and construction. Incredibly, the entrance passage was built to align with the setting of the midwinter sun, when the light illuminates the tomb's interior. Norse crusaders broke into Maeshowe in the mid-1100s, 3,000 years after it had fallen from use. They left a fascinating legacy: today you can still see runic graffiti carved all over Maeshowe's walls. Maeshowe is part of the Heart of Neolithic Orkney World Heritage Site, where you can visit stone circles, villages and burial monuments – places where people lived, worshipped, and honoured their dead. Remarkable survivals from that distant age not far from Maeshowe are the Stones of Stenness, the Ring of Brodgar and Skara Brae.

Open year round, excluding 25, 26 December and 1, 2 January. Access to Maeshowe is by guided tour only, advance booking recommended. Tours depart from the Maeshowe Visitor Centre (at Stenness).

Hermit's Castle
Achmelvich

This diminutive poured-concrete fortress was created in 1950 by David Scott, an English architect. The often-repeated story is that Scott worked on the project for at least six months, but left after spending only one night inside. The stark interior is never wider or taller than 2 metres, and contains a concrete bed, hearth and shelving. Despite the name 'Hermit's Castle', the building has never housed a hermit or an army, but it can provide shelter as a bothy (although the windowpanes and door are now missing). The miniature Highland castle, tucked in among the rocks, is a 15 minute walk from Achmelvich Beach, which itself is a four mile drive down single-track roads from Lochinver, in Assynt – an area notable for its rugged landscape of mountains, lochs and coastline.

Stanley Mills
Perth

For 200 years, this spectacular mill harnessed the power of the River Tay. As demands for textiles changed and technologies developed, buildings were added, adapted, expanded, destroyed by fire, rebuilt, shut down, reopened and demolished. Machinery came and went, powered initially by water wheels, and latterly by electricity generated by water-powered turbines on the site. Built in the 1780s, the mills provided employment for many before they finally closed in 1989. Visitors to Stanley Mills can uncover the stories of these workers (mainly women and children) and experience the clamour of the factory floor through interactive displays in one of the best-preserved relics of the Industrial Revolution.

Open daily from 1 April to 30 September, 9.30am to 5.30pm
Open daily from 1 October to 31 October, 10am to 4pm

Forth Bridge
Firth of Forth

The Forth Bridge, spanning the Firth of Forth from South to North Queensferry, is an internationally recognised icon of engineering and Scotland's newest World Heritage Site. Only 20 minutes from Edinburgh's Waverley Station, the cantilevered steel bridge is owned and operated by Network Rail. Opened in 1890, this is no relic – with 200 trains crossing the Forth each day, the rail bridge still fulfils its original purpose by connecting the north and south of the country. You can admire the bridge's incredible lattice of red steel from numerous viewpoints on either side of the Forth, from the two road bridges, on a boat trip or kayak down the Forth – or by simply taking a train journey across the bridge itself.

Bothwell Castle
Uddingston

Bothwell Castle sits in a beautiful and dramatic location above a winding curve in the River Clyde. Built in the late 1200s, the castle has frequently passed back and forth between English and Scottish hands. Such hostility – in particular Edward I's great siege of 1301, which brought 6,800 soldiers and a huge siege engine to the castle – meant the structure was never completed to its original plan. Nevertheless, Bothwell is one of Scotland's most impressive medieval strongholds. The ruined castle has many fascinating features to be explored, including the imposing circular keep tower known as the donjon, a grim medieval prison and an impressive fourteenth century chapel.

Open daily 1 April to 30 September, 9.30am to 5.30pm
Open daily 1 October to 31 March, excluding Thursday and Friday, 10am to 4pm
Closed 25, 26 December and 1, 2 January

Kinneil House
Bo'ness

The 200-acre Kinneil Estate provides a fascinating snapshot of Scottish history, with traces of the Antonine Wall, a medieval church, and the workshop where James Watt created his prototype steam engine. But at the centre is the 15th century Kinneil House, once the residence of the wealthy and powerful Hamilton family. The house was being prepared for demolition in 1936, when rare 16th century wall and ceiling paintings were discovered. These were of such significance that the house was preserved. Look out for Kinneil's ghost, Lady Alice Lilbourne, said to have jumped to her death from the top floor of Kinneil House to escape her unhappy marriage.

Special open days are held at Kinneil House throughout the year. The surrounding Kinneil Estate is open daily year round. Kinneil Museum is also open all year, excluding Tuesdays, 12.30pm to 4.30pm.

Kinnaird Head Lighthouse
Fraserburgh

This extraordinary lighthouse began life as a castle in the 1500s. With its exposed position overlooking a rocky coastline and the stormy North Sea, the castle was sold to the Northern Lighthouse Board, with a lamp lit on the castle roof from 1787. Kinnaird House Lighthouse was adapted over the years, with a spiral staircase running through the centre of the original castle – a unique combination of old tower house and new lighthouse. Visitors to the lighthouse can marvel at this lifesaving piece of engineering, and the dedication and courage of the lighthouse keepers. Although a small, unmanned light now fulfils the role of beacon, the Kinnaird Head lantern remains in working order.

The Museum of Scottish Lighthouses at Kinnaird Head provides tours of the lighthouse. From the end of March until the end of October, tours take place hourly from 11am to 4pm (with the 12 noon tour dependent on demand). From November to the end of March, tours begin at 11am, 1pm, 2pm and 3pm.

Crookston Castle
Glasgow

Crookston Castle was built in the 1400s, but is set on top of older earthworks dating back to the 1100s. The only surviving medieval castle in Glasgow, Crookston is located on a hill south-west of the modern city, in the midst of the large Pollok housing estate. It was once at the heart of an entirely rural landscape, which was swallowed up by twentieth century housing built to relieve overcrowding in central Glasgow. The layout is very unusual for a Scottish castle, as it comprises a high central tower, with four square corner towers (although only the north-east tower remains fully intact). The castle was co-opted by the military in World War II – with the north-eastern tower used to watch for enemy aircraft during the Clydebank blitz.

Open daily 1 April to 30 September, 9.30am to 5.30pm
Open daily 1 October to 31 March, excluding Thursday and Friday, 10am to 4pm

Crossraguel Abbey
Maybole

The peaceful ruins of Crossraguel Abbey reflect the prestige and spiritual glory of the building's past. Founded in the early 1200s as a daughter house of Paisley Abbey (and possibly constructed on an ancient holy site), monks of the Cluniac order served here for over four centuries. Despite being a place of worship, the monastery could not avoid conflict, and was severely damaged in the Wars of Independence (1296–1356). Crossraguel survived and flourished in the following centuries, remaining in use even after the Protestant Reformation, though in a much reduced form. By 1617, however, the abbey was no longer functioning as a religious establishment. Visitors today can see echoes of the monastic way of life that thrived here, and appreciate the extent and complexity of a large medieval religious house.

Open daily from 1 April to 30 September, 9.30am to 5.30pm (excluding Sunday)

St Peter's Seminary
Cardross

The Modernist ruin of St Peter's has sat on a hilltop above the village of Cardross for more than three decades. Over that time the seminary, designed by Glasgow-based Gillespie, Kidd & Coia, has gained a cult-like status among architects, preservationists and artists. The Catholic Church only used St Peter's as a seminary from 1966 to 1979, and although briefly repurposed as a drug rehabilitation centre, the building was soon abandoned to decay and vandalism. Ever since, people have argued and puzzled over the future and importance of St Peter's. It was category A listed in 1992, and has been called both Scotland's best and worst twentieth century building. In 2016, the new owners of St Peter's, the arts organisation NVA, began the building's renewal as a cultural space with their inaugural event, Hinterland.

St Peter's is not currently open to visitors. NVA are developing plans to open the site to the public in the near future.

Edinburgh Castle

Dominating the city from the top of a plug of volcanic rock, Edinburgh Castle has witnessed many defining events in Scotland's history. Sieges were fought over the mighty stronghold. Royalty lived and died within its walls. Just the sight of the Castle Rock terrified and inspired countless generations. Today it is Scotland's leading tourist attraction and a chief element of the Old and New Towns of Edinburgh UNESCO World Heritage Site – while also remaining an active military base. The maze of buildings inside the castle walls includes St Margaret's Chapel (the oldest building in Edinburgh), and the Scottish National War Memorial. Among the national treasures on display are Scotland's crown jewels, the Stone of Destiny and the One o'Clock Gun. There are also breathtaking views across the city and beyond, a reminder of the castle's strategic importance.

Open daily 1 April to 30 September, 9.30am to 6pm
Open daily 1 October to 31 March, 9.30am to 5pm
Closed 25 and 26 December; open 1 January, 11am to 5pm

Mousa Broch
Shetland

Brochs are Iron Age roundhouses that exist only in Scotland, and Mousa is the best-preserved of them all. Thought to have been constructed around 300 BC, it stands 13m tall, a totem of Scottish prehistory. Mousa is unique among broch towers – it has the smallest diameter, but its walls are far thicker than the others. A stone stairway corkscrews between the inner and outer walls to the top, where visitors can appreciate the broch's commanding position. Mousa Broch appears twice in Norse sagas. Egil's Saga recounts how an eloping couple took refuge here after a shipwreck en route to Iceland in AD 900, while the *Orkneyinga Saga* describes the broch as 'an unhandy place to get at' for an attack. Today the main residents of the Neolithic tower are the storm petrels, which nest there during the summer months.

Open year round. Mousa is accessible by boat from Sandwick, 14 miles south of Lerwick.

Authors

Lin Anderson is the creator of the forensic scientist Rhona MacLeod series of crime thriller novels, and is co-founder of the Bloody Scotland Crime Writing Festival. Lin is a screenwriter, with a Celtic Film Festival best drama award for *River Child*. A movie based on her *Dead Close* story is going into production, and Lin is working with John Sinclair (former keyboard player for Ozzy Osbourne) on a rock musical. She divides her time between the Highlands, Edinburgh and the south of France.

Chris Brookmyre is the author of twenty crime and SF novels, including *Quite Ugly One Morning, All Fun And Games Until Somebody Loses An Eye* and *Black Widow*, which won the 2016 McIlvanney Prize for Scottish Crime Novel of the Year and was named the 2017 Theakstons Old Peculier Crime Novel of the Year. He is a regular visitor to Bothwell Castle, but they might not let him in again after they read this anthology.

Gordon Brown lives in Scotland but splits his time between the UK and Spain. In a former life Gordon delivered pizzas in Toronto, sold non alcoholic beer in the Middle East, launched a creativity training business and floated a high tech company on the London Stock Exchange. A co-founder of Bloody Scotland – Scotland's International Crime Writing Festival – Gordon is the author of five crime novels published in both the UK and the US.

Ann Cleeves is the author behind ITV's *Vera* and BBC One's *Shetland*. She has written over thirty novels, and is the creator of detectives Vera Stanhope and Jimmy Perez – characters loved both on screen and in print. She is a multi-million bestselling author and her books are sold worldwide in many languages. In 2006 Ann was awarded the Duncan Lawrie Dagger (CWA Gold Dagger) for Best Crime Novel, for *Raven Black*, the first book in her Shetland series. In 2012 she was inducted into the CWA Crime Thriller Awards Hall of Fame, and in 2017 awarded the CWA Diamond Dagger. Ann lives in North Tyneside.

Doug Johnstone is a writer, musician and journalist. His eighth novel, *Crash Land,* was published in 2016. His previous book, *The Jump*, was shortlisted for the McIlvanney Prize Scottish Crime Book of the Year. *Gone Again* was an Amazon bestseller and *Hit & Run* was both an Amazon top seller and a winner of the prestigious Fiction Uncovered prize. He's an arts journalist, Royal Literary Fund Consultant Fellow, musician, player-manager for the Scotland Writer's Football Club, and has a PhD in nuclear physics.

Stuart MacBride is the #1 *Sunday Times* bestselling author of the Logan McRae and Ash Henderson novels. He's also published a couple of standalones, a short story collection, two novellas, and a slightly twisted picture book for slightly twisted children. Stuart lives in the northeast of Scotland with his wife Fiona; cats Grendel, Gherkin, Onion, and Beetroot; some hens; horses; and a *vast* collection of assorted weeds.

Dubbed the Queen of Crime, **Val McDermid**'s novels have been translated into 30 languages, selling over 15 million copies worldwide. Her books include three main series: Lindsay Gordon, Kate Brannigan, and the Tony Hill and Carol Jordan series, the first entry in which, *The Mermaids Singing*, won the Crime Writers' Association Gold Dagger for Best Crime Novel of the Year. The Hill/Jordan series was adapted for the highly successful television drama, *Wire in the Blood*, starring Robson Green.

Denise Mina's 1998 novel, *Garnethill*, won the Crime Writers' Association John Creasy Dagger for best crime novel by a first-time author. She has now published twelve novels and also writes short stories, plays and graphic novels. In 2014 she was inducted into the Crime Writers' Association Hall of Fame. Denise presents TV and radio programmes as well as appearing in the media. She regularly speaks at literary festivals, leads writing masterclasses and was a judge for the Bailey's Prize for Women's Fiction in 2014.

Craig Robertson is the author of *Random, Snapshot, Cold Grave, The Last Refuge, Witness to the Dead* and *Murderabilia*. His debut novel, *Random*, was shortlisted for the CWA New Blood Dagger and was a *Sunday Times* bestseller. He started out as a journalist with a Scottish Sunday newspaper. During his 20-year career there he interviewed three Prime Ministers, covered major stories including 9/11, Dunblane, and the disappearance of Madeleine McCann. He lives in Stirling.

Sara Sheridan is an Edinburgh-based novelist who writes two different kinds of historical novels. One is a series of cosy crime noir mysteries set in Brighton in the 1950s – the Mirabelle Bevan series – and the other is a set of novels based on the real-life stories of late Georgian and early Victorian explorers and adventurers – *The Secret Mandarin*, *Secret of the Sands* and *On Starlit Seas*. In 2015 Sara was named one of the Saltire Society's 365 most influential Scottish women, past and present.

E S Thomson was born in Ormskirk, Lancashire. She has a PhD in the history of medicine and works as a university lecturer in Edinburgh. She was shortlisted for the Saltire Society First Book Award and the Scottish Arts Council First Book Award. Her first novel in the historical Jem Flockhart series, *Beloved Poison*, was a finalist for the McIlvanney Prize Scottish Crime Book of the Year 2016. Elaine lives in Edinburgh with her two sons.

Louise Welsh's first novel, *The Cutting Room*, won several awards, including the 2002 Crime Writers' Association John Creasey Dagger, and was jointly awarded the 2002 Saltire Society First Book Award. Louise was granted a Robert Louis Stevenson Memorial Award in 2003, a *Scotland on Sunday*/Glenfiddich Spirit of Scotland Award in 2004, and a Hawthornden Fellowship in 2005. In addition to her four subsequent highly acclaimed novels, she is a regular radio broadcaster, has published many short stories, written for the stage and has contributed articles and reviews to most of the British broadsheets.